Thieves & Lovers

K WEBSTER
J.D. HOLLYFIELD

Thieves 2 Lovers

ISBN-13: 978-1973704478
ISBN-10: 1973704471

Cover Design: All By Design
Photo: Adobe Stock
Editor: PREMA Editing
Formatting: Champagne Formats

Dedication

This book is dedicated to two friends who are thick as thieves…*us*.

Dear Reader,

We hope you love Linc and Reagan's story! Writing together, as usual, was a blast. As with both *Text 2 Lovers* and *Hate 2 Lovers*, one of us took the hero's POV and the other took the heroine's POV. If you've read the first two books, you'll remember! We'll also tell you at the end.

It is best if you've read *Text 2 Lovers* and *Hate 2 Lovers* so you'll understand the dynamic of the characters in this story. Plus, you don't want to miss out on all the fun of the first two books!

Enjoy and we'll see you on the other side!
K Webster and J.D. Hollyfield

"I realized I'm in love. It's always been right in front of me."

—*Richelle Mead, The Indigo Spell*

Chapter One

Linc

Let's Not Be Weird Anymore

It's been three weeks since I pulled my best friend into my lap and kissed her like she should always be kissed. Hard. Passionate. With all the intensity in the world.

It was the best kiss of my life.

Sexy as fuck. Sweet. Perfect.

But it was also a royal mistake. Things went from normal to…*weird.* Reagan went from spending every free moment with me to throwing herself into her and Chase's relationship. Of course, I didn't help matters. When I woke up the next morning, my head pounding from a hangover and my heart pounding with regret, I bailed without so much as a goodbye. Aside from the occasional text, I haven't spoken to her and it's driving me fucking crazy.

I've had too much time on my hands.

Time, for me, is never a good thing.

Time has always gotten me into trouble.

"*Oof!*"

Which is exactly why I'm tied to a chair getting my ass kicked by a wannabe thug who should have never trusted me with two grand and a sketchy errand.

"Where's my money, asshole?" the loser demands, his chest heaving with exertion. Maybe if he ever left his mom's basement, he wouldn't be so winded over an old-fashioned ass kicking. I mean, I'm not even able to fight back for fuck's sake.

"I lost it," I lie.

When I grin, blood coating my teeth, he screams at me. "You need to fucking find it!"

Narrowing my eyes at him, I let my smile fall away. "Untie me, and I'll go have a look-see."

"You'll bolt," he snaps. "I'm not stupid."

But he is stupid. He gave two thousand dollars to a tattooed punk he barely knew to go purchase some weed from a supplier. I'm a thief not a druggie. I'd have gotten away with it, too, but apparently this thug is social media savvy. And thanks to Reagan and her obsession with checking in everywhere on Facebook, I led this asshole right to the Dairy Queen I visit at least three times a week. *You get a discount for checking in*, Reagan said. *It'll save you money*, she said. What she didn't say was that it'd get me whacked over the head with a baseball bat and then dragged into some fucker's basement to get my ass kicked.

"I'll get you the money but I can't do it from this chair," I grumble, my words irritated. "It's at my place."

"The one at 2334 South Lyons Avenue?"

My body stiffens and I wonder how the fuck he knows where I've been staying. "I don't know what you're going on about, dude. Just let me out of here, and I'll get you the cash."

The guy, Larry or Lenny or whatever the hell his name is, glares at me. "I see you going in and out of there all the time. I see the geeky guy, too. Wouldn't want to have to fuck him up to get my repayment. Kid looks like he'd break the first time I punched him."

I suppress a growl. The "kid" is my mom's best friend's son, Keith. Keith is actually my age and was nice enough to give me a place to stay when I got back into town after spending eight months in New Jersey. The last thing I want is for him to get involved in my mess. "Man, just let me out. I'll get you the damn cash by tomorrow."

He stares at me for a long time before he works on untying me. "Don't fuck me over again or you're going to piss me off."

Clenching my jaw, I give him a clipped nod before stalking out of his shitty house. How the hell do I end up in these situations?

Shame coils in the pit of my belly like a snake as I pound on Reagan's door. Chase's shiny sports car sits in the driveway, and I hope I'm not interrupting a boring fuck fest. On second thought, I'm hoping to rescue her from some snooze sex. Earlier, I confided in Keith that I'd gotten myself into a mess. He showed me his gun—which I may or may not have stared at in shock—and then proceeded to tell me he could take care of himself. He also told me I was no longer welcome.

I refuse to move back home with Mom and my stepdad Roger.

And my usual landing pad is no longer an option. Andie is no longer a single chick ready to take in her brother at a moment's notice. She's married and has a brand-new baby to deal with. I'm certainly not high on her list of priorities. Not that I'd ever make it past her fuckface husband anyway.

"Linc," Reagan greets, shock lacing her voice. Her shoulder-length brown hair is slightly tousled and her lips are swollen. I interrupted something. "Did you get in a fight?"

I wince at her words because what happened earlier today was not a fair fight. It was an unfair beat down.

"Something like that."

"Well, get in here," she says. Worry flickers in her eyes. "Tell me what happened."

She ushers me inside and my gaze falls to her ass. It always does. Reagan has one of those tight round asses you could bounce quarters off of. I should know because I've done it a couple of times, just to fuck with her. My dick still gets hard every time I think about our kiss—a kiss where my hands had the freedom to roam her perfect ass.

Chase sits on the sofa and tosses a look of irritation my way when he sees me. His hair is slightly disheveled. I still don't know what she sees in that Dave-Franco-looking motherfucker. And I cannot stand the fact that he calls her Pet.

She's not a fucking pet.

She's…perfect.

"Name your poison," she chirps as she starts rummaging around in the kitchen cabinets.

I drop my bag on the floor and saunter after her. Unable to stop myself, I mutter, "Fireball."

Her back tenses momentarily, and with a shaky hand, she pulls out the half empty bottle. Looks just like the bottle we downed that night. I love the way her throat turns slightly pink as if she's remembering.

"I think I'm going to head out," Chase grumbles as he enters the kitchen. "This"—he waves at me—"looks like it may take a while. I'll come by after work tomorrow. Maybe we can finish what we started." He grips her by the elbow and she yelps in surprise. My fist clenches with the need to punch this asshole. "I love you, Pet," he murmurs before giving her an obnoxiously wet kiss. My lip is still curled up in disgust when he throws a smug look my way—as if he's the better man between us. He probably is. "Later, *Lincoln*."

I refrain from rolling my eyes and simply offer him a head nod. Once he's gone, I stride over to Reagan to pluck the bottle from her tiny hands. She keeps her grip on it and stares up at me with a frown.

"Tell me what happened." Her brown eyes flicker with hidden emotion. I love the way her cute button nose flares with each breath she takes. And her mouth, Jesus, I'm such a fucking fan of her mouth. I'm fixated on how her bottom lip is slightly fuller than the other and pouts out. I remember just how good that bottom lip felt between my teeth, too. "Linc…"

I yank my beanie off my head and run my fingers

through my messy hair. She'd wanted me to grow it out. So, of course, I fucking did. Now my dark, almost black hair, hangs in my eyes when I haven't taken the time to style it. A small smile plays at her lips and she reaches forward to brush away a strand that's flopped in front of my eye.

"I like this," she says with a grin. "Looks good on you."

I wink at her and steal the Fireball while she's distracted. "I see Chase loves you now," I blurt out, a little bitterly I might add.

Her smile falls and she huffs. "He does."

I unscrew the cap and drink straight from the bottle. Fire engulfs my mouth and burns all the way down my esophagus until it reaches the pit of my belly. "Is the feeling mutual?"

"I don't know."

I laugh. "You'd know if it was."

Our eyes meet for a heated moment. I'm sure she's thinking about the same thing I am. The night I pulled her into my lap and kissed her like a man is supposed to kiss a woman. With his entire goddamned soul.

"Linc," she sighs. "You're avoiding the inevitable. Tell me who beat you up and why. Let me help you."

My heart aches at her words. *Let me help you.* Maybe that's why I connect so well with Reagan. She's everything I'm not. And somehow, that makes me want to be better for her. She *does* help me. Anytime I'm in her presence, I feel on top of the world. Like I could do anything as long as it involved her.

"My buddy Keith and I got in a fight. He kicked my

ass out." Not technically a lie. It just wasn't a fist fight. I don't want her knowing all the shitty details of my life. Reagan is untainted, and I'd like to keep her that way.

"I'm sorry," she says, her eyebrows pinched together in concern. "Do you need a place to stay? I have the guest room, you know?"

The thought of sleeping under the same roof as her has my heart thumping hard in my chest. It would be my favorite solution but probably not the best one. "I can call Andie and—"

She snorts and steals the bottle. "We both know Roman would not let you move in. Even temporarily. You know what a dick he can be." The bottle tilts up as she takes a swig. I find myself staring at her slender throat as she swallows down the liquor.

I step closer to her. Before the whole kiss screwed up our easy friendship, I touched her a lot. Purely platonic. So I told myself. My fingertips crave to touch her hair or to tickle her ribs. For now, I settle for invading her personal space.

"You really mean it?" I ask when she hands me back the bottle. I'm glad when she doesn't move away from my nearness.

"Of course I mean it. You're my best friend. Even if things were a little weird for a while," she assures me. "Speaking of weird. We should talk about the kiss. It was a mista—"

I cut her off before she says words that will cut deep. "It's fine. An experiment. I was just showing you so you could teach Chase because we both know that boy needs lessons. We're *friends*, Rey. Besides, it was like kissing my sister." Hurt flashes in her eyes. Quickly, I continue because I want to wipe that look right off her face. "Thick as thieves, remember?" I flash her a crooked grin she's not immune to and, thankfully, she caves.

"I remember," she says, smiling beautifully at me. "I'm glad we had this talk. And I'm happy we'll get to hang out all the time again."

God, I've fucking missed her smiles.

"You going to wash my laundry too, Rey?" I waggle my eyebrows at her.

She laughs and swats at me, the tense moment gone. "No, *Abraham*."

I arch a brow at her as I set the bottle on the counter. "Remember what I warned you I'd do if you called me that again?"

A squeal escapes her as she starts to bolt. I'm close enough and quicker. I easily toss her tiny ass body over my shoulder and haul her into the living room. She screams at me the whole way.

"Let me go!"

"Nope."

"Yesss!"

"Ain't happening, sweetheart."

I throw her on the couch and pounce before she can get away. She weighs hardly anything, so I overpower her within seconds and pin her wrists to the cushions with one hand as I straddle her thighs. Her entire body trembles and squirms.

"I'm sorry," she pants, her eyes frantic. "Do not freaking tickle me."

I smirk before digging my fingers into her most

ticklish place. Her ribs. The laughter that comes out of her is fucking adorable. I tickle her until tears stream from her eyes and she's uttering curse words I've never heard leave her mouth before.

"Stoooop," she screeches.

Grinning, I slow my movements. "Like this?"

Her eyes are filled with heat when they meet mine. My fingers are no longer tickling her but stroking her instead. When my thumb grazes along the sliver of flesh that's visible between her shirt and the waistline of her yoga pants, she shudders.

"Does that tickle?" I ask, my voice husky.

A whine escapes her as she lies. "Y-Yes."

My cock is hard in my jeans, but she's not looking there. Right now, her eyes are locked on mine. So many words flash in her gaze. I wish I knew how to make them escape.

"I missed you," I blurt out, my tone sad.

She swallows and nods. "I missed you too."

"Let's not be weird anymore," I tell her, my fingers slipping under her shirt slightly. Her gasp makes my dick throb. "Let's just be us again. Reagan and Linc."

Her eyes flutter closed when my fingers dare slide farther under her shirt. My longest finger grazes along the underwire of her bra.

"Linc," she breathes out. "We can't do this."

My hand trails back south, away from her breasts. "Why not?"

"I have a boyfriend." She reopens her eyes and sadness flickers in her gaze. "Please. Just don't. I can't…I can't…"

Releasing her hands, I pull away from her and sit at the end of the couch. She sits up on her elbows and her lashes bat against her cheeks before she lifts her eyes up to meet mine. Now that we're no longer separated because of the stupid kiss, all I want to do is touch her. I fucking missed her.

Running my thumb along the bottom of her bare foot, I take a moment to enjoy having her again—even if it's only like this. "Want to watch a movie? I kind of miss all those lame chick flicks you made me watch. Three weeks is a long time to watch fucking football."

A giggle escapes her as she climbs off the couch to go put on a movie. Once it's started, she grabs a blanket and settles on the sofa with her head in my lap so she can see the television.

I can't help but stroke her hair. That's platonic, right? She seems to think so because she lets out a contended sigh. This close, I can smell her hair. She smells sweet. Whatever shampoo she uses is my favorite.

"I'm sorry you fought with your friend," she murmurs. Her head tilts up and our faces are just inches apart. I could lean down and kiss her. Right now, I could claim her beautiful mouth. Instead, I shrug and look away before I do something idiotic, like make out with her again.

"It's fine. I'll sort out my shit and be out of your hair," I tell her, my voice gruff.

Her palm reaches up and touches my face in a soothing manner. "Don't rush. I kind of missed you being in my hair."

We both chuckle, and the tension seems to seep

away. Soon, her breathing evens out as she falls asleep. I slide my palm down her shoulder over her shirt and graze my fingers against the bare skin above her elbow. Her skin is soft, and I want all of it pressed against mine.

But I'm not about to fuck this up again.

With a groan, I lean my head back against the sofa and close my eyes. Chilling here with her in my arms is perfection. Nothing whatsoever feels wrong about it.

Is it possible to be madly in love with your best friend?

I'm pretty sure I am.

And I don't know what to fucking do about it.

Chapter Two

Reagan

Never, Devil Woman

JUST FRIENDS.

Just friends.

Just fr—

"Oh, frickity frack. Who am I fooling?" I toss the throw pillow in its rightful place, and poke at the couch cushion. I can still see Linc's imprint on my sofa, and it needs to go away. Like right now. How did I fall asleep on the couch? How did *he* fall asleep sitting up? We managed to stay that way the entire night until my phone started going off this morning with scheduled reminders. Linc must have felt my body tense at the realization of the position we slept in, because we were both up and out of each other's arms in no time. He claimed he had to meet a guy and I claimed…well, I claimed work. I had to go to work.

I'm dressed in only a towel after the shower I took to scrub his scent off me—a shower where I attempted to also wash away all the wrong thoughts that were swarming in my head caused by said smell. Which didn't work, I might add. I'm trying to get rid of any sign that Linc spent the night so my boyfriend won't be upset. One more bash to the pillow and I look at the time realizing I have to abort mission. I have a meeting in thirty minutes. I snatch the Febreeze and hesitate before mentally smacking myself and taking aim at my furniture. Must delete any sign. *He knew Linc came over, Reagan.* But I'm sure he didn't expect for him to never leave. "Delete, delete, delete," I repeat, then gag on the now overwhelming amount of spray choking me and toss the bottle.

I hurry into my room and snatch up a pair of suit pants, a blouse, and a blazer. It takes three attempts to get the buttons right before I lose my patience, rip off my blouse and end up in a light sweater. They turn the air too high in the office, anyway. I throw myself in the bathroom and begin brushing my teeth as I get a good look at my outfit. It's then I realize the sweater I put on is the same one I had on the night Linc kissed me. And, well, I kissed him back.

Oh, God, did I ever kiss him back.

His lips were soft, his tongue inviting. The taste of him was like no other. He was just… "Shut up. Shut up!" I jab myself in the mouth with my toothbrush. I gag, not thinking that through and almost throw up spit and toothpaste. But that needed to be done. I need to shut my brain down. All these thoughts I'm having about Linc are ridiculous. We're just friends. *He also compared kissing you to kissing his sister.*

That reminder causes a tiny slump in my shoulders. And here *I* was thinking it was the best kiss I've ever experienced. I shake my head and spit, rinsing my mouth out and exiting the bathroom. I shouldn't dwell on it, anyway. We're friends. He's my *best* friend. Keeping our distance from one another over the last few weeks was miserable. I missed him terribly. I missed how much I laugh when he's around, our talks, the peaceful silence when we can just chill and watch television for hours without a single peep between us. Without him around, I felt…lonely.

And that also makes me feel like a huge jerk. Because while Linc was avoiding me—or maybe I was avoiding him—I tried to fill that void by throwing myself fulltime into my relationship with Chase. I thought that by not thinking about Linc, I could focus on what was missing in my real relationship. But as time dragged on, nothing really changed. Chase was still just…well, Chase.

I never grew the balls to ask him to experiment with me. Possibly because every time I thought about it, it only brought up that night, and I could never get in the mood. Linc's comment weighed so heavily on my mind. The way I should always be kissed. And, by golly, I wanted that. The first time Chase was over after the Linc fiasco, I practically mauled him, driving my tongue down his throat. I tried to kiss him hard and passionately, hoping for that spark I felt with Linc. But it never came. And in the end, Chase pulled me off him, reminding me there was a golf tournament on and asking if we could table our plans for later.

If I wasn't such a pro at putting a smile on my face and acting the happy-go-lucky part, I would have broken down and told him to leave. Cried myself to sleep or gotten drunk and called every single ex-boyfriend I'd ever had, asking them what was so wrong with me that they couldn't see what I wanted them to see in me. What Linc possibly saw in me. I wanted to be loved. Cherished. I wanted to be swooned over like in those darned movies. I just didn't know what I was doing wrong. And the whole time, all I wanted to do was talk to my best friend. But he was MIA.

I don't know when Chase caught on that something was wrong. Maybe he realized that our relationship wasn't all about me smiling and nodding while he talked about himself, feeding himself more compliments than he did me. And let's not get too excited about the ones he *did* offer. Because the more they came, the more I realized they were two-sided. Telling me I'm beautiful, but saying my hair would look better down and not in my childish ponytails. He loved my body, but I shouldn't hide it behind all my frumpy clothes. They weren't compliments—they were ways to make jabs at the things he didn't like about me. And maybe Linc was right. I needed a man who would take my breath away every single time he looked at me. I wanted that. And I was about to demand it.

That is, until Chase—casually over a crab dinner at Shaw's—told me he loved me.

He assumed when I choked, it was over the large piece of food I put in my mouth and advised me that I should really learn to take smaller bites. It would help with balancing portion control, he said. But in reality, I choked because of his bullshit words.

He loved me?

Since when?

But then again, I've had boyfriends tell me those three words for less. After I gagged down my bite and smiled back, I didn't know what else to say. I knew I couldn't say those three words back. Did *I* love *him*? My mother loved him. My brothers loved him. Everyone else loved him. But me? I was just so confused. But, being the people pleaser that I am, I smiled back and shoved another bite in my mouth.

We came home, and Chase fell asleep instantly. I laid in bed thinking about my night. My life. In the beginning of our relationship, I pictured exchanging those special words with Chase. I could see a future. A life. I was content with what we had. I didn't need all the extra bells and whistles. I had so much love around me that it didn't seem necessary to worry about all that extra stuff for myself. But as I laid in bed, I thought about what I was truly missing out on. The tingles that never came when seeing Chase at work. The sex that had started becoming a lie since I was faking my orgasms. And the small insults veiled thinly behind his compliments.

I didn't want to give up on us, but sometimes I think I already have. Chase was busy and successful and he gave me what he could. And maybe it was me who needed to work on being better. Maybe I was being too needy. Maybe I was being insane about that whole kink idea. I vowed that night that I was going to try and be better in my relationship. Try harder. And so my focus was on my relationship.

Until I opened that door last night. And I saw Linc's beautiful wounded eyes staring back at me.

And all I wanted to do was help *him.*

But we were friends. Thick as thieves as he liked to call us. Maybe that was for the best. Seeing him again made me realize that I needed my best friend. Which maybe meant burying any feelings that had secretly been festering. I couldn't have both. He clearly didn't *want* both. But we both wanted one thing. Our friendship. So that's how we would remain.

Thick as thiev—

I turn the corner to exit my bedroom when my body slams into another surface. Instantly, I scream. The moment my voice rings out in terror, the other person screams, too. My eyes, which were squeezed shut, re-open to see Andie holding on to me, screaming along with me.

"Jesus, Andie, what are you doing? You scared me to death!"

"I scared *you*? I've been calling your name, and when you finally come out of your room, you barrel into me and start screaming bloody murder!"

"You were calling my name?"

"Yeah. I heard you talking to someone, so I came back. Is Chase here? Ew, did I interrupt something?"

I agree with her on the *ew* part. *Shame on me!* No, I *don't* agree because that would make me a bad girlfriend. *Ughh…* "No, he's not here. I was…um, talking to my-self. I have a huge meeting today and I was just going over some key talking points. What are you doing here, anyway? Is everyone okay? Is my brother okay? Where's Molly?"

Andie starts looking at me confused. Shoot, did I

forget something?

"Honey, Molly's with your mom. I'm picking you up for work so you can ride home with Roman. You said you could babysit Molly while Roman and I attempted a date, remember?"

Oh my God! I totally forgot.

"Oh no! I totally remember!" Kind of a lie. "I miss my little princess and I can't wait to eat her up. Not literally. Oh! And I bought her more tutus!" I turn back to my room and grab the shopping bag in the corner from LuLu's Baby Emporium. How could I forget tonight's plans? I'm a horrible aunt. Spending all this time worrying about myself and my stupid problems, I forgot about family.

"Hey, if you can't, it's no big deal. Roman thinks that we don't have to wait six weeks to be cleared to have sex but he's insane if he thinks I'm going to let that big ole monster inside me. Do you know how many stitches I got after Molly's giant head ripped through me?"

"Um. Yeah, twelve. The same amount of times you've told me." I laugh.

Andie grumbles, and we both walk out together to her car. "Well, still. I need the time off, but renting a hotel by the hour and sleeping sounds more romantic than dinner and a movie. God knows neither of us are going to actually watch the movie. There is no reason why Roman picked a three-hour movie, other than to take a damn nap during it."

I laugh at how well she pinged my brother. Andie is still home on maternity leave, but Roman is back in the office, though he looks like crap. He claims he's fine, but he is definitely behind on at least three weeks of sleep.

"Well, maybe you should just take it slow. No need to jump right back into your old ways, ya know?"

Andie turns to me as she buckles her seat belt and gives me her infamous *Are you serious* look. "Reagan. That man looks at me like I'm a goddamn steak dinner. I could have vomit on my tit and he'd still suck it off just to get at them. He's a ticking time bomb. If I don't offer my vag up soon, he's going to tie me up and find other ways to get off, and let me tell you, my mouth is still sore from the last—"

"La-la-la-la! Stop. He's still my brother. You can keep the details to yourself." I love Andie and her zero filter, but I have heard way more than I ever want to in three lifetimes about my brother's privates and what he does with them. The first time I met Andie, she didn't hold back from telling me the things my brother can do. It took me almost three days to be able to look Roman in the eyes again.

"Sorry, you're technically my sister, best friend, and confidant all in one, so you have to hear it. Plus, when we get to the office, I need you to tell me if I have a hickey on my left ass cheek."

Thank goodness I don't live far from the office. I love my sister-in-law dearly but if I have to hear one more thing about Roman's sex addiction, I'm going to claw my ears off. Walking into the office, I get lucky because my new assistant Clara grabs me, rattling off my schedule, allowing me to get out of hickey patrol duty. I wave to Andie, who enters her husband's office and shuts the door. Assuming *he's* going to be doing the hickey patrolling, which I'm sure he's okay with, I enter my own office.

"Your eight o'clock meeting just got pushed back. The finance team wasn't ready to present and the client had a hold up with their accounting team. They rescheduled for tomorrow morning. Your nine o'clock is already here, but is getting a tour from Ram. Apparently, they're really interested in a marketing campaign Ram just launched. You had a lunch scheduled with Chase, but he was here earlier looking for you. Told me to tell you he had to cancel but would see you after work." Clara continues rambling, as a spark of disappointment settles in my stomach. This is the third time in a row Chase has cancelled our lunch plans.

"Did he tell you why?" I pretend to act unconcerned when deep down, I worry that he may think something is up between Linc and I. The comment he made before he left now sits on my mind.

"No, just that he would see you later. He looked quite handsome today, too. You sure are lucky to scoop up a looker like him." I turn to Clara and she's smiling.

"Yeah. Lucky me."

Just then, Ram walks into my office, alone. "Hey, sis."

"Hey." I smile brightly at Ram. "I thought you were with Legend Piping Corp?"

"I still am. I have them in the creative room with Henry. They're getting the complete tour of all the programs we use. Mr. Jensen looks like a pig in shit right now. We'll have a signed contract by the end of the day."

I smile proudly at my brother. He has worked so

hard to make this company successful. I step closer and wrap an arm around his middle.

"Woah, what's the hug for?"

I squeeze him tight, then release. "I'm just proud of you. Dani is the luckiest girl alive."

His face lights up with the sound of his future wife's name. Anything Dani related makes my brother tick. And in three short months we finally get to welcome her into the Holloway family. "Well, I'll tell her you said that. Right now, she may not feel that way since I accidently washed all her leggings in hot water, making them wearable for Molly."

I can't help but laugh. The mad version of Dani is like a cute little kitten who can't reach her toy when it's rolled under the couch. I pat my brother on the shoulder and turn, heading back to my desk. "Well, I'm sure she'll forgive you."

Sitting down, I look back up to find Ram already on his phone. Those two and their texting. At least when Dani wants to share her sexual escapades, she keeps it G-Rated, unlike my other sister-in-law. Then again, my brother Ram is just like our dad. The romancer. The gentler Holloway who has always worn his heart on his sleeve. That's what makes him and Dani so perfect. I sigh watching his smile spread, knowing Dani probably responded with something cute, trying to be sexy, but always failing since she still refuses to borrow Andie's kink book.

"Anyway, I saw Chase this morning. Cool dude, Reagan. He invited us all to the golf club this weekend. Not that I play golf, but I may take Dani to show her off." He stops to think about something then continues. "But then I might lose her to those caddies who hand out towels at the entrance. Well, either way, I'm sure Roman will take him up on the offer. You going to go?"

This weekend? Chase promised to help me till the dirt for the garden I've been dying to put in the backyard. "Hello, earth to Reagan…"

Right. "Sorry, um, I don't know. I was going to visit Mom and then do some stuff around the house. Maybe."

Ram shrugs his shoulders and jams his phone back in his pocket, "Well, I'm sure Mom would love to see Chase, too. You know her. Always wanting to know when her baby girl is going to settle down and marry."

The mere thought of getting married right now sends an eruption of heartburn up my chest. I can't even get my boyfriend to commit to lunch, how am I going to get him to commit to marriage? And, oh God, who's even thinking about marriage?

"I have to meet back up with Legend Piping. Oh, and invite Chase over for dinner sometime. You know Dani loves you two together. Catch you later."

And Ram is gone.

I fall back into my office chair, blowing a strand of hair out of my face. *What am I doing wrong here?* Never in my life has my entire family agreed on someone I dated. Lord, *I* haven't even agreed on my choices, but now, everyone seems to be gaga over Chase. Everyone besides one. *Me.* The one person who *should* be the surest just isn't all that sure.

I throw myself into my work, keeping busy enough that my mind doesn't shift to other things, or people. I work through lunch, because just like Ram said, Legend Piping Corp. was eager and ready to sign. It took all afternoon to finalize the details, but with Ram's smooth convincing, they were willing to sign at any cost. And that made Holloway Advertising very, very happy.

It's just past five and the sounds of sweet gargling get my attention. I hear a squeal followed by the cutest little laugh ever, and I know Andie's back and she has my favorite little princess with her. I close down my computer and grab my stuff to head out. My phone dings and I grab it from my purse to see Linc sent me a text.

Abraham L: Hey, Roomie. Hope your invitation to crash still stands. If not, maybe the cereal, Fireball, and the bag of salt and vinegar chips I bought will sway you. Want me to scoop you from my sister's later?

I can't help but laugh at his text. He despises those salt and vinegar potato chips.

Me: Offer still stands, but you have to eat the chips with me.

Abraham L: Never, devil woman. Those are Satan's chips.

I shake my head, laughing.

Me: Fine, no chips, but you do have to help me till my garden this weekend. It's part of your rental agreement.

Abraham L: Deal. What time should I come for you?

My heart beats faster at his last text. Of course my mind takes me to that place where Linc comes and saves me from all my stressors and problems and brings me back to my couch and kisses me senseless. Then I grunt because *I* have lost my marbles and need to knock it off. We are friends. And I need to focus on why my boyfriend seems to be pulling back.

Me: Come for me around nine, kind sir.

But after I catch a harmless ride home with my roommate.

Chapter Three

Linc

What's Tumblr?

I CRACK MY NECK AS I WIND THROUGH ANDIE AND Roman's neighborhood. Sleeping like a fucking statue last night sucked, but at least it was with Reagan, which made it so worth it. Even if I do have stiff joints today. When I woke with goddamned morning wood that was doing its best to stab her, I had to bolt before I did something stupid like poke her between her pretty pink lips.

My dick twitches at the thought and I groan. With a huff, I steal another French fry from the sack in the passenger seat. Despite that dumbass wannabe drug dealer looking for me, I still picked up dinner from our favorite place. I just didn't check in this time to get my ten percent discount.

When I pull into Roman and Andie's driveway, I stare at the big house in the dark for a long moment. My sister deserves a nice life. A man—*albeit a motherfucker*—who is good to her. The expensive house. The baby.

I'm proud of her. Sadly, it's a reminder that I can't even compete when it comes to my own life. What I wouldn't give to be able to offer this entire happily-ever-after package to some woman one day.

Not just any woman.

Reagan.

My chest aches. She's on the fast track to having this life with Chase. I don't necessarily hate the guy…I just don't like him. She can do better. Better than him. Better than me.

Pushing away my brooding thoughts, I snag our Blizzards and burgers. I trot up the steps and the door flies open as I reach the top.

"You came and, oh my God"—she groans as she snags a sack from me—"I'm starving."

"So happy to see you, too, Rey," I tease as I follow her inside. "Where's my niece?"

"Sleeping," she says quietly. "No wonder they needed a date night. That little girl is so fussy. I was ready to rip my hair out." Her hand dives into the bag and she retrieves a fry. "You're here early."

"I figured you might be hungry," I say with a shrug as I help her pull the food from the bags.

She lets out a moan of happiness as she takes a huge bite of her burger. I can't help but grin at her. The girl loves her Dairy Queen. Once she swallows, she smiles at me. "Thank you. I didn't eat anything all day."

I frown. "I thought you had lunch with Chase today."

Her cheeks turn pink and she nibbles at a French fry. "He cancelled."

"So you didn't eat?" Irritation flickers through me.

So maybe I *do* hate the guy. "Why didn't you call me? I'd have brought you something."

She waves me off as she devours another bite. "It was fine. I survived."

My broody mood returns and we eat in silence. It isn't until we've finished and cleaned up that she hugs me suddenly. Hugs for us come easy. Just another simple part of our friendship.

But this time I don't hug her briefly.

This time, I embrace her tightly and inhale her delicious smelling hair.

When she starts to pull away, I don't let her go. I *can't* let her go.

Her chin lifts so she can meet my gaze. Heated brown eyes seem to dance with different emotions as that brain of hers works overtime. I think I see need in them. Maybe guilt. Also happiness.

At least I'm not the only one who feels conflicted.

"You still up for helping me till the garden on Saturday?" she questions, her voice hoarse as she desperately tries to steer the conversation elsewhere. Neither of us makes any move to separate from our embrace. "Maybe we can dig the holes, too, if time allows."

"Can we make one of them big enough to bury Chase?" I tease.

She laughs. "Very funny. I'm planting cucumbers, among other things. Mom says you can't plant anything this time of year, but I'm going to do it anyway because I'm dying to do something with that part of the yard. Chase promised to help but…" Her smile fades. Yep, I most definitely hate that motherfucker.

"Chase promises a lot of things and never delivers."

Her throat bobs as she swallows down her emotion. "Anyway, he's decided to play golf with my brothers instead."

A stabbing sensation makes my chest ache. Another reminder that I'm not "the one" for her. Chase is Mr. Country Club and he's friends with her brothers. I don't even know what the fuck a country club really is—aside from old fuckers golfing—and her brothers sure as hell don't like me, especially Roman.

Her bottom lip wobbles slightly. I can tell her feelings are hurt but brave little Reagan keeps it under a lid, like always. I'm about to lean forward and kiss her sweet mouth when something catches my eye behind her.

A golf bag leaned against the wall.

I pull away from her and saunter over to the bag. "Golf, huh?"

"Yep," she says sighing as I pull one of the clubs out.

"You think this one is important?" I ask as I run my fingers along the end. It's the only one that looks like the ones Andie and I would use whenever we'd go play miniature golf high as fucking kites as teenagers. "Looks important."

Reagan places her hands on her hips. "They all look the same to me." Her lip is slightly curled up as if she's annoyed just looking at the damn thing.

I reach out with the club and use the end to lift the hem of her shirt in a playful way. Shooting her a wicked grin, I say, "You think he'll miss this one?"

She swats away the club but she's grinning. I continue to poke and tease at her with the end of it.

"Should we steal it and see?" I challenge.

A squeak escapes her when I not-so-innocently run the end of the club between her thighs. She swats it away again but her breathing is heavier. "Roman would kill you."

"Roman tries to kill me every day. What else is new?" I smirk at her. "Here. Take it. I'm going to take the big one."

"He's going to flip out," she whispers and takes the club. "We can't take it. That is like a fourteen hundred dollar set of clubs!"

"We might need them to help us in the garden," I tell her. "We're *borrowing* them."

"Fine," she concedes. "But when he comes for blood, I'm blaming you."

Once we both have a club in our hands, I look around. "What else do we need for the garden?"

"We need a hand shovel." Her brown eyes gleam with mischief. "Hmm. I know just the thing." She starts rummaging around in the kitchen cabinet until she retrieves a mug that has ants painted all over it. "This is his favorite mug. Andie got it for him. Like I told him when I was a kid, ants belong outside, not in the house."

I snort and take the mug from her. "You're a naughty girl. I like you."

She bites on her lip thoughtfully. "Oh! I know what else we need." Reagan practically skips along through the house. Being a bad girl looks good on her. I follow her into Roman's home office and she points to some ugly metal piece of art hanging on the wall with her golf club. "That. My garden needs a lawn ornament."

We spend the rest of the evening hiding lots of shit Roman probably won't notice in my trunk. It's funny as hell because he'll be pissed when he finds out.

"We're home," my sister calls out when they come through the front door.

Reagan's face blazes red and she looks seconds away from blurting out her confession. I sling an arm over her shoulders and whisper against her ear, "Relax."

Her body loses some of its tension. "Did you guys have fun?"

Roman saunters in behind Andie, grinning like he just got his dick sucked. When his eyes find mine, it quickly morphs into a glare. Fuck, this dude's an asshole.

"It was great. Food was phenomenal. The orgasm in the car outside the restaurant was even better," she tells us, her blue eyes twinkling with delight. "*Dessert* was spectacular."

Roman grunts his agreement.

"Ew. TMI," Reagan says with a laugh. "Glad you guys had fun but I'm beat. Linc, you ready?"

Before I can answer, Roman's eyes narrow at the way I have my arm around his sister. Meeting my gaze, he asks her, "How's Chase?"

Reagan stiffens again and steps away from me. "He's fine. Just busy with the upcoming Masters tournament at the club."

"People with jobs and hobbies *are* busy," he agrees with a knowing smirk. "Remind me again, Linc. What do *you* do for a living? What are your hobbies, besides trying to get arrested?"

"Roman!" Andie bellows. "Stop."

I grit my teeth and shoot him a *fuck you* glare. He knows how to throw digs at me every time we speak. I'm about to tell him I'm doing his sister for a living—just to terrorize the shit out of him—when Molly starts crying upstairs. Andie points toward the stairs and gives him a stare that lets him know he's in trouble. Before he goes, though, he snags her in his arms and kisses her hard. All anger melts away as they all but try to make another baby right here in the living room.

Another pang shoots through me.

That is how I'd kiss Reagan every day if things were different.

She wouldn't have to settle for her Chasebot kisses.

I'd kiss her hard and passionately because that's what she deserves. She deserves to be made to feel as if she's the only woman on the planet. The best woman on the planet.

Fuck if I don't hate Roman, but he gives my sister exactly that.

And goddamn do I want to give *his* sister exactly that.

"I want that."

I frown in confusion. "The Chop Whiz?"

"No," she says with a laugh, turning away from the *As Seen on TV* commercial and looking over at me. "*That*. What Roman and Andie have."

"Pornographic sex 24/7?"

Her lips tug into a shy smile. "Apparently, they have the best sex ever. The stuff Andie tells me sometimes can't be real. I mean, anal beads? She has to be messing with me."

"They're real," I assure her.

"Whatever."

This time, it's me who's chuckling. "Are you serious right now?"

Her cheeks and throat burn bright red. "Anal beads are really a thing? I thought it was a joke."

"Not a joke. There are a whole lot more sexual things out there than just missionary sex with a robot," I tell her, an evil grin tugging at my lips. "What exactly *do* you look at when you go on Tumblr?"

"What's Tumblr?"

"Oh, Rey," I growl. "I don't know if you're ready for the dark side."

She crosses her arms over her chest and challenges me by lifting a sculpted brow. "Maybe I just need someone to show me the way."

Smirking, I pull out my phone and open the app. My tastes range from normal sex to St. Andrew's crosses and choking and everything in between. I pull it up and search for anal beads.

"See? Real."

She screeches, her hand covering her mouth, as she scrambles closer to me on the sofa. Having her warm body this close has me wanting to do so many dirty things to her. Instead, I scroll through the erotic pictures and gifs of people using anal beads.

"It looks painful," she admits, her palm resting on my chest as she leans in to get a closer look. "What if they get stuck?"

I laugh. "They don't get stuck. They use lots of lube."

"Have you ever used them?" Her curious eyes dart to mine as she questions me. Being this close to her face is dangerous. Fuck, I want to kiss her again.

"I've never been a receiver, if that's what you're asking," I divulge. "But I have used them on women before."

Her mouth parts open as she whispers. "Oh. Women…as in multiple?"

"Not all at once. Over time," I say with a laugh. "The beads are fun, but this is better." I find a home video of a couple having anal sex. Reagan lets out a gasp of shock.

"That looks extremely painful," she squeaks.

"Not as painful as this," I tell her and search for some BDSM videos. These videos are darker. The women are tied up and their tits are red and bruised from being hit.

"How can they like pain?" she demands, horror seeping into her voice.

"Sometimes pleasure is best when it's preceded by pain."

Her eyes narrow as she looks at me again. Skepticism dances in her eyes. "I have trouble believing that."

And I would *love* to prove her wrong.

Hell, maybe looking at porn wasn't the best idea. My dick is stone solid and her mouth is just too damn tempting.

"I wonder if I can talk Chase into trying that," she says absently. Her finger points to a woman with her wrists bound together and tied to the headboard while the man eats her out like there's no tomorrow. What motherfucker wouldn't be into "trying that" with Reagan fucking Holloway? I know I sure as hell would be first in line.

"If he's too busy, I could always fill in," I tease in a playful way, so she knows I'm kidding. But I'm not kidding. I could suck on her clit for hours.

"Don't be gross," she says with a laugh. "This is good research, though. Show me more."

We end up spending at least an hour scrolling through Tumblr. I load the app on her phone for her and help her add some of the people to follow so she can "research" it more later. She's practically in my lap as she holds her own phone while searching stuff. I've lost interest in the porn I'm looking at to spy on what's on her screen.

A guy choking a woman.

A woman riding a guy as he gropes her tits.

A woman taking two cocks at once.

She simply scrolls, fascinated by all the different stuff, but stops on one particular couple. The guy is broad shoulder and tattooed with dark hair. *Like me.* The woman has brown hair and sexy tits. *Like her.* They're fucking, but it's intense. *Like it would be if it were us.* He has her chin in a brutal grip so he can stare at her as he drives into her. It's fucking hot.

"He's so…" she trails off and swallows.

"Obsessed with her?" I finish, my voice husky. "Madly in love with her?"

Double meaning hangs thick in the air. She pulls out of her trance and scrambles off the couch onto her feet. "It's late. I should get to bed." She won't meet my eyes, and I hate that. My dick aches in my pants for release. What I wouldn't give to sink my cock into her tight heat.

"Goodnight, Linc."

She bolts and soon her bedroom door closes. I stare up at the ceiling for a moment to settle my cock before rising from the couch to go to bed. On autopilot, I lock up and turn off the television and lights. I'm just walking into the hallway when I hear it.

Buzzzzz.

Buzzzzz.

Buzzzzz.

Fucking hell. I walk toward the sound and lean my forehead against her door. If I were a braver man, I'd storm in there and get her off with my teeth and tongue so she wouldn't have to use her vibrator. If we didn't have a fucking Dave Franco twin as a wall standing in our way, I'd claim her as mine.

I know I'm not like him. Successful. Well-loved by everyone who meets him.

I don't have consistent money coming in. But I'm what you call an opportunist. I get by. I have means.

And maybe I don't have a house, but hanging with Reagan at hers is pretty cool.

I'd make up for all of my shortcomings in orgasms.

So many orgasms.

It would be a great fucking trade.

Buzzzz.

Buzzzz.

Buzzzz.

A moan comes from the other side of the door and my dick strains against my jeans. With no regard for the consequences, I unfasten my pants and push them, along with my boxers, down my thighs until my heavy erection bobs free. The moment I take it in my grip, I hiss. Her moans get louder and more ragged with each passing moment. With tight, quick tugs of my fist, I jerk off.

I imagine her tits. Wonder what her nipples look like. Imagine biting them until she squeals. I try to envision what her flesh would look like once I've properly worshiped her breasts. Would they turn purple and blue from the bruises I would undoubtedly give her?

She comes with a loud shriek. It's enough to have me groaning loudly—too loudly. My cum shoots across her door. I fucking wish it were her tits instead. With a grumble, I quickly yank my pants back into place but don't fasten the top button. Ripping off my T-shirt, I use it to clean up my mess. I've just fisted up the shirt to take to the laundry room when her bedroom door flies open.

Her oversized T-shirt doesn't even reach the middle of her thighs. If she were to lift her arms in the air, I could almost guarantee she'd flash me her panties. Or maybe just her pussy if she's not wearing any.

"Linc," she murmurs, her eyes lazily skimming down my chest. "Never mind."

If she knows I just whacked off out here in the hallway, she's not letting on, aside from the bright red tone of her flesh.

"'Night, Rey," I tell her, my voice husky.

"'Night."

She starts to close her door, but I stop her with my words. "You look so fucking beautiful right now." And she does. Everything about her is perfect, from her messy dark hair to her pouty pink lips to her bright orange-painted toenails.

Tears well in her eyes and she stares at me. Heartbroken. As if I've just said the worst thing to her. A second later, she slams the door shut.

I stalk over to it and lean my forehead against it once more. "I can't take it back," I say softly through the door. "I know it's out of line but I had to tell you. Because you *are* beautiful, Rey. Friends are allowed to say that."

When she doesn't respond and all I can hear is her sniffling, I let out a sigh and stalk to my bathroom where I intend on taking a cold shower to snuff out some of the raging fires blazing within me.

Moving in with her was a very bad idea.

I'm going to ruin our friendship.

One fucking compliment at a time.

The destruction is imminent, yet I still can't find it in me to stop.

I want her, no matter the consequences.

And fuck if I don't hate myself for being so selfish.

Chapter Four

Reagan

In It to Win It

I'VE HAD MY EAR PRESSED AGAINST THE DOOR FOR A solid minute and nothing. He must still be sleeping. Good. I take a deep breath and slowly and quietly open my bedroom door. I tiptoe out of my room, holding my breath, while I pass Linc's open door. *Don't look, don't look, don't…* "Oh!" I gasp, throwing my hands over my mouth and running past his door. Dammit! I told myself not to look, and who sleeps *naked* nowadays!? Jesus, how am I going to get *that* image of his perfect backside out of my head? I'm currently running on two hours of sleep since I spent my entire night tossing and turning with the image of Linc, shirtless on my mind. I don't want to acknowledge what he was doing outside my door or what he heard.

Nope. He heard nothing.

I'm sticking to that.

But, God, he is beautiful. Muscular. Full of tattoos and, man, oh man, I just wanted to lick him all over.

"Shut *UP*, Reagan," I scold myself. I shake my head, realizing that if I want to sneak out of my house without having to face Linc, I should probably stop talking out loud to myself. I grab my work bag and slip through the front door. In my car, I toss my bag and speed down my driveway.

I force myself to think of what I have on my schedule for work. How many black pairs of shoes I have in my closet. How many languages I can say hello in. Sadly, only two. I just want to jam my brain with anything that doesn't consist of a certain bare chest with tattoos. I fight to continue counting every time I ate tacos this month, but the specific tattoo over his heart keeps breaking through. A set of angry flames choking a bird. It was so beautiful in color—so visually stimulating. It was so angry. It made me want to know what it means. What *all* his ink means.

I'm sure if I asked, he would tell me. Because we are friends. I'm sure he would let me brush my fingers across his smooth skin and let me ask those questions. I'm curious why he has a scar just below his neck or why he has certain tattoos inked on him, and what they mean. I know Linc has led a rough life. A few times, when he's had too much to drink, he's opened up about the things he's been through. The trouble he's been in. And in those times, I wanted nothing more than to save him. To tell him he's in a better place now and I would always be there for him when he needed me.

Because we're friends.

Then why are you picturing his naked, tight butt lying on your sheets?

"Ugh!" I hit a stoplight and pull out my phone. I start scrolling through my pictures, pulling up photos I have of Chase and I. This is what I should be thinking about. My good-looking boyfriend. The one I'm dating who loves me and I… I… "Ugh!" I toss my phone back in my purse.

Last night was my own fault. I shouldn't have asked Linc, of all people, to enlighten me on anything sexual. I knew it wasn't going to lead to anything innocent. Sitting so close to him, looking at a couple get so deep and intimate. It made me think of us. Made me imagine that being him, gripping my hair and taking me roughly. I shouldn't have done that to him. Leading him on when clearly I have no intention of following through.

I did the right thing by going to bed. But there was no way I was sleeping until I released some built up tension. I probably didn't even need my vibrator to get off, I was already halfway gone. It only took a few minutes until my body got exactly what it was craving. I just wished I didn't feel so guilty imagining Linc between my legs.

I need to knock it off. And that's why when I get to work, I am going to throw myself at my boyfriend and wash any wrongful thoughts of my best friend out of my mind. That's it. That's what I'm going to do. I'm going to find Chase and do what Andie and Roman do all the time. Shut his door and seduce him. Show him that I am in it to win it. Maybe a little office head will make him realize how devoted I am. *Office head? Really Reagan?*

I make it upstairs and Clara is waiting for me as always.

"Morning, Reagan, I have your morning schedule.

It's pretty compact. Jenner Realty just signed and Ram needs you to go over the financial plan to make sure it looks accurate. I have Lindsay Tyson for you at ten o'clock regarding your *office head*."

At that, I trip. "What did you just say?" I turn to her, looking super guilty. How could she have—

"I said your interview with *The Herald*. Ms. Tyson is here to take your office headshots."

Office *headshots*. Dummy! "Yes, great, okay, what else?" Man, my mind really wants me to lose it.

"When are you going to *pound Linc* into next week?"

Another trip and this time my purse goes flying over my shoulder.

"Oh dear, Reagan, are you okay?" She tries to steady me, but I'm staring at her as if she's grown two heads.

"What did you just say to me?" I snap, more rudely than is appropriate.

"I said I've been hounding IT to get that link on your computer. They promised me next week. Are you sure you're okay?"

Clearly not.

Masking my delusion, I smile and grab the files she's holding. "That will be all, Clara. Thank you."

I've always been a levelheaded person. I don't have these malfunctions. I don't malfunction!

"Something wrong with the mailroom?"

I turn to see Roman standing outside his office. Great…now I've gone completely bonkers arguing with myself out loud. "I said malfunction… Oh, I mean, um, *yeah! Mailroom.* I, uh, uh, sent a package to an old friend. It came back. Stupid postage." I shrug, fighting to keep eye contact. *Don't look guilty.*

"Okaaaay," he drawls out, a scowl painted on my older brother's face. He scrutinizes me for a long moment before he continues. "I wanted to ask you. Any chance you messed with my golf clubs last night? I wanted to get them polished before golf with Chase on Saturday and I seem to have misplaced two of them."

Oh crap. Act innocent. Act innoc—

"*Golf*? As in clubs? Like the ones you hit balls with?"

Okay, I said act innocent, not dumb.

Thankfully Roman, laughs it off. "Wow, Chase has a lot to teach you. You're coming on Saturday, right? I think even Mom is. Heard they have a great buffet. You know our mother and her food. Probably going to end up in the kitchen taking notes."

If one more family member brings up this stupid golf weekend, I'm going to blow up. Inside I'm raging. But on the outside, I smile my normal casual laidback smile and respond. "Not really sure. I have a lot of stuff I want to do around the house, and you know me, I don't really care for golf." And that's because my own boyfriend didn't even invite me. He seemed to have made the effort to suck in my entire family, without asking the one person who should matter most.

"You okay?"

I must have gotten lost in my thought. I snap out of it, my smile back in place. "Yep! Just started thinking about all the stuff I have to do. Busy day." I wave him off before he sees through my lie or starts questioning me about other missing things in his house.

Now in my office, I toss my bag and rest my head

against my leather chair. When did my life get turned upside down? My boyfriend seems to want to date my family more than me, and I want to date my best friend more than my boyfriend. And, my *best friend* seems to think I'm beautiful and isn't sorry about it, which makes me *want* him to be *my* boyfriend. Gahh!

I throw myself into my work, pretending nothing in my life is awry. I get through the financial contract for Jensen and Co. and begin crunching the numbers for a new client Roman is interested in when my phone dings.

I look at my screen and see a notification from Tumblr.

LincLovesTheLadies is now following you.

I smile at his ridiculous screenname. Of course that doesn't stop my curiosity from swiping unlock on my phone and opening the app. I click on the screenname and his page pops up surrounded by a ton of gifs. I find myself scrolling, my eyes wide at the first few I take in, my lips parting once I get to a gif of a man choking a woman while he takes her from behind. I press my finger to the gif and it starts playing with sound. Before I can realize what's happening, moaning and flesh slapping against flesh blare throughout my office.

"Oh, Jesus Almighty! Turn off! Turn off!" I'm trying to click the *X* button to close the browser, but the only thing that happens is the increase of moaning and slapping. Sheer panic seizes me as I try shutting down my phone.

Clara walks into my office. "Everything okay in here—"

"Gahh, NO! I mean yes. Sorry, uh, Andie sent me

another birthing video, in case, ya know, if I ever…" I finally see the swipe option to shut off my phone. I shove it into my desk drawer and lift my head, trying to act nonchalant, which may be impossible because even *I* feel the crimson in my cheeks. "Sorry, ew, don't recommend those videos. Sounds painful." *Ugh, but she sure looked like she was enjoying it.* "Anyway, have you seen Chase today?" Now seems like a great time to attempt to ravish my boyfriend. That or I am going to, for the first time ever, need to go to the ladies' room and fondle myself until the buildup of what I just saw works its way out of me.

"Yeah, he's in. Looking sharp in that navy blue suit he wears." Clara winks at me and turns to head back to her desk. I quickly check my calendar and see that I have thirty minutes until my first meeting. Thankfully Chase isn't the long-lasting type, so that gives us plenty of time.

I fix my hair and stick a mint in my mouth before heading down to his office. As always, he's seated behind his desk going over résumés.

"Hey, sexy," I purr, trying to be just that. He lifts his head and regards me, then sticks his nose back into his stack of papers.

"Hello, Pet. Are you getting sick?" No, just me being seductive.

"Ehh, no. Healthy as a horse." He doesn't look up, so I turn and shut his door, clicking the lock in place. "So, I have thirty whole minutes before my meeting starts. Was hoping you and I could catch up. Maybe finish what we started the other night." I sway my hips toward his desk, not even sure how to sway. Since he's not even looking at me, midway, I stop the act and just walk up to his desk. “Did you hear me? I miss you.” I step behind his desk, and take a seat on top of the papers he’s trying to review.

“What are you doing? We’re at work,” he grumbles, sitting back in his chair.

I take the opportunity to slide off his desk into his lap, using my fingers to thread into his perfectly styled hair. “And since you’re head of HR and I’m the CFO, I think we can break a few rules here.” I lean in to kiss him, but he puts his hands up between us to stop me.

“Stop being ridiculous. This is not the time nor place.”

“Then when is the time, Chase? You’ve blown me off for lunch the past few times and we haven’t spent any time together in days.”

He rolls his eyes, regarding me like I’m some whining child. “And since when have you become so needy? Seriously, Reagan, I didn’t know I was dating an insecure child. The amount of time we spend together is fine.” He pushes me off him, causing me to throw my feet to the floor to stand in order to avoid falling off his lap.

“What about this weekend? You promised to help me with my garden. Now, apparently, you’re taking my entire family golfing? And when were you going to inform me? I don’t know, maybe even *invite* me?” I raise my voice—no sense in trying to hide the hurt in it. I cross my arms over my chest, waiting for a response.

“You should be thanking me for being so generous to your family,” he snips. “You know how much that will set me back? Having your *clan* tag along on Saturday? I’ve already had your mother call me three times about the food. For Christ's sake, isn't an invitation to the most elite golf course enough?"

I gasp at his rude statement. How dare he insult my mother, or my family! "You invited *them*! And please, my family has enough money to buy that stupid golf course," I spit back, feeling the anger bubbling up inside me. "And for your information, no one asked you to do this for them. You're dating me, not my family. You should be trying to impress *me*."

At that, he cynically laughs. "And how so? Shall I sit around drinking cheap booze with you? Watch those silly shows over and over? Maybe I should get a ridiculous tattoo on my body. Would that *impress* you?" I stare at him in shock. "Really, Reagan, knock off this act." He dismisses me and lifts up a piece of paper, going back to work.

I can't believe him. I can't believe *me*. What am I doing with him? I take a few more deep breaths to calm myself, but that fails. And I let my anger run its course. I open my mouth.

"I came here because I missed you. Because I had every intention of seducing you right here on your desk to show you just how much I wanted you. But you know what? That idea died the moment you opened your mouth." I turn to leave but I'm not done, so I turn back. "And one *more* thing, I enjoy drinking cheap booze, even out of the bottle. I love watching reruns, no matter how many times I've seen them, and for the record, you're too big of a pussy to get a tattoo!" I raise my voice. "And yeah, have fun kissing ass to my family. I'll be at home, spending time with someone who actually *wants* me around. Maybe I'll show *him* just how much I missed him—"

My words are cut off when Chase leaps out of his seat and startles me by wrapping his hand around my neck and pushing me against the closed door. "Watch it, Pet."

I've never seen him this angry—like, completely pissed off—not to this degree. His chest heaves as he glares at me.

"Ch-Chase, what are you doing?" I rasp in a calm voice. "Let me go."

He doesn't. His grip only tightens. "I've been really patient with your childish games, needing your *friend* around. But I've about had it. You want more of me? Get rid of him. He's a wrench in our plans, Pet."

I'm struggling to push him off me, but his alarming strength has me pinned against the wall. I feel his hot breath against my ear as he places a kiss to my lobe. "You're mine, Reagan. I have a plan and you're a part of it. The house. The yard. The white picket fence. And I think it's about time you make it known to that stray dog who doesn't know when to go away that he isn't a part of that plan. He belongs on the other side of our fence."

"Chase," I hiss. "Stop this."

"Stop what?" he snaps, his furious gaze meeting mine. "Stop wondering all the damn time if you two are screwing each other behind my back? So help me if you are—"

I try and lift my heel to kick him, when a knock resounds on the other side of the door. "Chase? I have those papers you requested," Sandy, Chase's assistant, calls out, and I couldn't be happier to hear her voice. Chase instantly releases me, and I grab for the knob and throw the door open. "Oh! Hi, Reagan. I'm sorry. I didn't mean to interrupt. I can come bac—"

"Nope, it's fine. I was just leaving."

"Reagan." Chase calls my name, and I force myself to turn and make eye contact.

"I love you."

Chills blast through my body. Feeling the cold rush of confusion, I don't know what to say. I know I don't want to send up any red flags in front of Sandy, so I nod and offer him a weak smile before hurrying back to my office.

I decided to cut my day short, claiming not to feel well, and go home. I was useless at work anyway. I just couldn't comprehend what had happened. I kept it together for most of the day, but the moment I got into my car, I broke down. How could Chase do that to me? I was never ignorant to his cocky side. I knew the moment we began dating that Chase was a kept man. But to put his hands on me?

I cry the whole way home. I make it into my driveway when I realize Linc's car is gone. Where is he? I need him right now. I need to tell him what Chase did. I can't tell my brothers because they would kill him. Linc may not be any better. But he'll listen. He'll hold me and tell me things are going to be okay.

I grab my phone and shoot off a quick text as I make my way into my house.

Me: Where are you? Can you come home?

It takes him longer than normal to respond. When I'm changed into my yoga pants and a tank top, I finally hear my phone ding.

Abraham L: I'm kinda tied up right now.

Like tied up or *tied up*? My stomach drops at the thought of him being tied up by a woman. How could he even be with someone right now? *Because he's not yours, Reagan.* I send off a reply trying not to sound like I'm prying.

Me: Are you going to need help getting untied or will she let you go once she's done with you?

My face doesn't show the humor I'm trying to show in my text. I need him right now, and for all I know he is with someone else.

Abraham L: Sorry, got this thing I need to take care of. I'll see you tonight.

No humor in his response back. He's definitely with someone. My heart breaks even more, even though I know it has no justification to. He isn't mine. I'm not his. I go straight to my kitchen cabinet and grab for the bottle of Fireball. I skip the shot glass and immediately take a strong swig instead. My eyes squint and my teeth grind at the burning sensation flowing down my throat—that first sip never gets easier.

It takes two more swigs until I feel warm and less likely to have a breakdown. I bring the bottle to my couch and sit, switching on the TV. The movie on is a Nicholas Sparks flick—go figure—destined to make me want to cry my eyes out. I change the channel to the next station, which ends up being golf. Fuck golf. I turn the TV off.

I spend some quiet time alone with my Fireball, trying to figure out what I need to do. I promised myself that after Jimmy in California, no one would put their hands on me ever again. I never in a million years thought Chase would be abusive, but then again, no one has *I suck* written on their foreheads as a warning. I take some time looking harder into our relationship. Chase has never really been the overly caring type. And if he ever leaned that way, it was when my family was around. When he'd be putting on his show. Why am I just seeing this now? I'm so angry with myself for being so blind. I always let men walk all over me. And every time I swear it will be different the next time, I fall back into the same relationship.

I refuse to be with someone like Chase. I deserve better. I deserve someone who tells me I'm beautiful and means it with such force that there's pain in his voice. The pain caused by the fact that he can't have me. I take another swig, the memory of Linc at my bedroom door weighing heavily on my mind. The sound in his voice. The ache in my chest that I felt after his words seeped inside me. I wanted to run to the door and throw myself into his arms. Confess all these feelings that have been festering since the moment I met him. I would tell him right now, if he were here.

But he would have to be here to do so. And he's not. Because he's busy. Another swirl of anger hits my chest as I take another pull.

"He's not mine. He can do what he wants," I say,

trying to convince myself that the burning feeling inside my chest is the alcohol and not jealousy churning inside me. I'm deep into the bottle when my phone starts to chirp. I look to the couch where I left it and see a notification.

DaddyWantsAKitten is now following you.

Who the… I grab my phone and unlock it. When I get into the app, it seems that I have a bunch of new followers. "Jesus, what is he *doing* with that?" I turn my head sideways, trying to figure out what hole that guy is shoving that pole in, when it starts over. *What's up with this five-second tease?* Surely people want to see more than five seconds. For research purposes, that is.

I move on, scrolling through my new buddy's interests. Seems to be the thing to use whips and ball gags. Not sure how that poor girl can breathe while her lover has his hand wrapped in her hair as he tugs on her scalp, stretching a device around her neck. I'm not sure if I find it disturbing or a turn on. I can't seem to take my eyes off it, so I'm going with the latter.

A few more posts down and I find myself becoming more comfortable on my couch. My tank top seems too hot, so I expose my stomach by bringing it up to just under my breasts. The next image is of a woman being taken by two men. Feeling bold, since I'm at home, I press on the gif so it opens full screen and the sound surrounds my living room. Her moans are hungry and with each grunt from her lovers, she is pushed farther into the bed, her glistening thighs spread wider by the man's large length.

"Ohhh." I accidently catch myself moaning as I

watch the other man's finger disappear into her back hole. I find myself feeling warmer, embarrassingly turned on by watching her be taken so aggressively. I stare at her large nipples, which seem to be covered by clamps as they bounce back and forth with each thrust. "I need to try a pair of those," I mumble, taking a swig, spilling a little bit down my shirt. I rub my hand over my chest to wipe up the spilled liquor when my nipples perk. I do it again, this time slower, and the sensation sparks a slow throb down below.

Just when her face looks like she's about to orgasm, the reel starts over. "Dammit," I grumble, shamelessly squeezing my breast through my tank. I know the Fireball is taking over, because I would never be so brazen to touch myself while watching porn on my couch, in the middle of the day. I quickly scroll, so I can find another video before I lose my arousal. I scroll past an advertisement and decide there's no harm in clicking on that, too.

It, to my disbelief, takes me to a site where there are no boundaries. I mean, they sell everything. With each click, I find something that intrigues me as much as it scares me. I imagine myself using the tools on myself or having someone use them on me and I find myself so turned on that I'm dumping item after item in my basket. "World of Kink, where have you been my whole life," I talk to my phone while I attempt to shimmy out of my yoga pants.

Enter your shipping details. "Sure thing, you dirty website." I chuckle, kicking off my pants. I'm having a hard time seeing the screen as I enter in my credit card information and shipping address. If it denies me, maybe it will be a good thing. As it is, I can't recall what I put in my basket but I could care less. I'll use every single darn thing.

Once my purchase is completed, I go back to Tumblr and a girl masturbating immediately pops up on my screen. Using a dildo quite aggressively, I watch her as she rams it inside her, her eyes closing with each thrust. God, this is so naughty, but so hot at the same time. I would never think that watching another chick masturbate would turn me on so much. It then gives me the idea to match her. I get up and sway to the right almost taking out my coffee table. I may have accidently drank a wee bit too much and my legs struggle to walk in a straight line. I close an eye and make it to my bedroom in search of my dildo. Once I find it, I rip off the rest of my clothes and throw myself onto my bed. I unlock my phone, and with the girl pleasuring herself, I begin to mimic her moves.

Until my damn battery dies.

Seriously!?

"Fudge. Fucken' Fudge," I slur and throw my legs off the bed. The rest of my body almost goes with them landing me in a face plant on the floor. I steady myself but knock my lamp over in the process. "Tomorrow's problem," I mutter as I stumble into my bathroom. I fall to the floor in front of my vanity and open my cabinet in search of my extra batteries.

"Where, oh where are you, vibrator battery stash?" I say with a giggle, pushing through tampon boxes and expired hair products. I take a break, because I have too much stuff in my cabinet, and lean against the wall. Inhaling a big breath of air, I tell my brain to sit up and get back at it. My new Tumblr girlfriend waits for no one.

But instead, I pass out against my bathroom wall.

Chapter Five

Linc

Linky, I Drinky

When I get back to Reagan's, I'm stressed as fuck. I've spent all day dealing with shit. Mainly, covering my tracks. There's no denying it now. Louie has sniffed me out all the way down from New Jersey to North Carolina. If he finds me, I'm fucked. Deeply and horribly fucked.

I mean, who steals from the mafia?

A wannabe bookie who doesn't follow rules well, that's who.

I scrub my face with my palm before entering her cute bungalow. If I were a smart man, I'd bolt again. Leave this hometown of mine and head west. But I can't. Not with Andie now married and with a baby. I'm a damn uncle, for crying out loud. I need to settle down and get my shit straight.

Plus, I can't leave *her*.

Rey.

My best friend, who I'm fucking in love with.

Jesus.

A quick scan of the street tells me Louie's signature gold-colored Town Car is nowhere to be seen. I'd been on my way to pick up lunch and swing it by Reagan's work in case she hadn't eaten, when I saw Louie standing in front of his car, talking to that prick who beat my ass the other day. Lenny or whatever the fuck his name was. I was so shocked they were speaking together that I slowed down and locked eyes with Louie's beady ones. His cigar nearly fell out of his mouth when he grinned at me.

I'd spent the rest of the day driving in circles. Not only was I trying to get them off my tail, I also had to think. First thing I did was trade in my car for something nondescript with tinted windows. When I'd taken off with twenty-three grand of Louie's money, I bought a car. I know he wants his money back. I'm not about to tell him I don't have it all anymore, though.

With a huff of frustration, I walk inside Rey's, whose door is unlocked. Irritation bubbles up inside me. Chase must have left without locking up. I'm going to have to have a talk with her about this—especially now that the fucking Italian mob knows I'm laying low in this town. Once I lock the door behind me and draw all the curtains closed, I'm annoyed to see her pants lying on the floor in the living room. An open bottle of Fireball sits on the coffee table that's been moved a bit.

They fucked in here.

She used her research and sealed the deal.

Congratulations, Chase, but you're still a fucking robot.

I drop my backpack to the floor and pull out the two yellow daffodils I'd picked from the car dealership's front flower bed and hunt for a vase for them. I know the perfect vase. With a smirk, I fill up the coffee mug we stole from Roman and then sit it on the table before sticking the daffodils in it.

They were the only two in a bed full of colorful flowers. But these two were unique and stood out among the rest. It reminded me of her and me. How I wish I could claim her and make her mine.

My gaze falls on the living room and I get pissed. *I* don't get her. *Chase* does. Fucking asshole. I grow angrier as I shut off all the lights. He doesn't deserve her. The fucker doesn't even know how to please her. She has to *show* him.

If she were mine, I'd tie her pretty ass up and do all the teaching.

I'm headed for my room, yanking my T-shirt off, when I notice her door is open and the lights are on. I kick off my shoes in my doorway and toss my shirt inside before sauntering over to her room. At first glance, I notice her bed is disheveled but empty. Some shit went down, all right. But not too much shit. If it were her and me, we'd tear up the sheets, not simply rustle them up a bit.

I'm smirking as I visualize having her beneath me when I find her lying on the bathroom floor. Naked. A dildo lying at her side. *What the actual fuck?* All lust-filled thoughts dissipate as I rush over to see if she's okay.

"Rey," I growl, worry making my heart speed up. "What happened?"

She moans and rolls over to face me, giving me a whiff of the Fireball that she's clearly plastered from. Her brown hair is messy and drool runs down the side of her face. I frown and swipe her face clean before wiping it on my jeans. She's naked, and of course she's a fucking knockout, but I'm more concerned about how out of it she is.

"Talk to me, sweetheart," I urge softly, stroking her hair away from her eyes so I can see her. "How much did you drink?"

"Linky, I drinky," she says before giggling. Her shaky hand reaches up and touches my chest. "My bird."

I grab her hand and kiss the back of it. "I need to get you to bed. You can't sleep on the bathroom floor, you nut."

She groans when I scoop her into my arms and buries her face against my neck. "Spinnn."

"Close your eyes," I tell her and kiss the top of her head.

It takes a second of yanking covers, but I finally manage to get her into the bed and cover her up. I'm just turning off the bathroom light and heading out of her room when she starts to cry.

"Linc," she sobs. She's drunk as shit but the way she says my name fucking breaks my heart.

"Yeah, Rey?"

"I'm c-cold. I m-missed you."

Groaning, I run my fingers through my hair and lean my forehead against the doorframe. All common sense tells me to just turn off the light and walk away. She'll sleep it off and forget all of this in the morning.

I turn off the light.

"Please."

Fuck. I've never been responsible. I saunter through the dark room and crawl under the covers beside her. I'd be more comfortable taking my jeans off but with her in her drunken state and me in my love-struck state, I don't trust that we'd just stick to sleep.

I start to spoon her, but she turns to face me, pressing her bare tits against the side of my chest, and sighs heavily. Her palm roams up my chest and settles at my collarbone. "I love you," she tells me and starts crying again.

"We're best friends," I agree. "I love you, too."

Her body relaxes. "You're n-not the k-kind of guy my family wants me to b-be with."

I tense and grit my teeth. Ain't that the fucking truth? "I know. I'm sorry I can't be what they want."

Her cries are soft but sad as fuck. I wish I were good enough for her. I wish I didn't make stupid decisions and try to outsmart the mob. I wish I drove a Beamer and made a six-figure income every year.

I would give her everything and more.

She'd be so happy. So fucking happy.

And I'd be elated.

Reagan is a dream come true. A walking fantasy. She's mine, but not in reality. In my dreams, I get to keep her. I'm surprised she hasn't noticed that every gif or picture on my Tumblr is of dark-haired women—women who resemble her. She's *all* I see. Hell, I haven't been laid since I moved back because I saw *her* that first day.

Reagan.

Wide brown eyes. Sweet and innocent. Adorable as fuck.

Plump lips I've tasted. Cinnamon. Hot. Intoxicating.

Mine.

God, how I wish.

I can't get her out of my head. I'm punishing myself but I'm okay with that. I'll have her in any capacity—even if only a purely one-sided platonic one.

"Y-You're the only person who sees the real me," she breathes, her hot breath tickling my neck.

I stroke her hair and kiss her head again. "I see you, sweetheart. Always. You're all that I see. And, Rey," I confess, "I don't want to see anything else."

She lets out a small sigh and then begins to snore softly.

In a dream world, I could have her in my arms every night.

In a dream world, I'm not a fuck up. I'm worthy of a girl like her.

Too bad I live in a goddamned nightmare.

I wake to the sound of Reagan's phone going off with an alarm. Grumbling, I swat the air. "Make it stop." My head is fucking pounding as if I have the hangover. I'm love drunk. It's real. She intoxicates, me and sometimes I sip too much from her. I get myself drunk on the what-ifs. Then, in the morning, reality stares me in the face and beats a damn drum reminding me I don't get the girl.

Sliding out of the bed, *unwillingly I might add*, I stumble to the other side of the bed to turn the obnoxious blaring off as I rub sleep out of my eyes. She has several missed texts from Chase. All apologetic. He probably stood her up again. Maybe last night they didn't have kinky sex. Who the fuck knows.

I glance over at her sleeping form. She's still curled up where I was just lying. The sheet has been pulled down to her hips and her bare back is revealed.

Stop looking.

Stop torturing yourself.

And yet, I stare at her until it feels creepy.

With a sigh, I stalk out of her room to take a much-needed cold shower. I'm just getting out when I hear someone ringing the hell out of the doorbell.

Louie.

Fuck.

I throw on my jeans from the night before without even drying off and slip out of my room to go meet my fate. If it's that prick, he can take me. Do his worst. I will not let Reagan get involved. Clenching my jaw, I open the door and wince, expecting a bullet to the chest. Instead, I lock eyes with a familiar lucky-ass pussy in a pink Polo shirt with a popped collar, holding the biggest vase I've ever seen. Full of red roses.

God, I hate this douchebag.

"Sup." I nod my head at him before abandoning the door so he can come in.

"Where's Reagan?"

"Sleeping. She didn't feel well," I tell him as I saunter into the kitchen to put on some coffee. She'll definitely need it to deal with Chase this early in the morning.

He sets the vase on the table right in front of the two

daffodils I'd stuck in the ant coffee mug we'd stolen from Roman. "You stayed the night?"

I guess she hasn't told him. I'm not ratting her out. If she wants me to be her dirty little secret, I'm cool. "Needed a place to crash. Going through some shit."

He snorts and my back muscles tense. "Aren't you always going through some shit?"

"Shittier than usual," I clip out. I cross my arms over my still-wet, bare chest and level him with a hard glare. I've got at least twenty-five pounds on the guy and several inches. If Reagan wouldn't kill me, I'd enjoy pummeling the idiot. "I don't think she's going in today."

Guilt flashes in his eyes. "Did she…did she say why?"

Fucker ought to feel guilty for always standing her up. "She drank too much."

At this, his nostrils flare as if he's annoyed, and I fist my hand. I'm seconds from hitting him in his perfect nose.

"Sometimes she's so irresp—"

He's cut off when Reagan walks into the kitchen while tightening the strings of her robe around her waist. Her gaze skims down my bare chest to where my jeans hang low on my hips. I'm not wearing any boxers, since I was in a rush, and when her cheeks burn red, I imagine they're hanging low enough to show her some dark hair.

"Good morning, Pet," Chase says in a sad, soft voice. "You're not feeling well?"

She cringes when he speaks and tears her gaze from me. "Uh. What are you doing here?"

He straightens and lets out a huff. "We don't have to be at work for another hour. I thought I'd come check on you. You know…" He trails off and shoots me a nervous glance. "After how awful I was to you yesterday."

Her eyes well with tears and Chase takes the moment to pull her into an embrace. I feel as though I'm intruding. When I start to go, her panicked eyes meet mine. She probably wants to know if we fucked.

"Nothing happened," I mouth.

A tear rolls down her cheek, and I can't look at her anymore. Not without wanting to rip her right out of his arms and into mine. I stalk off without a backward glance. Quickly, I dress, brush my teeth, and tug a beanie over my head.

"Text me later," I call out before slamming the door behind me. The last thing I need to hear is them having makeup sex. Fuck that.

I'm driving in circles when my phone rings. It's Ram of all people. I don't want to talk to him but I answer anyway.

"Yeah?"

"Hey," he greets. "Remember that time you drew a picture of Roman taking a cock in his mouth?"

I snort. "Like it was yesterday."

"Well, I kept the drawing."

Now, I'm laughing. "Whatever floats your boat, man."

"Can you draw other stuff or are you limited to cocks and my brother?"

"I designed all my tattoos. My mom's friend had me draw animals all over the wall of her grandchild's nursery. I just fuck around with it when I'm bored. Why?"

He lets out a heavy breath. "How would you

feel about doing some freelance work for Holloway Advertising?"

I frown as I drive. "Like what?"

"Hand-drawn logos. Some illustrations as needed. We're outsourcing it right now, but I hate the dumbass we use. He doesn't respond to my calls. I need someone I can rely on."

Rely on?

That's a first.

My chest thumps. I could do it. I'd answer my phone. It's drawing not rocket science.

"And you'd pay me?" I ask, astonished.

He chuckles. "Of course. We'd pay you by the hour. However long it takes. And if it worked out, we could always consider something full time." The line grows quiet for a minute. "Look, I know we all started off on the wrong foot, but you're family. We love Andie, and you're a part of that. I know Roman is a dick, but that's just his personality. I can design until I'm blue in the face but I need an actual artist on deck. I'd love to give you a shot if you're interested."

"I have a record," I blurt out, instantly hating myself for all my mistakes.

"So does Roman," he snorts. "And he's the CEO."

"What?"

"He does stupid shit when he drinks," he tells me, humor in his voice. "It's gotten him in trouble a time or two. Are you in? Can you stop by today and we'll meet up?"

I don't even realize it but I'm already heading to their building. "How about now?"

Ram laughs. "Eager. I like it. You show up here and after you leave, I'll tell Stu he's out. Lazy-ass motherfucker."

"Thanks," I tell him genuinely. "Thanks for giving me a chance."

"Everyone deserves their shot at something good." He laughs again. "Even fuck ups like you and Roman."

"Asshole," I grunt.

"Bring me coffee, and I'll tell you what he did," he offers.

"You're on, man. See you in twenty."

Chapter Six

Reagan

Dumb Girl. Dumb. Dumb. Dumb.

"LOOK AT ME." CHASE'S FINGERS GRIP MY CHIN, and I flinch as he tilts my head, forcing me to make eye contact. "I'm sorry. I don't know what came over me."

My nose stings as tears threaten. "There's no excuse for putting your hands on me, Chase."

"And you're right. I am a louse of a man for touching you like that. But my jealousy got the best of me. To think of someone else getting to touch what's mine—to imagine Linc and you behind my back—angers me. You're mine, Pet. Not his. Not anyone else's." He sighs and softens his stare. "Tell me you forgive me."

Jealousy is no excuse. He can't talk himself out of this one. "Chase…"

"Please, Pet," he begs. "I love you. Let me show you how sorry I am."

I close my eyes as he brushes his fingertips down

my cheek. I can't bear to look at him when he spits those tainted words in my face, like that's going to fix things. His touch feels cold, unlike when Linc had his hands on me. The way his chest felt pressed against my naked one. Pieces of last night have been slowly coming back. The way he carried me into my room. The way he confessed to always wanting to be with me. The comfort I felt knowing he would never hurt me physically or emotionally.

I shouldn't have asked him to stay with me, but I needed him. And waking up this morning made me realize that I may need him more than before.

"Chase, I can't—"

Chase places his thumb over my lips, silencing my words. "Don't make any decisions now. Think about it. Let me show you how much you mean to me. I promise, nothing like that will happen again." He motions for the roses. "I brought those as a peace offering—to show you just how sorry I was." Then he smirks. "Besides, you have to forgive me. What will your family say if they find out you broke my heart?"

His lame attempt at a joke has my mind churning with thoughts. What *will* my family say? My mother will be heartbroken that I let the best catch—in her eyes—go. My brothers will be mad, thinking I wasted a good thing. No one would believe me if I said Chase was the bad guy.

Perfect Chase.

I close my eyes, fighting back tears. He's right. My family would be disappointed in me.

"We can work through this," he assures me in his normal, reasonable Chase way. "Let's get some dinner later and we can go see that movie you've been dying to see."

Fight, Reagan. Fight for what you want. Don't worry about what others will think.

He leans in and places a small kiss to my forehead. "Maybe we can pick up where we left off that one day on your couch. Please forgive me." Another kiss to my nose. "This is me begging, Pet. Forgive me." He places one last kiss to my numb lips and pulls away at the sound of his phone chirping.

Pulling it from his slacks, he checks the message and steps away. "This is important. We will continue this later. Are we okay?"

I can't do anything but stare at him. How can he think we are good? We are most definitely not okay. But how can I just stand here and say nothing? Because I'm a forgiving person and everyone deserves a second chance. *Just like Jimmy and Phil and Josh?*

He doesn't wait for my response. He leans in placing a quick peck to my lips. "I'll see you at work. Love you." And then he is walking out of my house.

I squeeze my eyes shut, fighting back the tears of guilt, shame, disappointment that I couldn't just stand up to him. I couldn't tell him we were done. My fists squeeze tight, and I hold my breath trying to fight off the anger inside me. It's when I break that I know I can't take any more. I throw my head back and scream. I scream so loud, if my neighbors weren't old and deaf, they would be concerned.

Feeling no release, I turn, looking for anything in sight to destroy. I spot the exaggerated array of roses he brought, sitting in the middle of the kitchen table. A peace offering. *Well, I'm not feeling very peaceful.* Without thought, I storm over to them, and with one swift motion, I toss them off my counter and watch them slowly crash to the floor. The vase shatters instantly as the roses and water flood my kitchen floor.

I'm heaving, trying to catch my breath as I stare at the mess. I glance at the table where the flowers once stood and I notice the stolen coffee mug holding two vibrant yellow daffodils. I suddenly can't pull my eyes away.

Two beautiful flowers.

Immediately, I know where they came from. My heart begins to steady at the comforting thought of *us.* Reagan and Linc. Easy. Fun. Best friends. Safe. Thick as thieves.

The mug makes me laugh because we *are* thieves. For each other's heart. Why can't life be fair? Why does what I want have to be so complicated? Why can't everyone else see what I see? A man with such a big heart. Wounded by the mistakes he regrets and the dream to be someone better. I don't see him as the troubled soul he makes himself out to be. I see him as this kind man, who would do anything for the people he loves. A man who has suffered and is aching to be loved. He isn't your typical white-collar guy who strives for success, has his life together, or demands power. He's easygoing. He enjoys the simple things in life. Laughs at himself and doesn't take life too seriously.

He's the comfort I crave in a world where everyone expects something of me. To be perfect. Successful to make the right choices, not the choices I want.

The tears start to flow, causing the vision of these beautiful flowers to fog. "I just want you," I whisper, admitting it to the ghosts in the room. I want Linc. I want him to be the person I wake up to, the person who makes my days brighter. The one who tells me to be who I want to be and makes sure I stand by it. I want him to be the person who makes me feel whole. And I know he would do just that.

But I just don't know how that would affect the people around me. I begin to cry harder, knowing how unfair life is. Will my family accept my decision? Will Linc even accept me? I bend down, not paying attention to the shattered glass, and I try picking up the mess. Red begins to cover my fingers from the sharp edges of the glass, and I don't even realize the pain until the noticeable amount of blood begins to cover my floor.

I finish cleaning up the mess, and before walking out of my kitchen, I press my nose to the daffodils, taking in their sweet scent. I have to make a choice. I can't keep being the person everyone expects me to be. If I do, it will cost me my happiness. Am I willing to sacrifice my own happiness to meet everyone else's expectations?

I drive to work in a fog. My eyes burn from crying. My palms sting pressed against my steering wheel from the cuts I got from the glass. I should have called out sick. For all people know, I'm sick. But then again I *am* sick. Love sick, heart sick, decision sick.

I get into work and make my way to my office. Passing Ram's office, I hear laughter. Two familiar voices. I backtrack and lean against the open doorframe while I watch my brother and Linc, my two best friends, laugh and cut up, pointing at some drawings.

I don't make myself noticed as I watch them interact with such ease. As if they've been friends for a lifetime. Ram compliments Linc on an idea he makes while Linc beams with pride. I swipe the tear that rolls down my cheek just before Ram lifts his head, catching me as I attempt to sneak away.

"Hey you," my brother calls out, concern flickering in his eyes. "Spying on us?"

I take in a deep breath and plaster a smile on my face. "Of course not. Making sure you two are behaving."

Ram seems to examine me and doesn't miss a beat. "Have you been crying?"

At that, Linc's shoulder tense. He's on alert, and I know he's about to bolt from his seat to come to my rescue. I quickly offer him the silent, *I'm fine* look, so he'll stay calm. "Yeah, I was listening to some sappy audio book. Got to the best part just before I got to work. Stupid romance novels."

I know Linc doesn't believe me. He knows me better. So does Ram. My brother continues to scrutinize me, as if he will get more answers from continuing to assess me. I flash him a wide smile, hiding my emotions. "Okay, well onwards to work I go! Have fun, boys!" I turn to leave but Ram calls my name.

"Reagan, by the way, Dani is really excited for Saturday. Seems like your beau is going to show us a good time. I think if you don't marry him, Mom is going to." He chuckles, but I can't find it in me to find any humor in the situation.

I make the cruel mistake of glancing at Linc. His jaw is set tight, and I can see his hands forming into white fists.

I can't do this.

With a wave to them both, I turn and rush to my office.

I hide in my office for the rest of the day. I tell Clara that I do not want to be disturbed for anything so I don't have to face Linc when he leaves my brother's office. I fill my schedule with fake meetings, so when Chase tries to make lunch plans with me, he sees how terribly busy I am.

And I *am* busy. Busy trying to figure out my life.

So far, the best plan is to move to Antarctica and become a deep-sea fisherman, where I don't even need to worry about having a sex life, because I will smell like raw sea life. *Ew.* Lesbianism crosses my mind. My new Tumblr girlfriend would make a good companion. But then again, I would probably want more after a while. Five seconds just wouldn't stay fulfilling forever.

I go as low as debating internally on marrying Chase and making my whole family proud of me. That only causes me to start crying all over again.

I think about a life with Linc. A life where my family disowns me and we pick up and travel, doing whatever the heck we want. I venture far enough into my fantasy to where we are naming our three kids when Clara buzzes in, letting me know my two o'clock is ready for me.

I end up making it through my day, avoiding all my problems, but I know it will be impossible to avoid them once I get home. One reason being that I temporarily live with one of them. Not that Linc is a problem. He is a solution in so many ways. I just don't know how to make the equation result into a positive one.

When I finally get home, and see his car isn't here, I grab some food from my pantry and lock myself in my room. Hours later, I hear him come home. I'm curious where he's been, but I refuse to give in to my temptations. If I do, I will end up pretending I am dying of an illness and ask to sleep in his bed… Naked because… well, because of the illness.

Knock. Knock. Knock.

I'm startled from thoughts of us tangled naked under the sheet when he bangs on the door. A quick glance at the clock tells me it's after nine. I throw my covers over my head so he won't hear me breathe. As if he has ultra-sensitive hearing.

A few minutes pass and I hear him go into his room, shutting the door. Disappointment settles in my chest as I turn to my side and peek out from the covers. I stare at the wall we share. Such a simple barrier. Even though I refuse to face him right now, a small part of me wishes he'd just bang down my door to see me.

I swear, a girl's mind is never sane.

I lie with the covers pulled to my chin, listening for any movement. I'm curious as to what he's doing. Is he going straight to bed? Wondering about what I'm doing? Using his fist to work out all the tension we've seemed to build between one another since he moved in a few days ago? *Okay, perv!* My self-reprimanding still doesn't stop me from thinking it. Maybe I can set my vibrator to low and get off too—

The chirping of my phone interrupts my grand plan. I grab it off my nightstand and see Linc's name across my screen.

Abraham L: I did something today. It was naughty. But also self-fulfilling.

My emotions jam into my throat. If he is going to share a sex story about him and some woman with me, I don't know if I can handle it.

Abraham L: I wanted to show you, but you're sleeping. If you wake up and want to see it, text me. But I must warn you... Once you see it, you will be considered an accomplice to my naughty ways.

Now he's got my attention. I'm unsure if showing me some pictures of him doing something raunchy would make me an accomplice, but now I can't stop thinking about what it might be. Forgetting I'm *sleeping*, I send a text back.

Me: Let me have it.

Abraham L: Ahhh, Sleeping Beauty is awakened by the lust for being bad. Acknowledge that you are just as naughty if you see it.

Jesus.

Me: I acknowledge, just show me.

Abraham L: No closing your eyes after you've seen it. You can't pretend you didn't see.

I roll my eyes as the small smile spreads across my face. Always making such a production.

Me: Promise. I'm just as naughty as you are.

Okay, maybe I should have rephrased that last text.

Ugh. I toss myself onto my back. Why did I just have to write that—

Just then the chirp sounds, notifying me of the incoming text. I brace myself for what I'm about to see. If it's him with another chick, then I'll probably cry myself to sleep and realize that whatever fantasies I have are just make-believe and move on. I will maybe marry Chase or move to Antarctica, where I can live the reminder of my life in sorrow. I take a deep breath and swipe open the text.

Abraham L: <PHOTO ATTACHED>

The gasp, then sound of my laughter, echoes throughout my room. The picture is of Linc holding a miniature statue. He *did* not steal that.

Me: He's going to kill you if he finds out you stole that. My mother gave that to him.

Abraham L: Well then, he kills us both. Accomplices remember? #thieves

I can't help but giggle. My mom gave Roman a porcelain statue of a mother and son holding hands for his thirtieth birthday, because yes, he is a big baby. And Roman being the momma's boy he is, *loved* it. I swear I even saw a tear when he opened the darn thing. If I'm not mistaken, the real reason his last secretary got fired was because she knocked it off his desk, almost breaking off the son's head.

Me: You're so bad.

Abraham L: I'd like to consider myself thoughtful. It's important a garden has a good array of trinkets. Just doing my friendly part for Saturday's extravaganza.

I almost forgot about Saturday. The day I've been looking forward to ever since I coerced him into helping me. I should cancel. I shouldn't make him help me when I just plan on moving across the world before the plants even sprout. All that work for nothing. It's also probably not a good idea for us to be so close to each other. In the September heat, getting dirty as he digs holes shirtless, with his muscles flexing and his tattoos on full display.

Yeah.

Bad idea.

Cancel, Reagan.

Me: Glad you don't want to disappoint me. I have high expectations for Saturday.

Dumb girl.

Dumb.

Dumb.

Dumb.

It's clear I enjoy torturing myself. Not only did I *not* cancel my off-the-record date with Linc, but I spent the remainder of the week egging it on! I did my duty of avoiding both men on Thursday and Friday. But at night, I would lie in bed while Linc sent me text messages of plants he'd researched or trinkets he'd thought would look best for our masterpiece. I about peed myself when he sent over a picture of Roman's electric shaver—not even wanting to know how he snatched that—and scolded him for the bath toys he took of Molly's. I made him put those back, not caring how he did it, but after a good lecture, he said they were no longer part of our plan.

Now that Saturday has finally rolled around, I can't stop feeling so antsy. I'm nervous about our day. I can't explain why. It isn't a date or anything. It's just two buddies planting a garden. But it is also the first time I have seen him since Wednesday morning. He was gone when I woke up this morning, claiming that he had to run an errand. It allowed me the time to change my outfit a trillion times, fix my hair double that, and apply four different colors of lip gloss.

What is *wrong* with me? I need to calm down.

But I can't.

I'm so nervous.

And for some completely silly reason, I want to impress Linc.

I adjust my new peach summer dress—debating on whether or not it's *the one*—when I hear his car pull into the driveway. "Oh, heck. You're being ridiculous." I pull myself away from my mirror and greet him at the door.

As soon as I open the door, his green eyes skim over my appearance. A dimple forms on one side as he grins crookedly at me. God, that smile always does me in.

"Well, look at you," he says and winks at me. "A blossoming peach on a hot summer day." Linc gives me a playful whistle as he carries in a tray of coffee and a bag of donuts from our favorite small café a few blocks from my house.

"Oh, this thing? It's old and I didn't want to ruin any of my good clothes."

Linc shrugs his shoulders as he saunters into the kitchen. "New or not, it looks sexy on you."

I can hear the appreciation in his voice and it's

anything but joking. Heat floods through me. I blush at his back, the compliment making me practically dizzy on my feet. I begin walking after him when I see something hanging from my side. My eyes widen, a small cuss word leaving my lips as I rip the store tag off the dress. I crumble it up and stick it in my pocket. "So… Um, what should we do first? I assume start tilling."

Linc drops the items on my counter and pulls out one of the delicious-looking donuts from the bag. He turns offering me his dangerous, dimpled smile, the one that probably burns the panties off all women, and slowly stalks over to me. My heartrate quickens and my body temperature sky-rockets.

What is he doing?

He's now so close to me that I can smell his cologne, which makes my nipples perk. Bending down to meet me at eye level, he lifts his hand, and brings a donut up to my lips.

Oh, God.

This is not sexual.

This is just *a donut.*

I am just *opening my mouth to take a bite. Of a donut.*

Focus, Reagan.

My lips part as he places the mouthwatering old-fashioned glazed donut on my lips, allowing me to take a small bite. All harmless.

Until I moan.

His gaze darkens and drops to my mouth. "Perfect," he says, his voice husky. "Right?"

I have a feeling there is double meaning all over that comment. I take a step back. "Uh, yeah. They sure know how to glaze a donut."

His jaw clenches as he stares at me with heat-filled eyes for a moment longer than a best friend should. With a shake of his head, he sticks the donut in his mouth, taking a large bite, and turns back, grabbing the coffee before heading toward my back door. "We're burning daylight, Rey. Let's go get dirty." And with that, he's out the door.

God, dirty doesn't even describe my wrong, *oh-so-wrong*, brain right now.

We are two hours into our garden day and I'm kicking myself for not setting up a secret video camera in my backyard and recording Lincoln Carter getting dirty. I've taken about a gazillion breaks to get water because I needed to cool off. As in cool my body temperature by fanning my darn lady parts. I've imagined jumping on him, tearing his pants off, clawing at his skin, using the garden hose in the crudest of ways and last, but not worst, having him shove me into our freshly tilled soil and getting me so dirty that I die of the best orgasm of my life.

It's settled.

I have major issues, and it's a good thing I'm moving to Antarctica.

I do want to point out, for the record, that Linc is not so innocent. That bastard knows what he's doing. He knew what he was doing when he took his shirt off, claiming he didn't want to dirty himself any more than he'd planned to, and that my eyes would take interest in his bare chest. And he knew what he was doing when he asked me to stand in front of him to "block the sun," because that was merely so I'd have a front-row view to his bulging muscles as he pushed the tiller through the soil. It was as if he was tempting me to lose my control and attack him. Some friend he was being.

We took a break to eat lunch, where I made us some turkey sandwiches. We ate on the lawn while chatting about this and that. I commented on him having a different car, to which he explained he was just bored with it and wanted something different. I brought up him meeting with my brother, but he just brushed it off, saying it was nothing and if it turned into something I would be the first to know. Lastly, I tried prying into where he goes all day but he seemed less than willing to fork up that information. I told myself it was none of my business so I let it go.

One day, I'm going to make him tell me everything.

But since I'm carrying around my own little secrets, I can't exactly demand he divulge all of his.

Once we finish and clean up, it's time to plant.

"What the hell is all this shit, anyway?" Linc asks while picking up a tray of red peppers. "Are you planning to live off the land for the rest of your life?" He smirks at me. "Or are you just wanting to plant this crap so you can take a selfie and hashtag something eco-friendly for all your friends to know you love your earth? #CucumbersSaveLives."

I laugh and swat him with my hand held rototiller. "No, you nerd. Those are peppers and some are vegetables, some are fruits, and some are herbs. It'll help save money and trips to the grocery store for one tomato or a tablespoon of basil."

He's just staring at me like I've grown two heads. "Basil? For what? You don't cook."

"Yes, I do!" I reply, shocked. "I love to cook."

"You've never cooked for me," he says with a faux pout. "And pouring Fireball down my throat is not the same thing." At that, he snorts with laughter.

With my hands on my hips, I give him my best *you don't know what you're talking about* look. "Well maybe you never asked me," I argue. "Tell me next time you're hungry, and I will."

Sometimes I just want to stick my foot in my mouth. Because that just gave Linc the invitation to look me up and down, his eyes gleaming wickedly. "I'm hungry."

And I'm now as wet as a slip-n-slide.

"Well…n-no food until you finish." I break eye contact and bend over to pick up a tray of cherry tomatoes. I won't deny that it may have accidently given Linc a peep show down the front of my dress. I hand him the row and he grabs for it purposely brushing his fingers along mine.

Okay!

"I think I need a water break. I'll be right back." I drop the empty container and start hurrying towards my back door. It's then I feel the rigid coldness slam at my back. I screech as I turn. Linc is holding the hose spraying me. "What the hell!?"

"You said you needed a water break. I wanted to save you the trouble of having to go all the way inside. It's like the thirty-seventh time you've done that. It leaves me all alone, and I miss you."

My mouth is still in the O-shape from the shock of his move. I can't believe he would—

Another attack hits me when he sprays me directly in the chest, soaking my dress. "Linc!"

"Yes?"

"That's cold!" I bark, stomping toward him.

"Then it's doing its job," he says, his tone matter-of-fact. "Do you feel cool yet?" He sprays me again, but this time in the face. I scream, trying to block the spray, while I sprint toward him. He must forget that I was raised with two older brothers. I make it to him and jump. I tackle him, and he bursts out laughing in shock. My bold move manages to distract him into dropping the hose. It also manages to make him slide in the now-soaked soil and slip. We both go down, him turning so he takes the brunt of the fall. Once in the soiled garden, he flips us so I'm now in the mud, pinning my hands down so I don't try and harm him.

Our eyes meet for a heated moment.

Even the icy cold water can't cool me down.

"Good thing you wore that old dress. Would have hated to get such a pretty new thing so muddy," he says, his voice a little bit hoarse. *My* voice is stuck in my throat, unable to find any comeback. I can't stop thinking about how good his hard body feels on top of mine. And it's impossible not to acknowledge the hardness resting on my hip.

With nothing coming out of our mouths, it leaves us silent—with only our eyes doing the talking.

I want him to kiss me. I want with every fiber in my soul for him to place his lips on mine. I know he wants to. His eyes are on fire and they're blazing with need.

"Linc..." I say breathlessly. Out of warning or need, I'm not sure. I want this. Him. But I want it to be right. I don't want it to be while I'm not available, fully. "You're lying on my freshly planted peppers."

And our connection breaks.

He must have seen the battle in my eyes. I'm thankful and disappointed at the same time. He lifts his finger and slowly wipes a chunk of mud off my cheek. When he does the same to the other side, I realize what he's doing.

"Linc..." I say his name again, this time in warning.

"What? You'd make a good warrior. Princess Pepper Destroyer." His laugh fills my entire backyard as I lift my hand and sucker punch him in the ribs. He rolls off me, lying on his back in the mud, not giving a care about getting dirty.

I sit up looking around us.

"We're a mess." Literally and figuratively.

Linc turns his head to me. "Did you want me to spray you off?"

I give him an eye roll and stand. He laughs and joins me.

We silently plant the rest of the garden until the last tray of mint and basil are underground. I don't know where his mind is but mine is completely on him.

"It looks perfect." I slap my hands together, discarding the soil buildup on my hands. We're standing next to each other, observing our masterpiece.

Linc throws the shovel and swipes a layer of sweat off his brow. "We're not done yet."

I look around, not seeing anything else to plant. I'm

about to ask him what we missed when he takes off, returning with a handful of items.

My smile explodes across my face as I begin shaking my head.

"Don't shake your head at me, woman. Hold these." He hands me Roman's statue, the razor, and a few other random items he's seemed to steal from my brother along the way. Bending down, he takes Roman's nine iron and jams it into the soil. I begin handing him each item, and with each one, he places it sporadically throughout the garden.

I can't help but cover my mouth and giggle the whole time, until the last item is placed. Once complete, Linc stands wiping off his hands, and turns to me. "Now it's done. Garden of Thievery we shall call it."

I smile and nod, because I think it's perfect.

"Well, it's getting late and I'm hungry," he says, mischief dancing in his eyes as he rubs his dirty, sculpted abs. "I'm pretty sure you said all I had to do was tell you and you would feed me."

I smile at his obvious antics. "You're correct. For all your hard work, I'll feed you. Anything you want." Ugh, foot in mouth, *again.* "You grocery shop, I cook. Deal?" I try and save myself, which I do. I stick my hand out and we shake on it. His hand is warm in mine, and I don't want to let go.

But I do.

I always let him go.

We go inside and take our showers, separately of course, and when I make a grocery list filled with ingredients for the fettuccini Alfredo with sausage meatballs and spinach with grated Parmesan cheese he requested, I hand him my list and he's off.

After blow drying my hair and slipping into a pair of tight black yoga pants and a flimsy bright yellow tank top, I play around in my kitchen, pulling out pots and pans, searching for dry herbs and any random items I'll need for Linc's over-the top-meal. I get a good look out my kitchen window which overlooks the backyard and laugh at the golf club sticking out of the ground. "Roman is going to kill me when he sees that."

But for some reason, I don't care. It's worth it. I can't stop smiling at each and every memory of today. My cheeks burn thinking about the parts of Linc that shouldn't be on my mind. As I pull down the strainer from a cabinet, there's one thought that's playing on repeat in my mind.

Lincoln makes me happy.

The happy that everyone wishes for.

He's the first face I see when I have something important to share. Who I want to confide in. He's the person I want to spend my time with, laugh with, be with. I want to be with Linc. I know it and feel it so deep in my bones. If he feels differently, then so be it. But I can't continue living this lie. The one where I pretend *not* to be in love with my best friend. I hear my front door open and close. It's too soon for Linc to be back.

"Did you forget something?" I call out.

I turn and see Chase storm into my kitchen all decked out in his golfer garb. "Where the hell were you today?"

His tone startles me, causing me to retreat a few

steps back. Chase's normally calm features are contorted into an expression of rage. His face is bright red and his chest heaves with his breaths.

"I-I was here," I stammer. I'm completely caught off-guard by his intrusion. "I told you, I had stuff to do around the—"

"You *had* to be with me today," he snarls. "You stood me up in front of your entire family!" He raises his voice and his eyes darken. I'm reminded quickly of the Chase I saw in his office earlier this week and it begins to unnerve me.

"I'm sorry but I told you—"

My words get caught in my throat when he seizes me, both hands gripping my throat. Rather forcefully, he pushes me against the wall. He isn't easy on me. His fingers digging into my skin will undoubtedly result in bruising. "I did *all* this for you. You think I enjoyed carting your family around? You were supposed to be there. Showing your family how devoted you are to *me*!" he seethes, spittle spraying my face.

"Ch-Chase, let me go," I choke out. "You're hurting me."

His grip tightens to the point where I'm having trouble breathing. I claw at his fingers. "Good," he snaps. "Maybe then you'll understand that standing me up was selfish. You looked like such a child. A stubborn, petulant child." He takes my body and slams me against the wall. "Is that what you've become? A child?" Again, another slam. With each shove, he threatens to knock the wind out of me. I begin fighting in his grip. "Need someone to teach you how to behave?"

My breath hisses from me as I struggle to say my words that are filled with venom. "Let me go, you asshole."

He laughs but it's far from funny. His rage has intensified with each passing second. "The mouth on you now, Pet. Did you pick that up from your stray dog? Is he teaching you his filth?" He slams me once more against the wall, this time causing me to gasp for air because it feels as though he crushes my windpipe.

When he loosens his grip, I rasp out my words. "That stray dog is a billion times more of a man than you will ever be, you fucking piece of—"

His free hand raises and thrashes across my face, his knuckles cracking against my mouth. I wince at the searing pain in my lip, automatically feeling the wetness of blood as it runs down my chin. My knees buckle beneath me as stars dance around me.

At seeing his handy work, he quickly releases me and steps back. I grab at my neck, trying to suck in as much air as I can while trying not to collapse.

"Y-You do this to me," he stammers out as he spears his fingers through his hair, messing it up. His crazed eyes meet mine. "*You* make me do this."

I'm starting to shake. I wipe my chin and pull my hand away to find it covered in blood. When my eyes meet his, I shoot him the most hateful glare I can muster. *Be brave, Reagan. You deserve better.* "Get out of my house," I rasp out. "We're done. And if you're smart, you'll put in your notice before my brothers get wind of this." I stand my ground despite the trembling that overtakes me, hoping he backs down before I do.

He stares blankly at me as if he's still trying to process what just happened.

"I said GET OUT!" I choke out tearfully and point toward the door.

His brows furrow together. "We're not done here."

I glare at him until he turns and leaves.

The moment I hear my front door slam, my body begins to shake uncontrollably. I slide down the wall, collapsing onto the floor before breaking down in sobs.

I need my best friend.

I need Linc.

Chapter Seven

Linc

An Eternity of Not Enough

I STARE IN THE REARVIEW MIRROR AS I DRIVE FROM THE grocery store back to Reagan's. The same black Chevy Impala has been following me since I pulled out of the parking lot. It isn't Louie's usual ride, but I don't put anything past him. I'm tired of these fuckers infesting my damn town.

Speeding up, I weave in and out of traffic before quickly turning down a side road into a neighborhood. I whip down the street and double back the way I came. When I'm finally sure I lost the fucker, I hurry back to Reagan's.

Today has been perfect.

Just the two of us. Alone.

No stupid fucking Chase.

And despite her words, her expressions and actions spoke volumes. Reagan is affected by me. Whenever she looks at me, heat flickers in her eyes. I know the way I feel deep down about her isn't unrequited.

She wants me just as much as I want her.

One day soon, she will see it.

I'll be able to convince her we'd be good together.

I'm just so damn sure of it.

A smile plays at my lips as I plan on ways to flirt with her while she cooks for me. But as soon as I pull into the driveway, it's wiped right from my face. Chase comes storming out of the house, his face bright red and angry.

What the fuck?

I throw the car in park beside his and jump out, snagging my two sacks quickly. After I kick the door shut, I stalk his way.

"She's all yours," he sneers as his shoulder clips mine when he walks past me. "That is, until she stops throwing her temper tantrum."

I set the bags on the bottom step and storm over to him. He slings his car door open, but I grip the top before he can close it. "The fuck you say?" I demand, glowering at him.

He tries and fails to close the door. "I said she's all yours," he bites out. "Pet needs a pet. A dirty little stray like yourself."

"It's a good thing we're roommates then," I snarl, my tone mocking. "I like when she scratches behind my ears each night. Makes me want to lick her."

With a fury I've never seen before, he slams his fist on his steering wheel. "I fucking knew it! Not only is she a child, she's also a cheating whore!"

I'm so pissed that I nearly send my fist through the window, but a black Impala slowly drives by at that exact moment. I stare at the vehicle, trying desperately to see in the tinted windows, when Chase manages to yank the door out of my grip. He's already pulling out of the driveway before I can stop him.

He squeals off down the street, and I have half a mind to go after him. But right now, I need to see how Reagan's feeling after their obvious blowout. Chase is such a pussy. He better not have said anything mean to her, like he spewed at me. She doesn't deserve that.

I snag up the bags and stalk inside. I'm not sure who was in the Impala but I'm certain if it were Louie, my ass would be dead. Louie doesn't simply drive by. No, this was someone else.

"Rey," I call out. "Everything okay? I just saw that douchebag and—"

The first thing that reaches my ears is the sound of her sniffling. When I step into the kitchen, I have trouble processing the scene in front of me. Reagan lies sprawled out in the middle of the floor, sobbing as she clutches her neck. I slam the bags on the counter and drop to my knees beside her.

I knew I should have dragged that motherfucker out of his car and given him a beat down he'd never forget.

"Talk to me Rey," I grit out, my voice on edge as I stroke her dark hair from her face so I can see her. Her bottom lip is bloody. "Did he hurt you? What happened?"

Her entire body trembles but she doesn't respond. That's when I see the bright red markings on her throat that are quickly turning purple.

"THAT MOTHERFUCKER!" I roar, making her jump. "I'M GOING TO KILL HIM!"

She seems to snap into action and scrambles up, right into my lap, locking her arms around my neck. Her legs wrap around me as she squeezes me tight. "D-Don't l-leave me."

My heart sinks. She's so broken. That asshole broke her. I'm going to slaughter him.

I rub my palms up and down her back. My lips press kisses to her bruised throat as if I have the ability to make it all disappear. I would erase it all if I could.

"I'm so sorry," I whisper against her flesh. "I should have known."

She shakes her head but her sobs grow louder. It's true. The signs were there. The stupid-ass pet name. The emotional abuse of controlling her by standing her up all the time and making her feel bad if she complained. The goddamned terror in her eyes when he came over Wednesday morning. She wasn't afraid that something might have happened between us—she was afraid I was going to leave her alone with him.

I did.

I fucking left her.

Never again.

If the motherfucker even looks at her, I'm going to choke him with my hands. Then he can learn what it feels like when someone bigger than you exerts their strength over you. And I won't stop. I'll choke the life right out of him.

Just wait until Ram and Roman catch wind of this.

Chase is going to have a trio of raging bulls after him.

"Are you hurt?" I ask, my eyes closing as I kiss her

neck. “Do I need to take you to the hospital?”

She pulls away and shakes her head in vehemence. “N-No! They’ll find out!”

I stare at her in confusion as I gently stroke her battered throat. “Sweetheart, who? Who will find out? And who the fuck cares? You’re hurt.”

“No,” she says more firmly through her sobs. “I just…I can’t deal with their disappointment. I fucked up again. I mess up with every relationship. It’s my fault and—”

“This is not your fault.” My tone is deadly. “Pricks like Chase prey on nice girls like you. You were a victim, Rey.” I hug her tight against me. “Not anymore. I won’t let anyone hurt you ever again.”

She relaxes against me. “Thank you. Promise me you won’t tell them. No matter what. My brothers. My mom. Please.”

I frown as I pull away. “I won’t betray you,” I vow. “Let me get this food put away and then we’ll talk more. Okay?”

She nods and releases me as she slides to her bottom on the floor. I’m just standing when the front door slings open. If that motherfucker is back, so help me, I’ll ruin his pretty face. Red hot fury surges through me, and I fist my hands. I’m just charging away from Reagan when her two brothers walk into the kitchen.

Ram’s jaw drops open as he gapes at the scene before him.

Roman doesn’t take a moment to think. He just acts. His fist cuts through the air, and I don’t have a chance to block it. Pain slices across my bottom lip the moment he punches me. With as much force as he hits me—even for a pretty boy wearing a bright orange polo—I don't stagger away or fall down. I'm still too blitzed out on rage over Chase. I snarl like a beast.

"It's not what you think!" Reagan screams at Roman.

He's already rearing his fist back again when Ram yanks him back. Roman and I stare each other down.

"You fucking hit my sister!" he bellows, fighting against Ram's grip.

Reagan climbs to her feet and wobbles. I immediately slip my arm around her waist, pulling her to me to keep her from falling. This seems to infuriate Roman more because it's all Ram can do to keep him from killing me.

"Roman!" Reagan cries out, her fingers gripping my shirt tight. "I said it's not what you think. I-I…" she trails off. "I fell."

I close my eyes and my nostrils flare.

"Unbelievable," Roman hisses. "You're fucking covering for him?"

"Reagan," Ram barks. "You didn't fall. Tell us what happened."

She starts crying harder. I snap my eyes open and pin them with a glare. "Just leave her alone. She'll call you when she's feeling better."

Ram frowns, his eyes flickering with unspoken words. I can tell he's putting together a different picture than what Roman's seeing.

"No!" Roman growls. "You're getting the fuck out of her house. We're going to call the cops and have your carnie ass arrested! I don't care if you're my wife's brother. I don't give a goddamn because that's my sister you just crossed the line with."

"Leave," Reagan hisses at him, fire in her voice. "I love you, but you need to leave right now."

Hurt and confusion flash in Roman's dark gaze. "Reagan…"

"NO!" she screeches and breaks from my grip to shove at her brother. "I want you to go."

Ram frowns at me but his eyes don't hold the same accusatory stare as his older brother's. "You heard our little sis, man. Let's go. When everyone has calmed the hell down, we'll talk about this like normal adults."

Roman's chest still heaves but some of his anger at me seems to have dissolved. He's missing part of the picture and deep down he seems to know it. His gaze darts past me to the window.

"Is that?" he asks, confusion in his tone. "Is that my nine iron?"

"Please go," Reagan murmurs before pushing past them to head toward the front door.

Ram tugs at Roman and manages to drag him through the house. Before they leave, Roman jerks out of Ram's grip and points at me. "I don't know what happened, but mark my words, I will find out. And so help me, if you're the cause—"

He doesn't get to finish that statement because Ram pulls him out of the house. Reagan slams the door behind them and twists the lock into place. I stalk over to her and pull her into my arms.

"I'm sorry," she murmurs against my chest as I hug her. "He hit you…because I didn't tell him the truth…"

"I can handle Roman."

"I should have told them…" she trails off. "Dammit! I should have just told them. I was just…"

I smooth down her hair and kiss the top of her head. My lip hurts but it doesn't stop me from providing comfort to my girl. "It's fine, Rey. Tell them in your own time."

She sags against me. "I'm so exhausted."

"I know, beautiful. Let's get you to bed."

I slip my arm beneath her ass and scoop her up into my arms. She's silent, aside from the occasional hiccup, as I stride through the house to her room. When I reach her bed, I shove a bunch of clothes that were piled up onto the floor. Then yank back the covers. My shoes get kicked off before I'm climbing into the bed with her. Once we're settled, I bring the covers up over us.

She's on her back, her teary eyes searching mine as I lie on my side beside her. My gaze skims over her pretty face, lingering at her slightly swollen lip that now sports a small split, then down to her throat. I hate the purple marks there. He fucking choked her. And not even in the hot, I-love-you kind of way.

In the abusive way.

Fucking psycho.

Her palm touches my cheek, and the rage instantly cools several degrees. "Thank you."

"For what?" I demand, the anger back in a flash. "I didn't do anything."

"You did everything. You are…everything."

The need to comfort her is intense. She's mine. Never his. At least not in her heart. My lips brush against hers.

Our eyes lock and I can't help but touch her gorgeous face. Her skin feels so goddamned soft. So perfect. Mine.

Her heart always belonged to me.

It still does.

"Kiss me, Linc," she pleads, her voice soft.

I don't wait for her to repeat that request. My lips capture hers, a little too harshly, considering we're both suffering from painful, busted lips. I devour her with a kiss that has promise after promise wrapped up in it. When she lets out a moan, I deepen our kiss. Her taste is sweet and simply her.

My Reagan.

We make out desperately for what seems like forever and just a moment all at once. An eternity of not enough. Our hands are all over each other. Exploring feverishly. So long overdue.

"I need to touch you," I murmur.

Again, I don't even await confirmation before I'm pulling her yellow tank top up her body. She lifts up to assist me. I toss it away before cupping her full tit through her nude-colored, lacy bra. A moan ripples from her, which has me needing to be closer to her. I slide between her thighs and her legs lock around me. The moment my stone-hard cock rubs against her pussy through her yoga pants, we both groan like animals.

"I knew you'd be perfect," I murmur against her mouth. My hands roam all over her but it's still not enough. Now that I'm touching her like I want, I can't decide where to start and I certainly don't want to stop.

"Your jeans," she whines. "Ugh. Make them go away."

I chuckle against her mouth and sit up on my knees

to unbuckle my pants. Her legs remain wrapped around my hips. "Make your bra go away," I challenge back with a lopsided grin.

She smiles beautifully back at me as she fumbles to remove it. Seconds later, my shirt and jeans are gone. I peel away her yoga pants. All that stands between us are my boxers and her silky black panties. I pounce on her again. Once our mouths fuse together, I grind against her, loving the fact that I can now feel the lips of her pussy against my dick. I've dreamt about this moment for so long.

I want to make it last.

To hold on to it for as long as I can.

Lifting away from her face, I regard her pretty tearstained features. My palm cups her full breast in a reverent way. When my thumb drags across her nipple, she gasps. Desire and happiness and love shine her gaze. I've never seen her look more beautiful.

"Rey…" So many words claw their way up my throat. All I can do is say one. "Rey."

She smiles and runs her fingers through my hair. "Linc."

"This," I murmur as I push against her clit with my cock, making her hiss, "is a long time coming. You ready for something real, sweetheart?"

She nods. "I'm beyond ready. I've wanted this for so long."

That makes two of us.

"Are you *sure*?" I breathe. After everything she's been through tonight, I don't want to push.

Her eyes glimmer with understanding. "Absolutely."

"Before I put my big cock inside you, I'm going to taste you," I tell her, my voice husky. "You still owe me a meal."

She giggles and reaches between us. Her hand pushes my boxers down so she can grab my dick. Fuck, that feels good. "Maybe I want you to starve and fuck me instead."

A growl rumbles from my chest. I pounce on her again, my mouth attacking hers. This time, my cock is free and slides against her barely-there panties. "You feel so good," I praise. "Better than I could have imagined. I'm dying to push your panties aside and shove my cock inside you. What do you think about that, Rey? You like it dirty?"

She moans. "Y-Yes."

"Condom?"

"As long as you're clean, we can do it without. I'm on the pill and I always used protection in my past. This time feels different," she murmurs, her voice shy. "I want to feel all of you. I trust you, Linc."

I rest my forehead against hers. She stares up at me as if I'm everything in her world. I've never been looked at by anyone like that in my life. "I'm clean," I assure her, "but I'm about to get you very dirty."

"I'm counting on it."

"Pull your panties to the side, dirty girl. You need my dick inside you," I tell her, a crooked grin on my face. "I'm going to fill you up with months' worth of built-up need. Is that what you want?"

She nods and pulls her panties to the side. "I want to know what it feels like. Not with just anyone. With you."

I press a kiss to her mouth and then grip my dick. The tip of my cock slides against her hot, wet slit. It's practically jumping in my hand each time it throbs with need. Slowly, I ease into her. I've never gone bareback with anyone before. Couple that with not having had sex in so long, and she feels fucking amazing.

"Jesus," I hiss, my entire body buzzing with desire. "You're perfect, Rey."

She moans and her fingers dig into my shoulders. "So are you."

I've been called a lot of things in bed but never perfect. If I wasn't balls deep in the most gorgeous woman I've ever seen, I'd beat my fists on my chest like a damn ape.

But I *am* inside her.

She's mine.

She always was.

I kiss her hard and start to thrust inside of her. Nothing slow or smooth. Ragged and needy and rough. Her fingernails claw at me as we kiss desperately. Her pussy is soaked, but I want to send her over the edge when she's wrapped around my cock. Sliding my hand between us, I locate her clit. One swipe across it, and she jolts. A whimper tries to escape her, but I drown it with a kiss that promises her the world.

She's already given me more than I could ever ask for.

It's only fair I return that to her tenfold.

Thrust after thrust, I pound into her as I circle her clit with my fingers with firm motions. She squirms and thrashes as her orgasm nears. I know the moment it hits because her body seems to grip my dick tighter than my fist ever does. Lifting up, I stare at her as she loses herself to ecstasy. Her brown lashes flutter. Her cheeks turn rosy. And her mouth parts open as her entire body trembles.

So beautiful.

Before she comes down from her high, I drive into her hard and kiss her mouth again. She shrieks against my lips as another orgasm ripples through her right on the heels of the last one. It's so erotic, I come without warning. Hot and gushing. I pour everything into her in one sexy-as-fuck moment.

We're both panting heavily, and I'm still throbbing out my release inside her when I nuzzle her nose with mine. "Did you like that, Rey?"

"Better than anything I've seen on Tumblr," she pants before she starts to giggle. "Oh, God. I could have been having this all along? What is wrong with me?"

I stroke some of her hair away from her face and kiss her sweaty forehead. "Absolutely nothing is wrong with you. Everything is so fucking right. And don't you worry, sweetheart, we're going to make up for lost time. Now that I've had you, I'm never going to be able to let you go."

Her brown eyes warm as she beams at me. "Promise?"

"You fucking betcha."

I slide out of her and sit back on my haunches admiring her just-fucked, bright red pussy. My seed trickles out of her. So goddamned beautiful.

"I'm going to fuck you in the shower now, Rey," I tell her smugly, my lips quirking up on one side. "Then make me a damn sandwich, woman. I'm starving."

She snorts and throws her pillow at me.

We spend the next ten minutes rough housing in the bed—her trying to hit me with a pillow and me trying to tickle her. It isn't long before I'm hard and inside her again.

So much for the shower.

I prefer staying dirty with my girl any day.

My girl.

I like the fucking sound of that.

Chapter Eight

Reagan

Spaghetti Sauce Is Horrible

I ROLL OVER IN BED, A SOFT GROAN LEAVING MY LIPS. I can't remember the last time I was this sore. It had to have been when Ram challenged me to the 5k race, and I had no time to physically prepare. I couldn't move off my couch for almost three days until my strained muscles finally let up on me. But then again, that time was caused by physically running for almost an hour at a speed my body really wanted to kill me for, just to win the bet with Ram. This time around, it hurts in different places, all due to the way Linc had his way with me.

I sigh into my pillow, thinking about how insanely perfect our night was. How crazy it is to think that we actually…did the deed. I giggle and open my eyes, hoping Linc is still sleeping so I can spend some time ogling him and his solid perfection. To my surprise, he's not here. A note is left in his place. I sit up and grab for the piece of paper and read through the cute chicken scratch.

Ronald-

I had to run an errand. I didn't want to wake you because I would have eaten you raw and never gotten my shit done. You're beautiful while you sleep. And even sexier while you snore. Be back as soon as I can.

-Abe

After internally denying that I snore, I can't help but laugh. Linc hates when I refer to him as our former president, Abraham Lincoln. I decided one day to poke him by giving him all sorts of nicknames, until he pulled out the, *two can play this game, Ronald.* I lost my smile really quick, but before I could retaliate, he tackled me to the ground and tickled me until I screamed Uncle. And *not* because I was giving in. I was pretty sure I had peed my pants.

I press the piece of paper to my nose, as if it will smell like Linc, and close my eyes.

I can't believe it.

Linc and I.

We finally had sex.

We stopped hiding behind our feelings, and it was the best darn move we could have ever made. I grin as I turn to my side, staring at the still indented half of my bed. Man we are two big idiots for waiting so long.

I hear my phone chiming and flip, grabbing for it on the nightstand. I bet it's Linc checking up on me. I look at the screen and see it's Andie.

Immediately, yesterday's less-than-magical events pop into my mind. Chase, the fight, Roman making the wrong conclusion as to what happened. *Shoot.* I should let her call go to voicemail. I'm not ready to explain. The call ends, and I feel a wave of relief. Until it rings again. Darn it! I know she's not going to give up. That's not Andie's style. With a deep breath, I answer.

"Hey, Andie—"

"I want details. Now."

She wastes no time, I see. "I'm not sure what details you want. Are you trying to cook Mom's lasagna recipe again? Because you know that you can't—"

"Don't play coy with me. You know what I'm talking about. *Your* brother's pissy attitude and *my* brother's busted lip. Start talking."

It would be a lot easier if she just told me what Roman told her. A small spike of anxiety settles in knowing she's seen Linc already this morning. Did he tell on me? Does Andie know about Chase? About us? "Listen, it was clearly a misunderstanding. You know Roman, always—"

"Whatever, I'm turning onto your street. I want to see your face when you explain your *misunderstanding*."

Coming over? I sit up and look around my room. "Wait! You can't." Clothes are everywhere. Linc's. Mine. Some furniture is knocked over. Partially. When we attempted the shower for the second time, we still didn't make it and ended up having sex against the wall, next to the bathroom door. We got thirsty, and God only knows what the kitchen looks like. There's no way she can see inside my house right now. Oh my God, it probably smells like sex. I had sex with her brother all over my house and she's about to smell it!

"Why can't I?"

"Because! Umm… because I'm having my carpets

cleaned. There's nowhere to sit. Let's meet at Benji's Café. I'm starved and can use some coffee."

It takes a few seconds, but I know Andie is thinking about those Danishes. "Fine. Be there in fifteen or I'm coming for you." And then the line goes dead.

Saved by the Danish. I huff and throw myself onto my back. To be honest, I never really put thought to what Andie would think or say if she found out that me and her brother got together. Would she be mad? Would she take Roman's side and want to kill him or take my side and want me to be happy? She wants her brother to be happy. But for some reason, she always seems to be reserved when it comes to him. Like even *she* knows he may be a little bit of trouble. But maybe *she* doesn't know her brother that well anymore.

With thirteen more minutes to spare, I shelve that thought for a later time so I can get ready. There's no doubt Andie will show up if I'm not on time, so I hurry and throw on a pair of yoga pants, my Jon Snow's Ho tank top and wrap a fashion scarf around my neck to cover my marks. I grab Linc's clothes and toss them into the spare room then shut it. Another topic to avoid. My new roommate. It seems we both failed to mention Linc's new living arrangements. It was a mere accident on my part. On Linc's? I'm not sure. If Andie knew, she definitely wouldn't keep quiet, which means Roman would be banging my door down, trying to rip off Linc's arms to get him out.

With a deep sigh, I head out. The café is close, so I use my last four minutes to travel and step inside just in time. The aroma of coffee slaps me in the face, in a good way, and I inhale the addiction. I turn to our normal table and notice not only is Andie sitting, but so is Dani. Great. They're going to tag team me.

"You're thirty seconds late," Andie mumbles while taking a huge bite of her beloved Danish. I look at the time and see it's been exactly fifteen minutes. "I'm actually right on—"

"Start spilling. I filled Dani in. Well, what Ram didn't tell her."

I look at Dani who is offering me her sweet sympathetic smile. The one that says *we love you and it's going to be okay*. This is not going to be fun.

Sitting, I wave to Greg the barista, who knows my order, and he gives me the *on it* head nod. I turn when Dani settles her hand on my shoulder. "Honey, are you okay? Your poor lip. Did Linc do this to—"

"Dani!" Andie snaps at her.

I stiffen at the insinuation.

"What?" Dani whines. "I'm just asking. He was the only one there. And Reagan didn't seem to point blame at anyone else."

"Well," Andie huffs. "My brother might be a fuck-up but he would never hit a woman."

"Guys…" I try and interrupt.

"I'm not saying it was but who else who do such a horrible thing?" Dani turns to me. "What has Chase said about this?" They're both looking at me, waiting for an answer, but I clearly don't have one. I'm pretty sure saying Chase is a bastard control freak who decided to have it out with my face and neck wouldn't go so well with the *We Love Chase* squad.

"Listen, guys. Linc did not hit me."

"I told you!" Andie jabs her finger at Dani who throws her a Shhh look.

"I was… I was attacked in the parking lot getting groceries on Saturday." Oh, here we go. Sometimes the lies fall so easily when it comes to my life. Linc is the only one who knows the true me—not the one I try so desperately to present to everyone, even my best girlfriends.

Both women gasp. Dani jerks her hands to her mouth while Andie swears loud enough to earn a nasty glare from the old woman sitting three seats down.

Dani grabs my hand. "Oh my goodness, you must have been so scared. Did you call the police?" Yeah, the pretend police. I'm going to hell.

"No, I panicked and got in my car. I came home. Linc was there and he helped me."

Andie gives me the, *that's my brother the kindhearted fuck-up*, look. "Did you get a good look at the guy? Have Linc make a drawing? Roman would track him down and rip his balls off through his spine."

Well, yeah I got a good look. He was tall and handsome with a side of psycho. "No, I didn't. It all happened so fast. But, honestly, I just really want to get past it. There's no need to rile up my brothers or worry. Linc helped me get through it, and I'm fine now. Promise."

I wish it were that simple to just move on. But that damn Andie and her calculating looks. Just like her brother. Never gives up.

"Okay, so… There are clearly cameras in parking lots. Did anyone see? Help you? And why was my brother already at your house?"

Ugh.

*B*ecause we're secretly in love with each other and he now lives with me and, oh, by the way, I had sex with him a billion times in my house and left no surface untouched! "He has a key. He was watering my plants."

Okay, maybe that was a bad one. Especially since I have no indoor plants. But, dammit, those beady eyes are breaking me down.

"Reagan, I love you girl, but something seems off. Where was Chase? And why didn't you come to the golf outing? He sure seemed put off that you didn't show. You didn't even answer his calls." *Because he* didn't *call.* "It seemed kind of rude on your part."

Well, you see… I wasn't really even invited and my boyfriend, now ex-boyfriend, is a man-handler, and I wanted to spend my day with your steaming hot, fantastic-in-bed brother.

"It was just a misunderstanding. I had prior plans and Chase seemed okay with it. I'm fine. Can we talk about something else?" I turn to Dani. "Have you decided what you want to do for your bachelorette party?"

While Andie begins groaning into her coffee, Dani smiles from ear to ear. "Oh, yes. I thought of the perfect weekend. How fun would it be for us all to visit Silver Dollar City?"

Having no idea where or what that is, I look at Andie for guidance. She just rolls her eyes. "What exactly is Silver Dollar City?" I ask.

"It's a theme park in Branson. That's where the taffy shop is! Wouldn't that be great? You girls would love it. You can watch taffy being made and we can try the new seasonal flavors and they have competitions and sometimes, if it's not too busy, they allow you to help make the taffy!"

Wow.

I've never seen someone so excited before.

I've also never seen someone else look so miserable. Andie may lose it if she has to hear about one more taffy-related thing.

"Sounds super awesome, but wouldn't you miss Ram if we went for a whole weekend? I'm sure he would be miserable without you." Nice save, Reagan. Dani takes in my comment and it hits her. The realization.

"Yeah… You might be right. Well, shoot. Maybe next year."

Andie sits up, back to wanting to take part of the conversation. "Yeah, next year. So, I say we plan a girls' blow out. Strippers, drugs, lots of—"

"Andrea Holloway," Dani gasps while I bust out laughing.

"Dude, I was kidding. Why would I need to see stripper dick when I have her brother at home flinging his in my face twenty-four-seven," she says, jerking her thumb at me. At that I cover my ears. Too much…too much. "Anyway, what I was really going to suggest was that we have a small party at Reagan's. She has the perfect place for it. We can have it be joint, too. Because you know Rammy-poo will probably weep if he were away from you for a full night."

At the sound of Dani's cute little giggle, I laugh again. She knows her man gets the itch when he's away from her for too long. I've heard his sappy endearments when he calls her on her lunch breaks.

"I think that sounds perfect. Unless that's not okay with you, Reagan. I don't want to intrude on your home."

I swat the air, offering her my best *pffft* face. "Of course it's okay! I wouldn't have it any other way! And maybe just for you, we can have some taffy delivered in the spirit of Silver Dollar City."

And as I make number one sister-in-law status, Andie pretends to gag. Personally I don't care what we do, as long as the conversation shifts away from Chase and my apparent mugging.

"So, by the way," Andie turns her chair towards me. "Roman mentioned he swore he saw his missing golf club in your garden. Anything you want to get off your chest?"

He's going to get it.

Him and his stupid thieves prank. It's all fun and games until someone gets caught red handed. And guess who just had to lie through her teeth to get out of it? Me! If Andie believed it, then I would be surprised, telling her I had no idea what she was talking about and the pole in my garden was an old antique umbrella I brought at a garage sale. And if she believed *that,* she sure played it off. Because, *really?* An umbrella?

I pull into my driveway and see Linc is back. Good. He's about to spend the rest of his afternoon removing and discarding all of my new garden ornaments. I get out and slam my door. Stomping my feet like a child up my walkway and into my house, I call out for him.

"Linc!"

I don't get an immediate response, but the glorious smells coming from my kitchen momentarily distract me. I toss my purse on the couch and make my way into the kitchen. There, I find Linc surrounded by pots and pans, my island filled with plates of food.

"What are you doing?" I ask, looking at the discarded ingredients he picked up yesterday for me to make his special meal.

"I'm making you lunch." He pulls the pasta off the stove and pours it into strainer.

I watch Linc, who seems to sure know his way around the kitchen. Nothing smells burnt and the salad he prepared actually looks like it came from a restaurant. I frown in confusion. "Yeah, but I thought I was the one cooking for you? And since when can *you* cook?"

He turns, offering me that wicked smile he's perfected. "Who ever said I couldn't?" With a wink, he tosses the pasta in a bowl and picks up the pan of simmering marinara, pouring it over top of the noodles. Taking a fresh log of Parmesan, he begins shredding thin slices onto the readied dish and tops it off with some parsley.

"Is that…?"

"From your garden? It is. Didn't want to have to go to the store for a simple dash. Sit. Lunch is ready."

My argument completely forgotten, I force my legs to my kitchen table and sit. Linc serves me up a hefty bowl of pasta, and it smells divine. He bends down, and places a kiss to my neck, leaving a path of goosebumps in its wake, then makes his way to the other side and takes a seat.

"Eat."

So many questions are swirling in my head. But I should probably take a few bites before I start laying them all out. "Oh my God, this is *soooo* good," I moan, shoving another bite into my mouth. My recipe was going to taste *nowhere* near this good. Linc offers me a smile of gratitude and begins stuffing his face.

Sated like a fat pig, I sit back against my chair, rubbing my food baby. "Lincoln Carter, where did you learn how to cook like that?"

"Lana."

"Your mom? I thought you two weren't that close?" As soon as the words leave my mouth, I wish I hadn't said them. Before I can apologize, he cuts me off.

"At one point we were close. My dad was never around, so I never got into stuff like band or that jock shit like your brother." He winks as he makes a poke at Roman. "But when I was home, and bored, I used to watch my mom cook. It was dumb, I know. But after a while, I asked if I could help. And she let me. We spent a lot of time cooking together. She would teach me new stuff every night. I was horrible in the beginning and destroyed a shit ton of meals, but after a while I got the hang of it." He pauses to take a swig of his beer. His eyes are focused on the bottle, seemingly lost in thought. "One day, my dad just stopped coming home. Fucked up my mom. She stopped cooking, stopped pretty much a lot of shit she used to do. Before I knew it, I was the one cooking dinner for us. Not that she would eat it. That fucker made her so depressed, I had to call her sister to come stay with us. I was just a kid so I couldn't stay home with her. Well, I tried, until school started getting wind of my absences. Anyway, one day Dad showed up with divorce papers. Said he'd met someone else. Completely broke my mom." He takes another swig, this time finishing the bottle. Slamming it a bit harder onto the table this time. "That's when I broke him. Busted his nose in three places. Got arrested and thrown in juvi. Bastard actually filed charges against me. Spent three months in there until I was released and… well…" He pauses, realizing he just said a whole lot. "Well, the rest is history. Boring shit. Want another beer?" He gets up, avoiding eye contact. He places his empty bowl in the sink and grabs two fresh beers.

"Linc…"

"Don't, Rey. I don't want or need your sympathy. It was a long ass time ago. Him leaving was the best thing that ever happened to my mom. She met Roger shortly after and with him came Andie."

I stand and walk over to him by the island, praying he lets me comfort him. "But what about you?" I reach up and caress his crinkled brow, seeing the pain in his eyes. "You needed a dad."

"I didn't need him. Reagan, he hit my mom. I didn't even know it until later when she admitted it to me. I'd gotten into some trouble. I was out of control and my mom blamed herself. The asshole that I was, I didn't tell her she was wrong. I just let her believe it was her fault. I grew up in a fucked-up home. They always fought and then one day he just left. I had the nerve to blame her for him leaving too. That's when she told me. That the motherfucker used to hit her. Times when she said she fell in the shower, hurt herself at work. It was him." He pauses to catch his breath. His hands lift and wrap around my waist tugging me close to him. The hardness of his body, the warmth of his skin, he brings his hand to my chin raising my face so our eyes lock. "A man doesn't fucking hit a woman."

With the intense look in his eyes, I realize he's no longer talking about his mom and dad.

"Linc…" I say his name but he cuts me off, lowering his lips to mine. He kisses me gently, then pulls away.

"I'm in a battle right now, Rey. I want you to keep this from your asshole brother so it gives me free reign to find that fucker myself and pound his face in. But they need to know." He places his forehead against mine. I can feel his breath brush against my face. "I can't focus unless I know he's gotten what he deserves. But that may put me behind bars."

I grip his waist tighter, shaking my head. "Please don't do anything. I can't lose you now. I just finally got you. He'll leave. I told him to quit. It's only a matter of time before he's gone."

His tense body tells me he won't let it go. I worry Linc will do something that will take him away from me. I can't bear for him to put himself in danger for me. "Kiss me," I plead, needing him to focus on the now. On us. On what's important. "Linc, please."

He brings his hands up to cup my face, and with his eyes searing, he crushes his lips to mine. He kisses me deep and hard. My lips don't need an invitation as they part and our tongues collide in a beautiful dance around one other. Just as Linc increases the pressure of our kiss, we both groan slightly, forgetting our wounds. Linc chuckles, pulling away.

"What a pair we are," he says looking deep into my eyes.

He scoops me into his arms, carrying me out of the kitchen and down the short hallway to my bedroom. Not releasing me, he crawls onto my bed, laying me on my back.

He wastes no time pulling up my tank top, placing kiss after kiss on my navel, ribcage, working his way up my chest. My eyes are closed. The feeling of his wet lips touching my flesh causes a rush of wetness in my core. "No one is going to touch you again." He presses his lips in between my covered breasts, pulling down my bra to take my peaked nipple into his mouth. "No one will ever lay a hand on you again. I fucking swear it." His pressure increases as he sucks my nipple hard into his mouth. My back arches, while my hands find his thick hair.

"Linc…" I moan, wanting to address his recent comments but loving this feeling too much to get the right words out.

"I know, baby. I got you. Not a single hand on you."

"Linc… wait…" I throw my head back and moan when he bites gently on my swollen tip.

"I'm going to protect—"

I cut him off by pulling at his hair. He abruptly stops, lifting his head. "What? What's wrong?"

"Well, about the whole hitting thing…"

"Yeah, never again."

I think I shock him by the disappointed look that appears on my face.

"What's wrong, Rey?"

"Well, you said no hitting. And I thought… I guess I was still hoping that maybe…" *Say it. Don't puss out.* "Well, that you would still want to experiment. With me. Would spanking still be in?" I watch as his eyes darken immediately, the green irises that I dream about disappear behind his growing lust-filled pupils. His hands around me tighten and my heartrate skips in anticipation. He's going to give in. He wants this, too.

"You want me to spank you?" Now, seemingly amused, his hands work their way back down my ribcage and lock around the hem of my pants.

I don't want to come off too eager. The fantasies I've had of Linc having his way with me have been a bit, shall we say, X-rated. But to think that all I have to do is say yes and my wildest, dirtiest dreams can come true… I lick my lips and answer him.

"Very much so," I whisper, biting my lower lip while trying to play it cool. His bad-boy smile tells me he knows I'm nervous. Excited. Once he gets into my panties, he's sure to find out that I am also immensely turned on.

My answer does the trick because he slips his thumbs into my pants and tugs. A small squeal falls from my lips as he pulls once more, roughly discarding my pants, taking my panties with them.

"And why do you think you deserve to be spanked? Have you been a bad girl?"

I fight not to laugh. I can feel Linc's smile on my pelvis as he kisses alongside my pubic bone. He wants me to talk dirty. He knows it's on my list.

"I have been bad," I reply, my voice dripping with nerves, but also arousal. "I…didn't do the dishes after lunch." *Oh God!* What did I just say!? I throw my hands over my face, complete embarrassment washing over me. "That was so not sexy—*ahhhh*."

Linc cuts me off by taking a nip from the inside of my thigh. His lips are so close to my center, his breath like a torch to my flesh. "You naughty little girl, you. Not doing the dishes means I have to punish you." Linc's words cause me to laugh. He's playing along with me. And I'm grateful for that. I slowly uncover my face as I watch him lick my inner thigh, barely brushing my sex. He raises his head and winks at me.

Before I have a chance to offer him my thankful smile, his mouth is on me. Covering my sex with his lips, filling me with his tongue, and gripping me roughly with his strong hands around my thighs. He isn't slow as he eats me, sucks on me, plunges his tongue in and out of me, until my legs begin to quiver and my orgasm is about to burst through me. I feel my belly knot, and I know I'm done for. I'm going to come.

"Linc, I'm going to…" Just as I'm about to release, he stops. He grabs for my hips and flips me so I'm now on my stomach. I turn, wondering what he's up to, when he places his hands under my hips, lifting them so my butt is raised in the air.

"Naughty little girls who don't do the dishes don't get to come when they want," he says, taking the palm of his hand and rubbing the skin of my butt cheek. "What do you have to say for yourself?"

Oh God, this is so fun. I know it's ridiculous to

role-play about dishes, but right now, I find it to be the hottest thing. "I should be punished. Spaghetti sauce is impossible to get out once it's dried." I feel Linc's body tremble a little and I know he's laughing. I wiggle my butt, encouraging him to teach me my lesson.

Slap!

My body jolts, a small whimper falling from my lips. I don't have time to register his spanking because another strike falls on my cheek.

Slap!

"Tell me how sorry you are for forgetting your chores." He pops me one more time, before taking his hand and smoothing it over my stinging flesh.

I never put much thought into the pain of being slapped, but the arousal overrides it. I'm so wet between my legs, I can feel myself dripping down my thigh. I'm not sure how many more strikes I can take but I'm extremely turned on and want more. "I'm not sorry. I should be punished more." I tell him, pushing my ass into his groin.

Another chuckle, then a groan from Linc as he grabs my hips and grinds into me from behind. "Jesus, Rey, you're supposed to beg for forgiveness, not want more."

Oops. But whatever I have to do to get him inside me is number one on my list. I meet his movement, grinding into his hard-as-stone cock, knowing he won't be able to refuse me much longer. "I need you to fuck me, Linc. Take me roughly. I've ruined those dishes and I deserve no leniency."

That does it. I hear Linc swear under his breath. His hands are off me instantly. The sounds of his belt and pants being ripped from his body fill the air. He's back behind me instantly, rubbing the tip of his cock at the entrance of my sex. "You sure you want this, baby? I don't take lightly to a woman ruining my dishes."

I try and fight my giggle. I push back, urging him inside.

"You're so goddamned sexy like this, Rey." With one hand around his cock and the other gripping at my shoulder, he gives me what I've been craving. He slams inside me, causing a rush of dizziness to swirl through me. Pulling out, he thrusts home again, each time going deeper than before. "Fuck," he grunts, grabbing my hair and wrapping it around his fist.

"Yes, fuck me. Yes." What a brazen little hussie I am. I've never even said a swear word during sex—much less done any begging—but right now, it feels empowering, naughty, bold. I meet him thrust for thrust. Each time, he feels harder and harder. I'm panting like a wild cat, while Linc is grunting and swearing. His grip on my hair tightens as his other hand gives a hard slap to my ass.

"Jesus. The way your porcelain skin reddens with my touch. Goddamn…" Another one, and another one, each one a euphoric jolt to my center. His pace is quickening. Each time I feel my knees skid farther up the bed. My hands are digging into the sheets so I don't go flying as he pounds me into the bed.

Linc must know I'm fighting to stay in place, so he wraps his hand around my hip, holding me there. With close proximity, he reaches over and works my clit with his fingers, until I know I can't take any more.

"I'm, shit… I'm going to, oh God… Linc." Explode. I

explode. My insides grip around him so tight, he growls, slamming into me harder than before. With a hot surge rushing inside me, he comes hard with a groan.

We both collapse on the bed, fighting to catch our breath. It isn't until I can finally see straight that I break the silence.

"I am never doing the dishes again."

Linc's chest vibrates from behind me. He kisses my back and rolls over onto his, taking me with him and allowing me to snuggle up to his side. "Who would have thought that dried up spaghetti would have been so hot?" We both laugh because, seriously, I'll never look at spaghetti the same way again.

"Thank you," I say resting my head on his sweaty chest.

"For what? I feel like I should be thanking you. That was fucking amazing."

I sit up and meet his eyes. "For allowing me to experiment. Showing me this part of sex. Being my victim."

Linc smiles, reaching up and cupping my breast. "I highly doubt I'm a victim. Consider me willing and ready any time you spark an idea."

With that, I smile big, knowing I have exactly that.

His eyebrows raise. "What?"

"Well, I actually have an idea I wanted to explore. How exactly does a sixty-nine work?"

Chapter Nine

Linc

Nah, Motherfucker, I'd Rather Just Kill You Instead

Chase: We need to talk. Please.

I stare at Reagan's phone as she sleeps naked curled up against me, rage bubbling up inside of me. Men like Chase get away with hurting women like Reagan because they have money and clout and likeability on their side. They think they can come over with a dozen red roses and beg for forgiveness. That all will be forgotten because they "made a mistake."

A cold chill settles over me, despite the hottie pressed against me, and I glare at her phone. That day last week when he came over with flowers was *before* he roughed her up in her kitchen Saturday. I always knew he was an asshole but now I'm starting to wonder just how much she was hiding from me. Was that the first time he hit her?

With a furious anger surging through me, I scroll

through their texts to the beginning. At first, everything was normal. Then, Chase started blowing her off at every turn. Eventually, he started saying derogatory shit to her. The last several days' worth of texts are apologetic ones.

And in a few hours, she's going to walk right back into that office and be forced to work with him. Unbelievable. She still bears the bruises on her throat he gave her, for fuck's sake.

I can't let this happen.

"Rey," I grumble and roll her over to her back.

She pulls a pillow over her face. "Leave me alone."

I want to do just that. Hide away in her bedroom making love to her all day rather than letting her go to work where that motherfucker still has a job. That would be the easiest thing to do.

Trouble is, I'm not in an easy kind of mood.

I'm feeling hard. Like fist full of knuckles through a nose kind of hard.

It's high time Chase pays for what he did.

But then a small hand is lazily rubbing at my cock. All murderous thoughts dissipate as I become a different kind of hard. Like balls deep in my fucking woman hard.

"You're my girlfriend," I blurt out, my mouth finding her pink nipple.

She pulls the pillow away and regards me with a sexy, sleepy stare. "Is that right?"

"And guys do things for their girlfriends," I tell her as I nip at her soft flesh. She releases a hiss of breath.

"What kinds of things?"

"Bad things that good girls like."

She laughs as I kiss a trail down her flat stomach

to her perfect cunt. "Speak of these bad things…I'm curious."

I flash her a wolfish grin before running my tongue along her slit. She's already aroused and ready to go. When I slip my finger inside of her, she's positively drenched. I fuck her slowly with my finger as I worship her pussy with my mouth.

"T-This is good s-stuff," she cries out. "I thought you said you were going to do bad stuff."

I gently bite on her clit before pulling my finger from her. "Spread open wide and let me look at you, Rey."

She moans but obeys. Such a good girl. Now that her pussy is glistening and open for me like a pretty flower on a rainy day, I admire the view for a moment.

"Good girls turn bad," I explain, my voice low and husky, "when their boyfriends touch them here." She whines when I tease the tight hole of her ass with my now-wet finger. "You want to be bad, baby?"

She whimpers. "I think so. Will it hurt?"

"Guess you'll have to find out, huh?"

I begin pushing inside her. Her body is tight and I can feel it clenching in response.

Leaning forward, I flick my tongue out and lick her clit, causing her to jump. "Relax."

"O-Okay," she breathes.

I start sucking on her clit to distract her from the slow intrusion into her ass. It works because she moans loudly and grips my hair.

"This feels weird, Linc. Is it gross? Are you grossed out?" she whines, her self-confidence gone.

"It's supposed to feel weird," I tease, my breath on

her pussy making her shudder. "It's a place where things go out, usually, and not in."

"Are you going to…" she trails off. "Will your finger get…"

"Shhh," I say, chuckling. "Let me get you off. Besides, that's what they make showers for."

Her body relaxes again. I slip my thumb inside her pussy while my middle finger fucks her ass. She squirms and writhes but doesn't seem too keen on stopping.

"One day I'm going to put my big dick there, beautiful. What do you think about that?" I ask, my cock throbbing at the thought.

"I-I-I think I w-would like that—Oh God!" Her orgasm hits her violently. Both her pussy and her ass clench in response as pleasure ripples through her. When she comes down from her high, I slide my fingers from her and carry her scrawny ass to the shower.

It isn't until we're clean and simply holding each other under the spray that I ask her what's been gnawing at me.

"That wasn't the first time, was it?" My voice is quiet but sharp.

"Butt play?"

I clench my jaw and press my knuckle under her chin so I can lift her gaze to mine. "Chase hitting you."

Guilt flashes in her warm brown eyes, and I fucking hate what that look means. That she'd rather sweep it under the rug than to pull it out into the light for us to inspect.

"Rey," I say firmly. "I need to know all of it. If we're going to be in a relationship, I need to know what that motherfucker did to you."

Her nose scrunches. "But why? Can't we just forget about it?" Tears shimmer in her eyes.

"He works with you," I remind her. "This isn't something you can ignore."

She drops her gaze to my chest. I grip her jaw and tilt her face back up. Softly, I press a kiss to her sweet mouth.

"I don't know what to do," she admits with a huff.

I run my palm down her wet hair and nuzzle my nose against hers. "Just tell me everything from start to finish. Please."

Her shoulders sag and she nods.

Over the next several minutes, I'm blasted by a quick version of how Chase evolved from friend to lover to abuser. By the time she finishes, I'm furious. She must sense my fury because she grabs my cock and kisses me hard. I'm momentarily distracted from being pissed as fuck. I slide my hands to her ass and lift her. She wraps her legs around my hips and I drive into her hard enough to make her cry out. My mind is focused only on her as I fuck my woman. It isn't until I'm coming hard inside her that I have a plan.

It's a bad one.

"I'm taking you to work this morning." My forehead presses to hers. "And, Rey?"

"Yeah?"

"You know I can't sit on this." I brush a kiss against her sweet mouth. "I won't sit on this."

She swallows and smiles bravely at me. "I know. Thank you."

I hate to see her go but fuck do I love to watch her leave. Today she'd put on a fitted charcoal-grey pencil skirt that hugs her ass in a delicious way. Her pink silky shirt is nearly transparent and it makes my dick twitch. What makes me angry, though, is the fact that she's wearing a wispy white scarf to hide her bruises. It pulls me away from lusting after her as she hurries to her office with her head down because it reminds me why I'm here.

My head jerks to Chase's office. His door is closed. Motherfucker is hiding.

"Linc," Ram booms from behind me, scaring the shit out of me.

"Dude. Don't creep up on a man unless you want to get your ass kicked."

He snorts as he comes to stand in front of me. "Do you always resort to violence?" There's a challenge in his stare.

"Only when absolutely fucking necessary." I clench my jaw and steal a quick glance at Chase's office.

Ram lets out a sigh. "I thought so. Come on, let's chat. My office."

He's probably going to fire me from the job I haven't even really started. I grab the straps of my backpack and shrug. "Let's go."

Once we're inside, he closes the door behind us.

"Did you finish those drawings?" he asks, his eyes narrowed at me.

I unzip my bag and pull out my pad before passing it across the desk to him. He flips through them, nodding in approval. Despite the shit that went down this weekend, he hasn't killed me so that has to be a good sign.

"I like this one," he says, thumping the simplistic drawing of a basil plant. "I have a nursery client who might like this one. The illustration has an organic feel. Goes with their entire brand. I want you to make me a few others. Vary it up a bit. Try a few different plants. Keep them simple and black, though. I love that look. I'll scan them in to Illustrator and make some vectors for them to look at. This is good stuff, Linc."

I feel a stupid grin creep up my face. "Really?"

"Absolutely. I have another client, an edgy clothing boutique, that wants a hand drawn logo. I'm meeting with them next week to go over some preliminary branding ideas. I'd like you to come with me and sit in. Maybe even whip up a few mockups while we meet. It helps sitting in with the client and getting to hear firsthand what they need. What do you say? You own something nicer than that old Rancid T-shirt and those holey-ass jeans?"

I shrug. "Probably not."

"Before you leave, go see Reagan. Have her take you to get a couple of suits or at least some slacks and a few dress shirts. We have a company credit card she can use."

Nodding, I start to stand when he holds up a hand.

"Wait."

Fuck.

"Yeah?"

"I want to know what happened Saturday. The truth," he says firmly. "Not the bullshit people-pleasing story Reagan has probably concocted by now." He frowns and scrubs at his jaw with his palm. "I know she didn't get robbed at the grocery story, like Dani told me. Some shit went down, and I feel like you're protecting her. Not harming her like Roman thinks."

I let out a sigh of relief. "Man..." Fury burns inside my chest. "I'm going to fucking kill him."

Ram frowns. "Roman?"

Clenching my teeth, I shake my head. "Chase."

His eyes narrow but he doesn't argue. I watch his shoulders tense as he mentally starts piecing together a picture with that one part of the puzzle. "Go on."

"He's a piece of shit, Ram. From the get-go, I knew this, but she seemed into him. She's my..." Everything. "She's my best friend, and I just wanted her to be happy. Chase *appeared* to make her happy."

"And we all know how Reagan is about keeping up *appearances*," he grits out, catching on quickly.

"You guys didn't see them as much as I did. He wasn't good to her. Didn't treat her like she should have been treated. The asshole acted like he was the damn prize, not the goddamned angel he somehow lucked into latching on to." I whip off my beanie and run my fingers through my hair in frustration. "He called her Pet, man. Pet."

"What?" A muscle in his neck ticks.

"Pet. Like a fucking dog."

He fists his hands but his face is turning purple. "Go on."

"He'd stand her up all the time. The shit she told me..." I slam my beanie on the desk. "He manipulated her, Ram. He emotionally abused her. The motherfucker put his hands on her multiple times. She's got goddamned bruises around her neck."

He stands and starts pacing the office, a growl rumbling from him. I stand, too, because I'm too pissed to sit still.

"He didn't even invite her to the lame-ass golf shit but then had the audacity to come over and yell at her for not going. Mental head game bullshit. My girl—" I huff, deciding to stop those words in their tracks. "Reagan stood up to him. Told him it was over."

"He hit her." His voice is icy as he stares at the floor.

"He was bolting by the time I got there. I was trying to comfort her when—"

"Goddammit," he snarls. "I am so fucking sorry."

I hold my hands up. "Don't apologize to me. I know what it looked like, and Roman fucking hates me. I'd do the same if the roles were reversed and it were my sister with the bloody lip." I grit my teeth. "She was too ashamed to tell you guys."

His head whips around as he glares at me. "W-What? Why? We're her brothers."

"Everyone loves good ol' Chase, man," I say, a hint of bitterness in my tone. "She doesn't like disappointing people, especially her family."

"Fuck," he mutters. "Fuck."

"I know he's your employee and—"

"Not for long," he hisses, his nostrils flaring with fury.

Ram is typically a cool, relaxed dude. Today he reminds me a lot of his older brother.

"I need to talk to Roman and see how he wants to proceed. With him being our employee, shit could get complicated." His entire body trembles with rage. "What I *want* to do is—"

I cut him off. "Is something I *can* do."

Before he can utter a word of protest, I sling the door open and stalk for pussy boy's office. Talking about everything that Chase did to her did nothing but get me fired up again. I'm not going to feel better until I show him what it feels like to get knocked around by someone bigger than him.

His office door is shut but that doesn't stop me from barreling through it. The moment he realizes it's me coming through his door, he knows he's in deep shit. He flies out of his seat and holds his hands up in protest.

"S-Slow down Linc. We can t-talk about this."

"Talk about how you fucking hit Rey and choked her?" I scream, spittle flying from my lips. "Nah, motherfucker, I'd rather just kill you instead."

Snarling, I charge around his desk and snag him by the throat. Just the way he touched her. I grip hard enough that he turns a sickly shade of purple and weakly swings at me. His pussy punches aren't felt in my adrenaline-rushed state. I slam him against the wall before crushing my fist into his nose. The pop of his bones is satisfying, but I'm not done with him. I yank my fist back again but before I can deliver another brutal blow, someone grabs me from behind.

Fucking Ram.

"That's enough," he roars.

It's then when Roman pushes past us and stalks over to Chase as he holds a hand over his bloody nose. I expect Roman to help him or offer his apologies.

"You put your hands on my sister?" Roman demands.

"It's not what you think," Chase croaks out, fear flickering in his eyes.

Roman's chest bumps Chase's as he gets right in his face. "You have exactly thirty seconds to remove your shit from this office. And what isn't out of here by then, you can find in the dumpster." His body trembles with fury. "So help me, if you even think about contacting my sister, I will hunt you down, motherfucker. I will find you away from my goddamned office and give you what you really deserve."

Chase's eyes are wide with horror. Pussy looks ready to piss his pants.

"Come on," Ram grunts. "He's got this."

I stagger along with him out Chase's room. My eyes skim the lobby until I lock eyes with Reagan. She's barely peeking out of her office. I wink at her and am rewarded a thankful smile.

A promise is a promise.

I've got her back from here until the end.

"Lincoln Carter?" a deep, unfamiliar voice booms.

Jerking my head to the lobby doors, I frown to see a guy in a suit. His narrowed eyes are on me and he doesn't look happy.

Fuck.

Have one of Louie's men come to get me?

He flashes a badge and my blood turns ice cold. "Mr. Carter," he booms as he stalks over to me. "You're under arrest."

"What?" I demand, yanking myself from Ram's grip.

"You're a detective or something?"

"Something like that," he snaps. "Now come with me. Don't make me handcuff you in front of your friends."

My head whips over to see Reagan walking out of the office her hand covering her mouth, shock written all over her features. Going to jail for popping that asshole in the face is worth it. I'm just walking his way when a thought occurs to me.

"How did you get here so fast?"

He frowns. "Come with me, Mr. Carter. We'll talk at the station."

"Just go," Ram booms from behind me. "I've got your back, bro. I'll post bail as soon as I can. You're not going down for this. We won't let you."

The detective grips my elbow and guides me out of the building. When he storms us over to the same black Chevy Impala I saw driving past Reagan's house on Saturday, I know I'm fucked and I put on the brakes.

"Man, can I see your badge again?" I ask, unease creeping down my spine. "Don't you need to read me my rights?"

He snorts as he yanks open the door and shoves me inside. "You have the right," he says coolly as he withdraws a weapon from inside his jacket in a holster and points it at me, "to shut the fuck up."

Chapter Ten

Reagan

Never Have I Ever

"WHAT DO YOU *MEAN*, HE WASN'T THERE?" This is not happening. Why did I let Linc get involved? Now's he's in trouble because of me.

"Exactly what I said. We went to the station and he was never booked there. We waited, but he never showed."

I stare at Ram in shock. "Well, did you ask about the detective who took him? Did you give them his name?"

"Reagan, it happened so fast, I didn't catch the guy's name. No one did. I was busy holding Roman back so he didn't commit murder in our HR office."

Shame washes over me. This is all my fault. "I'm so sorry, this is all my—"

Roman steps forward, pulling me to his chest. I wrap my arms around him, the comfort of my big brother helping ease my worry. "Do not even go there. This is not your fault. That bastard had us all fooled."

"But I should have said something. And now Linc is in jail and Holloway Advertising? Will he try and sue us?"

Roman pulls me away so he can see my eyes. "Linc will be fine. The company will be fine. I dare that motherfucker to try a lawsuit."

I pull back and my worried eyes find Ram. "Where could he be? I'm worried. What if they hurt him? Why would he just go with that man?" The panic in my voice is clear. The suited man just walked into Holloway Advertising, quickly flashed a badge, and Linc went with him, no questions. I ran after Linc, but everything was happening so fast and Ram grabbed me, telling me to stay clear.

How could I stay clear? This was all my fault!

Ram had Clara bring me back to my office so they could deal with Chase. They wanted him out and fast. Ram made sure he didn't take any company files and that he left in one piece. Roman seemed to only see red and wanted to rip his arms off. Thankfully at least one brother was thinking about the company. They didn't want Chase to get a chance to speak to me, so I was told to stay in my office and not leave.

By the time Chase was escorted out, I was running to my car to head to the police station. That's when Ram stopped me and told me to go home. Ram confessed that Linc took the lead to keep Holloway Advertising out of a lawsuit, so he owed it to Linc to bail him out and clear his name. He didn't want me near a police station and said Linc wouldn't want that either, so he told me to wait for them at home. That was until my brothers showed up without him.

"I have no idea what's going on, but I'm sure Linc will fill us in when he—"

Just then the door opens behind us, and Linc strolls in. I waste no time in breaking away from my brother and running to him. I throw myself into his arms, and he catches me with ease.

"Easy there, killer." He hugs me to him, pressing his mouth to my ear and whispers, "Careful, Rey. All eyes are on us. Unless you want your brothers to murder me before we try number seven on your list, you better chill." He pulls away nonchalantly, and I drop to my feet. Our eyes meet in a quick understanding and I slowly nod.

"What happened? Ram went to bail you out and they said you were never booked?"

It takes Linc a moment to answer. He looks over my shoulder toward my brothers, then eyes back at me.

"Nothing. A misunderstanding."

What? "A misunderstanding? What happened? Why did they arrest you then? And who was that man?"

Linc shrugs his shoulders and walks further into my house breaking eye contact. "Like I said, a misunderstanding. They had nothing to book me on so they let me go."

Let him go?

"Then where have you been? It's been hours since you left the office."

Linc turns to Roman, who's asking the question. "They aren't very courteous about handing out rides, so I had to walk back to your office and get my car."

I gasp. "Oh Linc, you should have called me. I would have come and gotten you." I follow him into the living room where he plops onto the couch. He shrugs and allows me to sit next to him, throwing his arm over my shoulder.

"Who knows. Cops are fucking tools. I'm fine. Fill me in about that asshole. Is he gone?"

Ram sits on the love seat, addressing Linc's question. "He is. He won't be back." Both men nod at one another, as if they have a secret understanding.

Linc takes a look around the somber faces and shocking everyone, he starts laughing. "Man, I feel so loved by the Holloway family. By the way, if all three of you are here, who's running your company?"

I look at Ram who looks at Roman. It's then we all join in on the laughter as we respond in unison. "Clara."

Poor Clara, she's probably on the verge of a breakdown right now.

"Remind me to offer Clara a raise," Roman says, taking a seat in a chair opposite of Ram.

Linc sits up and pushes himself up to stand. Clapping his hands together, he grins. "Since everyone is playing hooky today, we might as well make it worth it." Turning to me he says, "Glasses or no glasses?"

"Never have I ever," Roman says, a wicked grin on his face. "Brought a girl home and fucked her while mom was in the house." He snorts. "But the yard is a different story."

Ram throws his hands in the air laughing.

I gasp. "Ew, Roman, in the yard?"

Roman shrugs. "What? When you got the moves you got the moves, and sometimes those moves happen between the azalea bushes at midnight with the neighborhood skank." He points at Ram. "Drink because I *know* you're guilty…"

I look over at Ram who takes a chug of the Fireball and hands it back to Roman. Roman looks at me, curious as to whether or not I'll take a swig. I know this is a setup to see if I ever did anything my brothers would disapprove of in high school, so they can go and lecture me. Pitiful for me, I have actually never taken a guy home and gotten farther than first base under Mom's roof.

I lift my hand, reaching for the bottle, and Roman's eyes widen. "You're fucking kidding me."

I bust out laughing and pull my hand away. "Sike. I have more manners than that." I shudder. "The yard of all places. Gross. No wonder why I'm Mom's favorite."

Ram laughs, offering us his dramatic, Holloway Pfft. "Hardly. Mom loves me the most." He sits up reaching for the bottle.

"This isn't even up for debate. Mom loves me the most. It's evident," Roman argues, snatching the bottle away from Ram and taking a swig.

Going back and forth, I realize that we have managed to get ourselves drunk in the middle of a workday. I look over at Linc, who's leisurely lying back on the couch with his hands behind his head. This is his fault. I shake my head at him, trying not to smile, but it's impossible with that sexy wink he offers me.

It makes me want my brothers to leave so I can have Linc all to myself. Thank him properly for coming to my rescue today and every day since we've met. I'm tempted to turn to Ram and Roman and fake sickness, until someone at the door starts banging and it flies open. Andie, holding a car seat, diaper bag, and a billion stuffed animals in her hand, walks in.

"Oh my God! Is that my little princess?" I squeal and jump off the couch to help her. I pass Ram, who looks a little too smiley, and Roman, who looks like he just got caught with his hand in the cookie jar.

"It is. She just fell asleep, though. Wake her and someone dies," she warns.

I giggle and snatch the carrier out of her hands. I peek inside at the most beautiful little girl on this planet. I've also had a few too many, so it makes sense when Andie kicks me for goo-goo, gaga-ing too loud.

"Sorry, but I just want to eat her up," I say with a sigh. "She's so cute and tiny and kissable."

Roman finally gets his drunk butt off the couch and greets his wife. "Hello, beautiful. How are my wife and daughter today?" Andie takes one good look at Roman and Ram before bursting out laughing.

"Are you drunk?"

Oh boy.

I bring Molly over to the couch and sit her between Linc and I while I get comfortable for the show. Ram is already turned and Linc is taking a swig, putting the bottle out there, clearly not helping Roman.

"No, baby. Just a few drinks. We were celebrating."

Andie looks at him curiously but also like she might

slap him. "Celebrating what exactly?"

"Well, Reagan admitted that that bastard Chase was hurting her, so Linc kicked his ass and we fired him." My brother can be a big oaf when he's drunk. So when he explains our afternoon *that* way, I simply smile and shrug when Andie's blazing eyes turn on me, offering me the *what the fuck* look.

"You better *ALL* fill me in right now. And do it quietly, because if you wake that baby she is all yours!"

Andie squeezes on the couch, smashing Linc into the arm of the sofa while I give her the short rundown. She cries when I tell her about my first incident with Chase and swears loud enough at the second one that she wakes up Molly. Everyone points to her saying she did it, but then everyone fights to get at the baby first.

"I'm so sorry this happened to you. And that none of us noticed anything was wrong. I'm glad you had my brother to protect you." We hug, and I know she's offering Linc her thankful eyes over my shoulder.

Once were done, she pulls away and gives her husband her crazy eye.

"You're sexy when you look at me like that," Roman says. "Did you want to go home and tell me a secret in the dark?" Everyone breaks out in laughter except for Andie. She just shakes her head at my brother, stands, and makes her way into the kitchen. "I know you have something besides that gasoline to drink."

We spend the next few hours gushing over Molly and enjoying the remainder of the day. Ram texts Dani to head over when she gets off work. The easiness of the conversations and the way Ram and Linc get along warm my heart. I know Roman still has reservations but I can also tell he's eased up on him. There is respect there for what he did for me. Even if Roman wants to be too stubborn to admit it. Once dinner time arrives, everyone throws out the idea to barbeque.

"Let's just go pick up some burgers and we can grill out," Roman suggests.

I am out of my seat like a fire was just lit under my butt. "No! No grilling."

Everyone looks at me. "Why not?"

"Um, I had a bad experience with burgers the other day. Plus, I'm not feeling the mess. Let's, uh, let's just order pizza. I'll buy." Everyone is looking at me peculiarly while Linc is fighting a smile. He knows exactly why they can't go in my backyard. Thankfully, Ram agrees to pizza and everyone follows suit.

Once we're stuffed and everyone is coming down from the daylong drink fest, Andie decides it's time to drag her drunk husband home.

"It's because you have something important to tell me, isn't it?"

Andie whacks him in the back of the head. "Yeah, that you're an idiot when you drink. Do I have to carry you to the car or can you manage?" Roman bends down kissing her on her head and stumbles out of my door. I hug Dani and Ram and give Molly butterfly kisses on her sleeping nose. "You're just the cutest little princess, and I want to snuggle you all night long."

"How about you snuggle her while I use your bathroom really quick," Andie says and hands me the carrier. I swing Molly gently back and forth just like she likes it. At first I thought Molly looked like Andie, but I can see Roman sneaking through. Her head is definitely Roman's, but her sweet eyes and lips are all Andie.

"Once the house is all ours, any interest in testing out number seven on your list?"

I lift my head away from Molly and smile at Linc. "But what happens if we break the couch? We will have nowhere to practice number eight."

Linc takes a step closer, allowing our thighs to brush against one another, as he dips down and whispers in my ear. "We're definitely going to break that couch. And as for number—"

"Jesus, Linc, why are your clothes all over the place? Not sure how Reagan allows that," Andie says as she steps in to take Molly from me.

"Doing laundry. My shit's broken," Linc replies, separating from me.

Andie stares at Linc with those speculating eyes, and then to me. *Stop staring at me. Stop staring at me.*

"Whatever," she huffs and waves at us. "I need to go before my husband throws up in my car. Love you both."

And she's gone.

The second the door shuts, I'm up and in Linc's arms as he carries me over to the couch. He sits down with me in his lap, allowing me to straddle him. "Now, I'll let you ride me like the good little cowgirl you want to be, but then I get to bend you over this couch and ride you. Got it?"

My legs squeeze around him, already feeling the wetness form. "Absolutely."

"God, you're so fucking perfect. Shirt off,

beautiful. Now."

With a giggle, I lift my arms and off goes my shirt. My skirt has ridden up my thighs, giving Linc easy access to my butt cheeks and panties. Instantly, his mouth is around my breast, sucking at my flesh.

"Fuck, I love your tits," he praises as both hands cup my breasts. My hands are in his hair—I love the feel of my fingers threaded through his thick mane.

"Kiss me. I need you to kiss me."

"Anything for you." And his lips are on mine. Crushing our mouths together, fighting to get closer. I moan, he growls. It's never enough. If I could climb inside him, I would. That's how much I need him.

"Linc, I want—"

"Hey, sorry I forgot my…holy *what the fuck* are you two doing?!"

I throw myself off Linc so fast, only to realize I don't have a top on and squeal, grabbing a pillow to cover my chest. "Andie, Jesus. What are you doing?"

"Um, me?" she asks in astonishment. "You want to know what *I'm* doing?"

Shit.

I feel like now is the right time to start swearing. Because *shit*! I look to Linc, who doesn't seem like he knows what to do any more than I do.

"Listen… it's not what you—"

Storming over to us, she snaps. "Not what I think? Okay, so you half naked on top of my brother is not what I think. What *should* I think then, Reagan?"

Oh God, she's mad. She looks super mad. She turns to Linc. "I told you not to mess with her. I told you she was not one of your conquests. Dammit, Linc! Why? She's my goddamn sister-in-law!" She ends on a yell.

Linc hasn't moved, and neither have I. I can't tell who she's really mad at. I go to open my mouth, but Linc beats me to it.

"Because she isn't a conquest to me," he bites out, his tone dead serious. "She's my fucking everything."

I think Andie and I gasp at the same time.

"I know you don't approve, and I love you, sis," he huffs, "but it's none of your business. I would kill myself before I ever hurt her. I'm in this for the long haul. If she'll allow it."

I turn to Linc, the tears welling in my eyes. "Oh, Linc. I feel the same way." With the pillow still covering my chest I lean in and kiss him.

"Umm, I'm still here," she screeches.

We break apart guiltily.

"Listen…" I start, unsure of how this is going to go. "This started after Chase. I know that question is running through your head. But what we have is something that I've never wanted more. I know you may not understand. And neither will my family. But for right now, we want to keep this between us. To enjoy *us* before my brothers find out. Please. I know you might hate me for what we're doing—"

Andie quickly grabs my hand. "Hate you? Why would I ever hate you? My brother deserves happiness and if that's you then so be it. And I want *you* to be happy. You spend too much of your life worrying about others and not about yourself. If this is what you both want, then I'm all for it. Shit, one hundred percent. I can't predict how your brothers will take it, but I support you." She turns to Linc. "Both of you." The tears fully drip from my lids as I reach out and hug Andie.

"Okay, okay. As much as I want to bond over this, you're still topless, so…"

I laugh and pull away. Linc grabs my hips and hauls me behind him as if to shield my nakedness. Andie shakes her head at him, but not before he receives the smile of approval. "I'm just going to say that I am not shocked at this. Just that it took this long for you two to get caught."

Now *I'm* the shocked one because I didn't think we appeared to be anything more than the best friends we were before last weekend.

"Oh, give me a break," she says rolling her eyes. "Why do you think Roman really hates Linc? It's because he sees the way you two look at each other. He would have to be a dummy not to notice. Anyone would be. I doubt he'll be shocked when he hears the news. But either way, your secret's safe with me." She walks away then realizes why she even came back in. She turns and picks up the stuffed animal lying next to the couch. "Mr. Pickle. Molly's favorite. Nighty night, you two."

And then once again, she's gone.

We stand there for a few minutes, trying to take in what just happened.

"I think that went well," Linc says in my ear as his lips close around my earlobe. And surprisingly, I think it did, too. I was super worried about what Andie would think and to get her approval means so much to me. He sits on the sofa and pulls me down beside him. I take the lead and straddle his lap.

"Maybe we should get back to you telling me just how perfect you think I am."

And with that, with his lips, fingers, and cock, Lincoln Carter shows me exactly what he thinks of me.

Chapter Eleven

Linc

Bull Honkey

Over the past three weeks, Reagan and I have developed a bit of a routine. We wake up, we fuck. She goes off to work, and I spend the day sketching for Ram. I meet her for lunch, we fuck. Then, I pick her up from work, come home and cook her something that makes her start moaning…which makes us fuck. We end up spending the rest of the night playing around, experimenting with things she's curious about, which leads to more fucking.

Fuck. Fuck. Fuck.

I never saw myself as a goal-oriented kind of guy but I know now that I want to do this every day for the rest of my life. Goal-oriented as fuck.

Reagan is just…

"A walrus."

I jerk my head to stare at the client who sells baby gear and organic shit. "A walrus?"

"Walter Ruston. Get it?" The guy with the receding

hairline and trendy black-rimmed glasses grins at me. "My husband thinks it's clever."

Ram scribbles something down on his pad. "Actually, that's *really* clever. We could launch an entire brand around your name. 'Walter *Walrus* Ruston.' I like it. Give me a few days to come up with some ideas and slogans. Linc, you got any ideas rattling around in your head about logos?"

I focus on my task rather than my fuck-hot girlfriend. Sitting up in my chair, ignoring the stiffness of the navy dress-shirt Reagan insisted on getting me, I start sketching. The shirt looks all right on me, I guess. A far cry from my normal attire. She rattled out words like corporate and sexy, and the next thing I knew, she was on her knees in the dressing room, showing me just how hot she thought I looked.

I smirk as I sketch the walrus. When I draw on the same black-rimmed glasses Walter is wearing, he squeals and claps his hands. Ram chuckles behind me. After a few minutes, I push the pad over to Walter.

"This is art," he sighs, clutching his chest with one hand. "I can already see this logo on price tags and shopping bags. I love it."

Ram claps a hand on my shoulder. "Good work, man." Then he turns his attention to Walter. "I'm going to work up some mockups for you for your website and maybe even throw the logo on a couple of shopping bags, so you have an idea. This is going to turn out awesome, Mr. Ruston."

"I completely agree. Do you mind if I take a picture of this to show my husband? He is going to freak out," he exclaims, his smile wide.

Pride fills my chest that I can do something easy as shit and make people happy. This gig is actually kind of fun. I've gotten to know Ram a lot better during these past three weeks, too. Not all the clients want hand drawn logos but many do. Everyone wants to be different and stand out from the rest. It's been fun being a part of the process. I never dreamed that drawing could actually lead to a career.

And it *is* a career.

Ram handed me my first paycheck and I nearly shit a brick. Took my girl out for some celebratory steak afterward, too. After a lifetime of being a fuck up, I'm finally finding some solid ground to stand on. I feel like my life is coming together.

Only problem is, Reagan and I are still keeping our relationship a secret. My sister made good on her word and never spoke of our relationship to Roman or anyone else. As much as she likes to blab her big mouth, I think she knows how Rey's brothers, especially Roman, can be. We don't like each other, bottom line. I don't need to give him another reason to hate me. We're not friends but we tolerate each other. That's the best relationship I could ask for with him.

"We'll keep in touch," Ram says as he stands, offering his hand to Walter.

"I knew you guys were going to help make this real." Walter beams at us. "It's real. It's really real." He starts fanning his face. "My mother is going to go bananas once I show her this logo, too."

Ram and I both chuckle at the man's excitement.

Once we're finally in Ram's Mustang, he tosses his bag in the backseat and we gun it through town. I lose the tie and unbutton the top button so I can breathe.

"Want to go to Bender's and celebrate? Lunch is on me," he says with a grin.

"I could go for a Bender Bacon Burger."

While we drive, I text Reagan.

Me: Hey, beautiful. Small problem.

She responds immediately.

Rey: Oh no!! Did you not land the client? What's wrong?

I'm grinning like a fucking idiot. Ram side eyes me as if he's curious as to who I'm talking to.

Me: Actually, the client loved my logo and Ram has a pretty fucking cool branding idea he's going to work on. The client was excited. But, your brother wants to take me to Bender's to celebrate.

Her response is quick.

Rey: OMG! GO!!! Don't worry about me. Andie just came into the office with Molly anyway. When she leaves Roman's office, I can flag her down and grab lunch with them. This is great, honey! I'm so proud of you!

Once again, pride fills my chest. Reagan never fails to make me feel good about myself. When we're not fucking like two bunnies, we're still the same ol' best friends. Linc and Rey. Thick as thieves.

Me: Thanks, babe. I'll make it up to you later…

Rey: How? Tell me. In detail.

I jerk my gaze over to Ram but he's drumming on

the steering wheel as he jams out to something on the radio that has to be at least twenty years old.

Me: I'd take this fucking tie you made me get and gag you with it while I had my way with you.

The three dots are moving as she replies.

Rey: OMG. I just shut my office door. Tell me more because now I'm feeling hot and bothered.

I snort because I can almost imagine my beautiful girl fanning her face. Those high cheekbones painted crimson. Her perfect bottom lip caught between her teeth as she anticipates what's to come.

Me: Then, I'd bend you over your desk and push up your sexy as fuck skirt so I could see your ass.

"Tuesday special is half-priced draft beer and appetizers," Ram says as we pull into the parking lot.

When I look back down at my phone, Reagan has replied.

Rey: Would you spank me?

Me: Would you deserve a spanking?

Rey: Yes. <PHOTO ATTACHED>

I nearly choke when she sends me a picture of her wet fingers. Fuck. And I'm stuck having lunch with Ram.

Me: YES. A hard spanking. One that will make you scream so loud everyone in the office will know you've been a naughty girl. You're supposed to save yourself all for me. Now you're being greedy…

"You going to text your girlfriend all day or are we

going to go eat?" Ram asks with a lifted brow. "Who's the chick, anyway? You're kind of silent about it. I probed Reagan and she didn't know either."

Gritting my teeth, I jerk the handle open and stalk to the bar. Over my shoulder, I say, "Nobody. Just a friend."

"You seem to have a lot of those," he says with a chuckle. "Friends."

With my phone stowed away in my pocket, I try to focus on placing my order with Brent at the bar. Ram and him cut up back and forth about Dani and Andie. It gives me a minute to check my phone.

Rey: Bad for you. You like it when I'm bad…

Rey: <PHOTO ATTACHED>

Fuck.

Me.

She's taken a picture with her panties slid down to her thighs just below her skirt as she sits in her chair. I can't even see her pussy but it has to be the most erotic thing I have ever seen in my life. My cock is hard and I can't begin to think straight.

After Brent leaves, Ram babbles on about Walter Ruston and another client we are going to see tomorrow. I'm nodding, all the while, desperate to check my phone again. It keeps buzzing, and I am dying to know if she sent more bad-girl texts.

Brent sets down our burgers when a woman screams behind me. Ram and I turn to see an older woman patting her husband on the back. He's a sick shade of purple. Tossing my phone on the bar, I slide off the stool and stalk over to them. The man is choking. I guess those bullshit CPR and first aid classes they made us take while in juvi are coming in handy just like they told me they would because I don't think, I act.

I grab the man under his arms and lift him right out of his seat. Remembering vaguely what I'm supposed to do, I clasp my hands and hit him on the chest in an upwards motion. It takes four times before a big hunk of hamburger shoots from his mouth and lands in his wife's tea glass with a splash.

"Oh, my heavens," the woman cries out. "You saved my Morton!"

The old man coughs but turns to look at me. "Thanks, kid."

I'm about to back away to go eat my burger when the woman comes over to hug me. "Don't you dare run off, sweetheart. I need to tell all my bridge friends about the guy from *Prison Break* who saved my husband. Let's take a selfie."

Prison Break?

What the fuck is she going on about?

"Morton," she hollers, "grab my selfie stick from my purse."

Selfie stick?

"Ma'am—"

"Oh, dear. You sound just like Michael Scofield, too."

Morton rummages through her purse, grunting. "Dammit, Belinda, you have too much crap in here. I can't find the damn thing."

She exhales loudly. "Honestly, Morty. Wear your bifocals when we go out in public. How many times have I told you?"

"Listen," I say. "It was nice saving your husband's life

and all, but my burger is getting cold."

"Bull honkey," she chirps. "I need proof that Mr. Scofield saved Morton's life. They'll never believe me otherwise."

"I'm not Michael Scof—"

"FOUND IT!" Morton yells.

Just wait until I tell Reagan about this shit.

Reagan.

Fuck.

I jerk my head over to where Ram is sitting and he's glaring at me. His jaw is clenched and my phone is in his grip. He's not looking at it, thank fuck.

"I really need to—" I start.

"Hold still," Belinda chides. She fiddles with her phone and connects it to a stick. Then, with way too practiced efficiency for an old lady like herself, she extends the stick out in front of us. "Say cheese!"

I smile because I just want to get the hell back over to Ram before he sees something that might scar him and Reagan both for life.

"Well, hold on," Belinda grumbles. "My hair looks horrible." She fusses with her white bangs for a moment before ordering, "Say cheese!"

Morton stands there staring at us with disinterest as if this sort of thing happens all the time.

"This is a wonderful picture, Mr. Scofield. The ladies will be so green with envy. I can't wait to put this photo up on the Facebook."

I give her a nod and wriggle from her grip. "If you don't mind—"

"Not so fast, mister," she huffs. "Let me give you

something for saving his life."

While she roots around in her purse, I shoot another worried glance over at Ram. He's chewing on his burger but his brows are still furrowed. I'm definitely fucked.

"Here you go, sweetie," Belinda coos. "A little something for your troubles. I know you're a big Hollywood man but I know sometimes it's nice to have a little pocket money for when you're out and about trying to blend in."

She hands me a crisp five-dollar bill and grins.

Reluctantly, I take the bill so she'll leave me alone and wave at them both. "Thanks for the, uh, money."

I bolt back over to my barstool. Ram sets the phone down face first and slides it over to me.

"There are some things a man should never see. And I mean never." His voice is hard. "'Just a friend,' my ass."

Turning to him, I let out a sigh. "Look, man—"

"I'm not done talking," he snaps.

Clenching my jaw, I glare. "So talk." I'm not backing down on this. I fucking love Reagan. I'm not letting Ram or anyone tell me I'm not good enough for her. She's mine.

"How long?"

"Since after Chase."

He picks up his beer and gulps it down. "Are you good to her?"

"Of course I fucking am," I growl.

His stiff shoulders relax a bit. "Good. Now as much as I did not want to see my sister's boobs…" He shudders and makes a little gagging sound.

I'm just irritated she sent a shot of her boobs and I didn't even get to see them yet.

"I'm glad she's happy," he says, his tone hoarse. "I knew something was different with her. At first, I thought it was because she broke up with Chase and felt free. Now I realize it's because she's been with you. What kind of plans do you have with my sister?"

"The forever kind," I tell him, my tone dead serious.

His brow lifts and he smirks. "I knew you had a good head on you, man. Despite what Roman says about you." Then he scowls. "But you hurt her, even if it's fucking emotionally, I will gut you."

Reagan has always been closer to Ram than Roman, so I know he means every word.

"I wouldn't dare," I vow. Pinching the bridge of my nose, I let out a loud sigh. "Can you…can we keep this between us?"

"Well, Reagan already knows I know," he grunts. "I thought it would be funny to send her a picture of you being treated like a celebrity. I'd just snapped the picture and sent it when she replied immediately after with a picture of—" Another gag. "Her fucking boobs. Goddamn, can you two try and not leave that shit around for people like me to find?"

I groan. "Duly noted. Thanks for…"

"Not killing you?" he quips.

"Yeah, that."

He shrugs. "I figure Roman will think of a thousand ways to murder you the moment he finds out."

I pick up my burger that's now cold with one hand and my phone with the other. "Let's make sure he doesn't find out."

He snorts with laughter and then launches into an

animated conversation with Brent when he comes to refill his glass. I scroll through the texts I missed.

Rey: What would you do to these?

Rey: <PHOTO ATTACHED>

Gorgeous goddamned tits with perfect pink nipples. Then, it shows where I sent her a picture of me with Belinda. Immediately followed by Ram losing his shit.

Me: WHAT THE FUCK, REAGAN?! YOU AND LINC?! SEXTING?!

Rey: Ram! Oh crap! Omg!

Rey: Omg.

Rey: Omg.

Rey: Oh. My. God.

I chomp on my burger while I text her.

Me: I'd put my dick right between your perfect tits and fuck you until my cum shot you on your neck giving you the prettiest pearl necklace anyone ever did see. Don't say I never got you jewelry.

Rey: Oh, thank God. You're back. How bad is it? Does everyone know? Is Roman on the warpath? And FYI…how do you make something so nasty and dirty seem romantic?

Laughing, I reply back.

Me: Ram is good. I'm not allowed to hurt you or he's going to disembowel me. No biggie.

Rey: Gawwwwd. I am so sorry.

Me: I guess you should get your pretty ass ready for your spanking then.

Rey: I deserve it. Let me make it up to you…

I'm still grinning like a fucking idiot when I get

another text.

Detective Dickhead: Almost time.

My blood runs cold. That day Chase got fired and I got hauled away by a fake-ass cop, I learned exactly what this asshole wanted me to do.

Only *I* would manage to get the motherfucking Feds on my ass just as I've started to put my life back together.

Me: Waiting on instructions.

Detective Dickhead: Good dog.

The murderous scowl is wiped right off my face when my phone pings and it's from Reagan.

Rey: <PHOTO ATTACHED>

Chapter Twelve

Reagan

Cock Exercises

"IF YOU DO NOT STOP, WE ARE NEVER MAKING IT TO dinner." I laugh as Linc does another—as he calls it—helicopter with his privates. He doesn't seem to care that we're already running late when he does another swing, sending me into a fit of laughter. "Seriously stop. You have to be hurting that poor thing."

"He likes it. Cock exercises."

I fall over onto the bed, holding my stomach. He is ridiculous. "Oh, and what would you call what we just did three times?" Referring to the extremely difficult *Erotic Accordion* position that I found online earlier.

"I call that fucking Olympic training." We both laugh until Linc finally cuts it out and climbs onto the bed, pushing my shoulders back so he can crawl on top of me. He presses his lips to mine slowly, never taking his eyes off me. "You're beautiful. You know that, right?"

I smile against his lips. "So are you." And it's the truth. He is beautiful inside and out.

Linc bites gently at my lip, and pulls. “Thanks for the compliment but I would appreciate more of a hot, sexy, beastly over beautiful. Guys aren’t beautiful, babe.”

I smile up at him. “But you are to me.”

“But I’m also sexy as fuck, right? Rock your world with my manly cock. Muscles that scream all man, not beautiful?”

My grin widens and I can’t help but chuckle. “I think you’re all those things, but no matter what you say, you are beautiful to me. Your heart is so big. The way you make me feel. I’ve never felt like this. And if beautiful is how to describe it—along with hot, muscles for days, and a super cock all other men should be jealous of—then you *are* beautiful. To me.”

I barely get a glimpse of the emotion in his eyes before he slams his lips to mine. He’s done with the sappy talk. At least done showing me that soft side of him. I know that in times like these, he struggles to find the words, so he shows me physically how much I mean to him. His reply to my confession is rough and full of meaning. With his tongue dancing around mine and his hands touching me in ways that make me feel wanted, he is showing me that he feels the same way. That what he does to me, emotionally and physically, I do to him. I sigh, spreading my legs, knowing exactly what comes next. And I also know that we are going to be more than a little late to dinner.

“Babe, if you don’t walk faster, your brother is going to come looking for you and I would rather not die tonight.”

Linc is practically dragging me down the sidewalk to the restaurant. I would be moving a lot faster if my inner thighs weren't so darn sore. I mean, I work out. Okay I don't, but I clearly do now since I've never been so sore. Sex is physically exhausting!

We got down and dirty, then took a shower together to help save time. It didn't help that we got down and dirty in the shower, too, which meant we didn't save *any* time. Now we are practically running to the restaurant where we're supposed to meet my brothers, Dani, and Andie to talk about the upcoming coed bachelor/bachelorette party and we're forty-five minutes late. "Linc, I swear I think I pulled my groin when you put my leg into that spreader. No joke. You may have to carry me the rest of the way."

Linc stops quickly, and I slam into his back. "I'll carry you, but I'm going to warn you. If I put you in my arms, I'm going to probably get hard as fuck and carry your ass back to the car. Then I'm going to have to fuck you in my back seat because I think you would look hot all crammed back there, screaming my name."

I go to smack him, because how can he seriously think about sex right now? We are two yards away from the restaurant, and honestly, if I don't give my poor vagina a break, she might fall off.

"Fine," he concedes. "I'll slow down, but I hope you say something nice about me at my funeral. Preferably about my super cock." He smiles, then ducks as I take another whack at him.

"Oh, goodness," a familiar voice greets. "There you two are. Everyone is waiting. Roman is kind of hangry right now, and Andie won't let anyone order until you two get here."

We both turn to see Dani standing at the entrance of the restaurant. With just one look, I can tell she's had some wine. More than one glass, too.

"Sorry. Car trouble." We meet Dani at the door, who offers me a long hug. Having to pull her away, she says her hellos to Linc and walks us to the table.

"Lookie who I found!" she exclaims ending on a giggle. She goes to sit on Ram's lap, instead of her own chair, and Ram, rather than getting annoyed, coddles her in his arms, kissing her neck.

"So sorry guys. Bad traffic."

"I thought you said car trouble?" Dani pipes in.

Shoot.

"That too. Man I need a drink!" I refuse to make eye contact with anyone. I know Andie is calculating and Ram, well, I'm not sure because Ram and I aren't able to look each other in the eyes just yet since the whole sexting incident. Roman is probably too busy staring down Linc, thinking about what gun would kill him faster. So I play it safe and keep my focus on Dani. "Super cute top, by the way!" I divert the eyes away from me, and everyone joins in on complimenting the bride-to-be.

"Can I get you two something to drink?" A waitress comes behind me with her pad. *Sure, she can.* "Yeah, I'll have what she's having." I point to Dani, wanting to feel as bubbly as her and fast. I turn to Linc. "What do you want?"

"Nothing. You have fun. I'll drive us home."

"Drive *us* home?"

My back stiffens. *Ugh.* Of course Roman would catch that. I turn to my brother. "You know what he means." I scoff as Andie kicks him under the table. "Roman, knock it off."

"What?" he grumbles. "It's just a simple question."

"What Linc means, grumpy guardian," I start, "is that he's going to stay sober and make sure I get home, like the caring person he is."

Andie kicks him again because Roman grunts. "Leave it alone, Roman, or your shins are going to pay the price." Roman quickly shuts up, and I offer Andie a thankful smile.

"Okay so, now that everyone's here, let's discuss plans." Andie jumps straight into business. My wine is placed in front of me, and I thank the waitress and whisper to keep them coming. If I'm not driving, I'm surely going to take advantage of my sober driver. Then when I get home *really* take advantage of my sober driver.

"What's so funny?"

I turn to Andie who's apparently stopped talking.

"Oh, um nothing. Sorry. Okay so plans, yay! What's on the agenda?" Andie wants no part in knowing what I'm laughing about, which is good, so she continues.

"I was saying that since Reagan offered up her house, we should utilize the entire day. Girls do our thing at Reagan's. Boys, you can do what boys do and we can meet up later for a barbeque. Unless Reagan still isn't feeling it, and then we can do a taco-themed fiesta."

Everyone seems to be pondering the idea. I'm not sure Dani even heard her since her and Ram are whispering to one another. Ram finally chimes in. "Well shit, then why don't the guys go golfing? Linc, you ever hit some balls?"

At that I choke. If he means has he ever used a nine iron to jam into my garden, then yes. I gulp down my wine in an effort to look not the least bit interested in this idea. I'm really hoping Linc is smart enough to suggest another idea.

"Nah, but man, I'd love to try. Bet a nice set of clubs would help my swing." He turns to Roman. *Fuck.* "You got a set I can practice with? Heard you have the best."

I'm going to kill him.

If Roman doesn't first, judging by the look on his face.

"I do, but a few went missing. You wouldn't happen to know anything about that, would you?" I choke again on my wine, at the same time Roman grunts, assumingly from another kick, while Linc just laughs.

"Knock it off, Oaf," Andie huffs. "My brother wouldn't steal your golf clubs!"

"Then how can you explain what I saw?" he challenges.

She rolls her eyes. "It was an antique umbrella you jackass. Don't you know anything about garden flare?"

The waitress places a new glass down in front of me—great timing—and I go straight for it.

Linc smiles at my brother and gives me a quick wink. He seriously wants to get us killed.

"Okay, that boring shit is settled. Now, what should the girls do?" Andie asks, and this time, Dani perks up. I see Andie fight the eye roll because we all know what's coming. It wouldn't be typical Dani fashion if she didn't give it her best try.

"Well, I was thinking…since we can't make it to Silver Dollar City that maybe we can attempt to make some taffy at Reagan's! Like homemade! I have a whole board of pinned recipes. We can put them in the gift bags for the wedding!"

Her and her darn taffy. I swear she should just be a spokesmodel for the damn stuff.

"Fine. Sounds like a great idea. I can look up some girly drink recipes and we can get all the bags ready. We can do gifts and maybe play a few bridal games," I suggest, finishing off my second glass like a champ. Linc looks at me curiously. Probably wondering why I'm drinking so fast. But, let's be honest. I've had a stressful week. It's not easy running a business and trying to keep your smokin' hot relationship secret. Roman practically caught us three times this week at lunch, and one time, I swore we were both toast. If it weren't for him being tired from being up all night with Molly, he probably would have caught on.

There's also the stress of just wanting to come clean with the truth. Let them know. Tell Roman that I'm with Linc and just wait out the fireworks. It's *my* life. He isn't my dad, even though he tries to be at times. But then again, I think of Linc. And what he would have to endure. I know he can take my brother, but I don't want to see him go through that just because of me. I shift in my seat and moan a bit at the tightness of my inner thighs. I pout, convinced that I pulled a muscle down there.

Everyone is going back and forth about what drinks to get when my phone vibrates on the table. I reach for it to see Linc texting me.

Abraham L: Want me to rub that out for you? You know I have magical hands.

I laugh, and shoot off my reply.

Me: No. It hurts too bad. You'll only make it worse. And behave. I want to see you with all your body parts still intact later tonight.

Abraham L: Meet me in the bathroom. I'll rub out the muscle. Promise, you'll be as good as new.

God, it's tempting. But nothing is as innocent as it seems with Linc. Just like when he asked if I wanted dessert the other night and failed to mention *I* was the dessert.

Me: As much as I want this pain gone, we can't. You need to behave.

Abraham L: I swear, Rey. Just a rub. Magical hands.

Ugh, he's right. He *does* have magical hands. And this hurts. Every time I move the muscle threatens to tear into two. I take a few seconds to think it over.

Me: Fine. Meet me by the women's restroom.

With an innocent, dimpled grin that makes my panties wet, Linc stands up. "I need to make a call. Be back." And then he's gone.

I'm not sure how long I need to wait to not look suspicious. The wine is hitting me, which means my carelessness may also kick in. I can feel Andie's gaze boring holes through me so I make it a point not to make eye contact with her. "Geez, I drank those fast. Gotta pee now. Order me one more if she comes back. Thanks."

And avoiding all eyes, I get up and make my way to the bathroom.

Linc isn't by the women's restroom, so I figure maybe I'll just go pee really quick. When I step inside, a hand wraps around my bicep and pulls me into the first stall. Before I can scream, I feel Linc's hand over my mouth.

"Calm down, beautiful. It's just me."

"Jesus, Linc. You scared me. I thought you were a kidnapper!"

"Ahhh, that sounds like another fantasy we should try. Me accosting you. You screaming through duct tape as I pound into you from behind. My little prisoner tied up in my dungeon, ready and available at any moment."

"You don't have a dungeon." I go to jab him in the ribs but groan as my muscle flares.

"Here," he breathes against me, warm and delicious. "Let me rub it." I lie back against the closed stall while Linc works his magic. I shut my eyes at how good it feels. Just the way his fingers dig into my skin, I can already feel the tense muscle letting up.

Of course with my eyes closed, I miss his subtle attack. His mouth is on my neck, pressing wet kisses down my skin. With his hand on my inner thigh, so close to my sex, it's hard not to become aroused.

"How does this feel?"

"Good. Great. Perfect." His mouth is on mine, and I completely forget about my thigh. When Linc kisses me, everything else in the world goes mute. My body craves his. He pushes himself against me so I can feel how hard he is. So much for behaving—

"You ran off in such a rush, I wanted to check up

on…holy mother of, what are you *doing*!" Dani squeals as she rattles the stall door and peeks through the crack. Panicked, I push Linc off me and he trips, almost falling into the toilet.

"Oh my, oh my, oh my…"

Oh God, I think I just broke Dani. "Dani, calm down. Take a deep breath."

"I can't! I'm an accomplice now," she shrieks, her eye that's still staring through the door wide with panic. "If I tell Ram what I just saw, he will tell Roman, and then Roman will kill Linc, then kill me for just knowing."

Linc starts laughing, and I turn, shooting him a glare. "Linc, I got this. Go."

"But I want to hear—"

"Out!" I bark and he nods, making his exit out of the stall. Turning to Dani, I rush out, "Dani, listen. I'm sorry you just had to see that, but it's not what you think."

"Oh no, was he taking advantage of you?" Her face screws up in horror.

"No, honey. He wasn't taking advantage," I say with a small, devious grin. "I definitely wanted what he was offering."

Her nose scrunches in confusion. "Wait…are you two…"

"Yes. We're a couple. We've been one since after Chase." I watch her eyes begin to tear up. "Linc is the one for me, Dani. I need you to know that. I know it's probably a shock, but… I'm in love with him."

That does it and Dani begins to cry. "Oh my God, I knew it. I knew there was something special between you two. The way he looks at you. It always reminded me of how Ram looks at me." I'm so touched by her comparison that my own tears threaten to fall. "Oh Reagan, I'm so happy for you both."

"Thank you. That means a lot. But we're trying to keep it secret for now, so I would appreciate it if you kept this to yourself. You know my brothers. They may not be as welcoming to the idea as you are. And Linc and I just want some time to enjoy each other before my family's claws come out."

Dani pulls me in for a hug. I squeeze her tight, thankful that she is about to be my sister soon. "Secret is safe with me, promise," she says when we pull apart. "You deserve happiness. And if Linc is it for you, I approve."

"Thank you. We, uh, we should probably get back out there so no one starts asking questions."

She nods and we make a pit stop at the mirror to fix our makeup before heading back to the table.

"Everything okay?" Ram stands to greet his fiancée when we return.

"Perfect," Dani responds and lands back in my brother's lap once he sits back down. I take my seat, ignoring Linc's amused grin. I know my brother is assessing, along with Andie, so it's best I keep my focus on anything but them.

"What did I miss?" I ask.

"Well, I was going to suggest strippers for after the barbeque," Linc says. "Possibly a cowgirl and a naughty robber."

I nearly choke on my wine, drawing the attention of everyone at the table.

Dammit.

"Sorry, wrong pipe."

Linc is so dead. I am never playing cowgirl for him ever again.

Andie tosses her olive at her brother. "Dude, this isn't *House Party*. No strippers. Don't make me go into my story about when Rom—"

"NO!" We all say in unison, knowing the story about Roman and his attempt at stripping for Andie when he knocked over the billions of candles he had lit, setting the rug on fire, and almost burning his junk off by trying to put it out. The mental picture of his privates practically on fire caused me sleep issues for months.

"Geez, I wasn't going to bring it up," Andie says dramatically and her lip curls up in disgust. "But the smell of burning pubic hair is nasty."

Ugh.

Thankfully, the waitress shows back up and refills all our drinks. We drop the stripper and burned body hair talk and chat about flowers and matching bow ties. The girls *aww* at the plans Dani has for the moms and the guys give Ram shit for the song they have to walk out to.

By the time the check comes, I'm pretty toasty along with everyone else at the table, minus my sexy sober driver. We're all heading toward the exit when Dani grabs my hand, swaying into me. "I am soooo happy for you. Love is *wonderful*," she slurs, resting her head on my shoulder but slipping and giving me a head butt to the boob.

"Happy about what?" Roman asks, tugging his wife along with him.

Andie smacks him. "Happy that she's in the wedding,

you big oaf." She looks at me and winks.

Dani tries to stand on her own but wobbles. Ram is by her side immediately. "Yes, that too. I just can't wait for it to be her day. It will be soon. I bet you and—"

"*Speaking* of weddings," Ram interrupts, "I should get my future bride home. Thank you all for the fun night." He escorts Dani out of the restaurant and into the night. I turn to Linc, carelessly gawking at him. Before I can even paw at him, my brother steps in front of us.

"Are you sure you don't want us to take you home? It's on our way." I look at Andie who is shaking her head and mouthing *no*.

"Like I said before, I'm fine. Linc hasn't had a drop. Safe as can be." I slap Linc on the shoulder.

"Geez, woman." Linc groans, rubbing at his shoulder.

Roman takes the opportunity to throw a jab. "See, he doesn't look okay to drive." He points to Linc. "Can't even take a little slap from a girl."

Throwing his arm around me, Linc taunts Roman. "You're so cute when you're drunk, man. But I have to hurry and get your sister home. Got to get to robbin' some homes after I drop her off." At that I bust out laughing. If Roman only knew.

I wave to Andie and pull on Linc to take me home. I can't wait to play cops and robbers and test out the handcuffs he brought home last night.

He helps me gently into the passenger seat before taking his own and we begin our drive home. I can't help the smile on my face. It might be the five glasses of merlot I just had, but it's also because I'm just plain old happy. I look over at Linc. He looks happy too. Content. I can't wait to get home and show him just how happy he truly makes me.

Okay, so maybe I can't wait until we get home. I blame the wine. I lean over, placing a kiss to his neck.

"You're very tasty," I mumble while dragging my tongue down his neck. I scoot closer to him, bringing my hand to his thigh. My fingers slide to his inner leg and I can already feel his lovely man monster growing in his pants.

"What are you doing, beautiful?" Linc chuckles, trying to keep his eyes on the road.

"I'm trying out something else on my list." I reach over and try unzipping his pants. Damn, these things are harder when you're inebriated and in a car. I've never attempted giving a blow job in the car before but I think now is the perfect opportunity.

"Babe, I think this may not be the time to test out your road head skills."

"No way. We're doing this. I just need to get this zipper—"

Before I even get a good latch on it, someone crashes into us from behind.

Chapter Thirteen

Linc

Best Friends Until the End

"Fuck!" I roar and hit the accelerator.

Reagan shrieks and twists around to look behind us. "That person just hit us!"

"I know," I grumble as I switch lanes. The headlights behind me keep up with my every movement.

"Why aren't you stopping? Why are they chasing us?" she asks, terror in her voice.

"It wasn't an accident."

"W-What?"

Ignoring her question, I swerve between two cars and then haul ass when I get an opening. The car gets caught up between those vehicles but eventually makes it over. It gives me a little bit of a head start. I'm going nearly eighty miles per hour but I can't afford to slow down.

Louie.

That motherfucker and his men are thorns in my

side. I thought I'd done a good job of hiding from them. Apparently, they stop at nothing.

"Lincoln," Reagan says in a firm tone. "What is happening right now? What aren't you telling me?"

I hit my hand on the steering wheel and curse. "Just let me think. Please."

She sits quietly, and fuck if I don't hear her sniffling. Guilt consumes me, but I can't comfort her right now. I need to *save* her. If that car catches up to us, we're screwed.

"Rey—"

I'm caught off guard when the car speeds up and pulls up in the lane beside me. The car is most definitely one of Louie's. This is confirmed when the window rolls down and someone sticks their arm out. A gun points straight for us.

"Oh my God!" Reagan screeches.

I slam on my brakes and pull the steering wheel hard to the right. There just so happens to be an exit, and I take it. The other car misses the exit so it buys me some time. Weaving in and out of neighborhoods and backstreets, I finally make it to Reagan's bungalow not fifteen minutes later.

"Linc," she murmurs, her voice shaky. "Talk to me."

I grit my teeth. "Not here. In the house."

Climbing out of my car, I stalk over to her side to help her out. She's still drunk as shit, so I end up scooping her up in my arms so we can get into the house faster. Once we're inside, I set her down and make sure the doors are locked.

"You promised you'd talk," she reminds me. "That

was really scary. You're keeping something from me."

I palm the back of my neck and stare down at my shoes. Fuck, I can't tell her. Not in a million years. The less she knows, the better. If Louie ever got ahold of her…

Jerking my head up, I pin her with a firm stare. "I can't."

She gasps as if I've slapped her and her bottom lip wobbles. "What?"

"I fucking can't, Rey," I growl.

Tears quickly form in her eyes making me feel like a total asshole. "Tell me," she tries again, stepping closer to me. Her palms find my chest and she slides them around the back of my neck. "Please."

I close my eyes when she kisses my lips. I know what she's doing. And normally, when it comes to anything else she wanted to get out of me information wise, I'd fall into her trap and blab my fucking head off.

Not this.

"I can't."

"You can," she murmurs.

"Jesus, Rey," I snap. "I said no, okay?"

Her eyes find mine and a tear slips out. "Wow."

"Babe—" I start, but she pushes away from me.

"No," she hisses and points her finger at me. "I thought you were my best friend. I thought we told each other everything."

I scrub at my face with my palm. "Rey, it's not that simple."

"It *is* that simple. You tell me. I can handle whatever it is. I'm here for the long haul but I can't deal with this."

She waves at the window. "I've been through too much to have the person I care about most lying to me."

"Reagan," I bark, my tone making her wince. I soften my voice. "I just can't."

She blinks at me as her tears roll down. Without another word, she turns on her heel and stalks to her bedroom. Seconds later, the door slams shut. I pull out my phone and type out a text.

Me: Louie's men nearly ran me and my girl off the road.

The phone pings back immediately with a response.

Detective Dickhead: Good.

I clench my jaw and shake my head. I can't deal with this motherfucker tonight. After turning off the lights, I try Reagan's door but it's locked. I can hear her crying beyond the door. Leaning my forehead against the doorframe, I close my eyes and wish I could just spill everything to her.

I simply can't.

One day, maybe.

But not today.

With a sigh, I go into the guest room and take a quick shower. Looks like I'll be sleeping alone tonight.

I toss and turn until her crying stops.

Fuck this.

Throwing back the covers on the guest bed, I stalk through the dark house on a mission. In a hallway closet, I find what I need. With a long flathead screwdriver in hand, I make my way back to her door. I used to break into Mom and Roger's room all the time when I needed extra cash. Reagan's door is similar to theirs. I wedge the flat part into the crack of the door near the knob. Then, I jimmy it inside until it presses against the latch. It takes a few tries of simultaneously working the latch and leaning my shoulder on the door, but I finally pop it open. When I step inside her room, her soft breathing tells me she's still asleep.

I set the screwdriver on the dresser and make my way over to my side of the bed. Yeah, it's my side. Everything about her and her world is mine. We don't exist without the other. It's Rey and Linc. Always. Thick as thieves. This shitty fight we had is simply a blip.

She sleeps in nothing but a silky pair of panties. I'm wearing a pair of boxer briefs. So when I curl up behind her, our bodies meld together, and I can feel her every curve. A ragged sigh escapes her in her sleep. It's a sigh I know well. The contented kind. She feels safe with me, and goddammit, I want to keep it that way. This bullshit with Louie needs to go the hell away.

With my nose nuzzled against her soft hair and my arm curled around her in a tight embrace, I am finally able to fall asleep.

I wake when the sun rises and I'm glad she's still sleeping. After a quick piss and brushing my teeth, I abandon my boxers and crawl back into bed with her. Since she's still out, it gives me a chance to stare at her. Her chocolate brown hair is messy on the pillow and her plump lips are parted. She's lying on her back. The full, luscious tits I love so much are exposed and on full display.

"I love you," I murmur, my voice barely audible. I know she can't hear me, and it's probably the wrong time to say the words but I needed to let them out. One day I want to tell her those words as she stares at me with her big brown eyes.

I kiss her softly on her lips and then along her jaw. When I kiss her throat, a low moan escapes her. My lips make their trek down her neck to her collar bone. The moment my mouth finds her breast, she lets out another moan.

"Linc," she whispers.

I dart my eyes up to meet hers as I suck her nipple into my mouth. She bites on her lip as she watches me. One of her hands runs through my hair in that affectionate way I love so much. I continue kissing her tit as I let my palm slide down her flat stomach to her panties. Her breath hitches when I slip it underneath the silky fabric so I can touch her pussy. My tongue dances lazy circles on her nipple as I pleasure her clit.

"Take them off," she orders, her words almost a whine. When she lifts her ass off the bed, I grab her panties and pull them down her thighs. Once they're kicked away, she spreads herself open for me.

"I'm sorry," I murmur, my finger sliding deep inside of her wet channel.

"Mmmm."

I fingerfuck her slowly because I want to draw out this moment with us. It's just us. No tension between us.

"You're perfect, baby," I praise. I urge another finger inside her and use my thumb to massage her clit.

Her body jolts and jerks against my touch. When she comes with a shriek, I massage her as she rides out her orgasm.

"Linc," she pleads. "I need you."

I slip my soaked fingers from her and settle myself between her parted thighs. Her brown eyes are sad as she stares at me. Fuck if it doesn't make me feel like shit. I hold my throbbing cock as I inch myself into her tight heat. Once I'm settled inside my woman, I grab her hands, thread our fingers together, and pin her hands to the bed. Slowly, with my eyes on hers, I thrust against her.

We fuck.

A lot.

This morning, though, is different.

Deeper and full of unnamed emotions.

Our bodies connecting in a way they never have before.

I can't voice what I want to say to her but I hope my eyes convey that message. I hope she sees how sorry I am that I was a fucked-up loser in my past—that I only ever want to be good enough for her.

"Oh, Linc," she whispers, tears making her brown eyes look like melted chocolate.

"Shhh," I coo. "Let me love your body."

I lean forward to kiss her, my naked flesh pressing against hers, but I don't let go of her hands. My grip tightens. The message now is, *I'll never let you go*. Our mouths are greedy for one another. She's sobbing and it breaks my fucking heart. I kiss her with as much passion I can express. I kiss her and try to show her what love tastes like.

"Ohhh," she cries out, another orgasm trembling through her, making her heels dig into my ass.

I groan and my nuts tighten. A second later, I'm releasing my own blissful climax. My hot seed spills into her, and one day, I hope I can go the whole nine yards with this woman. Marriage. Babies. Forever. She makes me so fucking happy.

Our mouths break apart so I can lick away her salty tears. It's the least I can do. I put them there. Her arms are wrapped tight around my middle. I trail soft pecks along her cheekbone to her ear.

"I only ever want what's best for you. Always. I want to protect you, Rey. Always. Even if that makes us fight, it's worth it to me because it means keeping you safe." I sigh when she tenses. "Please trust me that if I could tell you, I would."

Her fingers thread into my hair. "Why don't you trust me? I would do anything for you."

My chest aches at her words. "I do, beautiful. Fuck, I do." I kiss her neck. "It's more complicated than that, though. My past…"

"Does not define you," she finishes. "You're amazing, Linc. You're amazing and mine. I want to share the bad parts with you right along with the good parts. How can you not see that?"

I lift up and stroke her messy hair from her face. "My past is embarrassing. I did a lot of shit I'm not proud of. Everything from stealing from my own mother to trying to set my principal's car on fire. One stupid ass mistake after another. If I didn't have Andie, I'd have probably done even stupider shit. My sister talked me out of doing some bad stuff. Problem is, she wasn't always around. Andie had a life and a future. I was just her fuck up brother."

Reagan shakes her head. "You're not a fuck up."

I drop a kiss to her mouth. "I was. I'm trying not to be anymore. When I met you, everything changed for me. I knew you deserved better so I was okay with just being friends at first. But then I realized how perfect you were and how much of a better person I wanted to be. I was captivated by you. Wanted to spend every waking minute with you." I rest my forehead against hers. My cock has softened but I'm still nestled inside her. I can feel our juices trickling out between us. "I didn't understand what to make of our friendship. It always felt like more. Now I know it is more. You're my life, Rey."

She palms my cheek. "You're my life too, Linc. Everything about my life has become happier since I saw you that first day, getting your ass kicked by my brother."

I chuckle. "Get your story straight…I was the one kicking ass."

"Not how I remember it," she teases.

We're both quiet and my thoughts drift back to the day we met.

"ROMAN!"

*I jerk my gaze away from this asshole who claims to be my sister's baby daddy, even though I've not heard a goddamned thing about it, and lock eyes with the prettiest woman I've ever seen. She stares at this prick—*Roman*—as* *if she's horrified at his behavior. He releases me and I blatantly stare at the woman. Her brown hair is smooth and silky. I can't help but wonder what it feels like.*

With confidence, she walks into the office with her hands on her hips. "What the hell is going on in here?"

I can't help but smile at her. I want to taste her, too, but smiling will do for now. "Just having a talk with Andrea's psychotic 'boyfriend.'" I take a step closer to her. "But I'd much rather talk to you."

Her brown eyes that seem to sparkle with interest linger at my mouth before she looks over at that growling beastly motherfucker. When her eyes flit back to mine, questions dance in her gaze. "You know Andie?"

I nod and fixate on her plump pink lips. "I do. And I love her." With a shit-eating grin, I flash Roman a triumphant look.

He charges like a goddamned bull.

But this tiny little thing steps between us. To defend me. Nobody ever defends me.

"Move," he barks at her.

She shakes her head as she squares off with him. My gaze drifts down her backside and I admire her round ass in her tight skirt. Fuck me.

"You move your ass right back over to your chair," she orders and points to his desk.

Who is this girl, and I wonder if she'll marry me? I've never seen anyone so fucking cute in my life.

Roman huffs and storms back over to his chair.

She turns to face me and stares up at me. Being this close to her, I can smell her. God, she smells delicious. I wonder if she tastes just as good. My guess, probably a thousand times better. I lick my lips just thinking about it.

"SIT DOWN, ROMAN!" she screeches at the fucker as he rises from his chair again before turning to regard me. "Everyone is going to calm down." Her voice is soft. Her eyes are soft. Jesus Christ, her mouth looks so soft. "Now who are you?"

"Lincoln Carter," I say with a lopsided grin that I know works on pretty much any chick I come across. I offer my hand in greeting. "You can call me Linc, angel." My smile grows wider.

She chuckles and shakes my hand. Warm but firm. I bet it would be creepy and I'd probably get my ass killed by that brute over there if I never let go of her. "Reagan Holloway. Nice to meet you." She leans in so close, her breasts brush against the front of my chest, making my dick wake right the fuck up. "And I'm immune to," she says as she pulls her hand from my grip and waves between us, "whatever this is."

"This is the beginning of something beautiful," I assure her with a panty-melting grin. "Anyone ever tell you your hair is smooth? Like unnaturally smooth. Like fucking Disney-princess smooth?" Like the creeper I am, I reach up and finger a strand of her hair before tugging gently on it. "I like it." Actually, I fucking love it. Baby steps, Linc.

After terrorizing this Roman jackoff a bit longer and seeing my sister, I let this little thing guide me back to her office. I'm thinking of all the ways I'd love to bend her over a desk and take her from behind. But when she takes me into an office that's clearly hers and I get a glance at the business cards that show her as the CFO, my confidence waivers.

This woman isn't a fuck-and-go type.

She's the type you latch on to and never let go.

And I definitely don't deserve that type of woman.

"Sit," she says and leads me over to a sofa in her office after she shuts the door.

I heed her instruction and am pleased when she sits close enough that her knee brushes against the side of my thigh when she turns to look at me. I'm having to think some seriously sick shit to keep my dick from pointing up right at her.

"Andie's brother, huh?" Her lips quirk up into a cute smile.

"Your brother and my sister, huh?"

She laughs. "They're an unlikely pair but they work. You know you can't taunt him like that. He's a hothead."

"And you're hot," I say with a smile. "Seems all this hotness runs in the family."

Her head shakes but she bats her lashes at me in a shy way. "That is something you can't do. He'll kill you."

I shrug. "Seems a good way to die."

She playfully slaps my thigh. "You're impossible, aren't you? A big ol' flirt."

"Can you blame me?" I ask and wink at her. "I've got a real live Disney princess sitting next to me. Of course I'm going to flirt."

"Okay, Prince Charming," she teases. "Down boy."

I reach over and tug on her hair again. So fucking soft. "I'm not Prince Charming. I'm more like the bad boy of this story."

Her eyes twinkle but she doesn't push my hand away. "I've never liked those dumb stories, anyway. Bad boys have more fun, huh?"

I flash her a wicked grin. "You have no idea."

She swats my thigh again. "Well, it's a good thing we're going to be friends then, right? I need a little adventure." She laughs and motions towards her office. "I mean, come on, I'm a numbers geek. You came at the right time, Mr. President."

Snorting, I release her hair. "An adventure you say? With me, you're in for a lot more than a little. I'm adventurous as fuck."

Her eyes roll but she's still beaming at me. "And arrogant too, hmmm?"

"A whole lot of other things as well," I say, my voice lowering, insinuating something darker and sexier. "What do you say? You up for some fun?" I rise to my feet and offer her my hand.

"W-What? Like right now?" she asks, astonished.

"No time like the present." I flash her an evil smile. "You ever snuck into a movie before?"

She gapes at me. If I'd known her for more than three seconds, I'd kiss that pretty mouth. "N-No. Never."

"I think what you meant to say," I tell her as I pull her to her feet but don't let go of her hand, "is that you've never done it until now. Come on. It's adventure time."

When I blink away the memories of the past, I find my future staring up at me. My dick is hard again and ready to go. I start thrusting inside of her and steal her mouth with mine. That day in her office was the beginning of us.

It's been a nonstop adventure ever since.

And I can't wait to see what else is in store for Rey and Linc.

Thick as thieves.

Best friends until the end.

The love of my fucking life.

Chapter Fourteen

Reagan

Three weeks later…

Orgasms 'R Us

D*ING-DONG!*

"Oh no, that was *not* the door."

Linc ignores me and continues his journey down my stomach. I knew we should have taken separate showers this morning. We woke up late, and I fell for the save-time-shower-together trickery that just led us to being even later.

Ding-dong!

"Ugh," I gripe. I'd much rather be spending time with him alone, but this day has been planned for weeks. Since *that* night. Despite being chased by God-knows-who and Linc hurting my feelings by keeping that information from me, I did let it slide. All he's ever done is make me happy. If he feels that he needs to hold on to that for now, I will let him. But one day, I will pull this information from him. I feel like he needs my help and I want to be the person to help him. I *will* be the person to help him. That's a promise.

Ding-dong!

"Staaaaahp!"

"Just ignore it. They'll go away." He latches his fingers into my panties, pulling them away from my skin. His mouth is already on my sex when the sound erupts again.

Ding-dong!

"Shoot! Linc, get off me. They're here! You have to go. Do something! Pretend you're doing laundry." I try pushing him off me, but that damn mouth of his. I grab at his hair, and fail myself by moaning. I need to be pushing him off me, and I just catch myself opening my legs, pressing his head harder into my sex.

"That's it, baby. Open up for me. The faster you give in, the faster I make you come, and you can open the door to the Laffy Taffy committee." I snort at his comment. Then follow it up with a long moan. *God, he's good with that tongue of his.*

I made Linc watch hours of endless videos with me on DIY, taffy-making techniques. As much as it makes everyone eye roll, I know Dani will love it, so it's important I got it right. I also dragged him around all last weekend to assist me in procuring all the materials I needed. He has officially joined the taffy eye rolling squad.

"Oh God, right there." I should be pulling him off me, *not* encouraging this. "*Fuuuu…*" Okay, maybe a few more seconds won't make a difference. I push on his head, encouraging him to go harder and faster. I know he's amused because I can feel his lips fighting a smile.

"Your eager cunt is my favorite." *Yeah yeah.* I call it on a time crunch. He works me fast and hard. His tongue doing things I have no idea how someone even learns, but it takes just a few more licks and bites before I'm flying. Arching my back, and pulling at his thick hair, I explode into his mouth.

"Jesus, that was amaz—"

BANG BANG BANG!

Okay. Reality check.

Just as Linc begins to sit up I see a shadow pass my bedroom window. Panicked, I lift my feet and catapult Linc off me. Paying no attention to the thump of his body hitting the floor, I fly up and grab my robe.

"Oh my God, you have to get out of here." Just then I see Andie peaking in my window.

"I see you! Answer your damn door!" She yells from the other side.

Shit. Shit shit *shit*!

"Sorry! I must have overslept. Coming!" *Overslept? Really?* It's eleven in the morning! Ugh! I jump up and almost eat the floor as I trip on Linc, who is still lying on my floor laughing. He grabs at my ankles and takes me to the ground.

"Linc, you have to let me—"

His mouth is on mine, offering me the sweetest, loveliest kiss. I know what he's doing. He's kissing me so I taste myself on him. Sexy bastard. He finally releases me with a pop of his lips. "Perfect, right?" I go to slap him, but our matching smiles cause my hand to stall. "Shouldn't you be getting ready?"

Damn him!

I jump off him and offer him a gentle kick with my foot. "Seriously, Linc. Get up and get out of my room. Pretend you're doing laundry or something. And... and...wipe the coochie juices off your chin for Christ's sake."

He snorts. "Coochie juices."

"Go!"

"Oh my goodness, this looks so pretty!" Dani squeals as she enters my house.

Andie looks at me and gives me a side hug, leaning forward and whispering in my ear, "Overslept my ass." Then pulls away. "Yeah, no wonder why you slept late. This place looks so cute!"

I take a moment to inspect my work as they do. Well, mine and Linc's work, since I forced him to help me all night. And thank god we decorated the entire living room and kitchen last night instead of this morning like I originally planned. Otherwise these ladies would be sorely disappointed.

"Thanks, it's just a few things here and there. Just wanted to make the day more special." Dani *awws* and comes at me, giving me her cute, snuggly hug. As the girls drop their bags and make themselves comfortable, my mind starts racing on what the heck Linc is doing. He can't just hide in the bedroom forever. And sooner or later he has to come out.

"So what's on the drink menu? Your mom has Molly till tomorrow, so I plan on taking advantage of it."

I start to panic, wondering if we ever got around to

picking up our clothes, which we quickly rid ourselves of. This was when we were trying to hang the bridal décor on the light, and Linc couldn't handle a simple, *hold my waist so I don't fall* task without it turning into a game of what sort of ways we could dirty up my kitchen island.

Andie gets up and starts making her way to the back when I scare her. "Wait! You relax, why don't—" Andie and Dani each know I'm seeing Linc, but they don't know he lives here. That's just one more story I don't want to have to explain right now.

"Rey, I used the last of your detergent. I'll replace it. Thanks for letting me finish my laundry." Linc walks out of the kitchen, holding a laundry basket with folded clothes in it. "Oh, hello ladies. Sorry to be in the way. Just finishing up borrowing her dryer." He lifts the basket higher for effect. I stare at him, hoping he understands my *did you pick up my bra and underwear* look, and thank God he looks back with that smile that I love. "All clean." He shakes the basket, and it's then I can see the hot pink bra I had on last night. Phew.

"Aren't you supposed to be with the guys? Roman left before I did." Andie addresses her brother, trying to take a peek in his basket. No doubt noticing, he doesn't wear hot pink.

"Yep. They're picking me up here. Needed a clean shirt for today." Andie gives him the whatever look. Linc smiles and walks back to the extra bedroom, forgetting he technically doesn't live here. Then, he walks back, still holding the basket. "Wanted to make sure I didn't forget anything. Just gonna put this in my car." And walks past me, exiting the house.

With a shrug and an eye roll, Andie pulls her attention away from her brother and back to us. "Anyway, so we brought our bathing suits, It's going to be gorge today, so I thought we could lay out in the backyard. Get some sun."

Speaking of backyard, *shooooot!* Linc was supposed to disassemble the garden décor before today. I nod, while trying to play it cool as I pull out my phone and shoot off a text to Linc.

Me: Garden. Now!

Abraham L: On it.

"Yeah, totally sounds fun. I can use some color myself." Dani chimes in and starts walking into the kitchen. *No, no, no.* Andie follows, and I'm at a loss on how to stop them.

"Okay, well first things first. Drinks. Did you get the peach schnapps and champagne, as requested? God, that stuff is *sooo* good."

Peach *what*? I watch as Andie starts digging in the pile of booze on the counter, right next to the window leading to the backyard. It's then I see Linc running back and forth.

"Over here!" I shout, causing both girls to jump. It does the trick because while Andie and Dani both stare my way, I am able to spot Linc running past the window with a handful of junk. "Now, um…listen. I just wanted to make a toast before we get started…" What exactly was that toast? While Dani is looking at me with such love, Andie is looking at me as if I've grown a second head.

"*Oookay.* Well, are you going to give the toast or

look at us strangely? Have you already been drinking?" Andie presses.

God, I wish.

"No, just that today is a special day for Dani. It marks the first event leading up to the big day, which means soon she will be my sister. And we'll all be related!" Phew! I save the day because both girls immediately get teary eyed. I actually fall for it myself because it's the truth. Before we know it, we will all have gone from friends to sisters. And I couldn't have asked for two better people to join my family.

Everyone is three drinks in, and the stories are flowing. Dani, being the lightweight she is, now has a loose tongue, sharing stories of her and Ram. I try and smile or laugh but I'm dying inside. When will these two realize I want to hear nothing about my brothers' sex lives? I'm tempted to start blurting out the size of Linc's junk just to see how Andie likes it, when my phone distracts me.

Abraham L: You owe me. I stepped on a garden rake and almost sliced my foot off.

Me: Teaches you to not steal people's stuff.

Abraham L: I stole your heart. Are you going to punish me? Or wait. Did you steal mine? Maybe we should punish each other. Wanna ditch these plans and meet in a parking lot? #carsex #markthatoffyourlist

At that I snort. The other day he suggested it, and I said maybe we should just do it in his car at night in my driveway so we wouldn't get caught. He gasped a little too theatrically, telling me I was a party pooper and that the whole fun was in the thrill, the excitement of possibly getting caught.

Me: No. Play nice with my brothers.

Abraham L: I want to play nice with you. Speaking of, did you clean off the island? I may have seen a little souvenir from last night. Don't mistake it for icing.

"Oh, Jesus." I gasp, realizing I also did that out loud. Both girls look at me. "I need another drink. These are darn tasty. Who else?" They both raise their hands, and I scurry to the kitchen. "I can't believe I'm looking for a blob of sperm," I mumble to myself, moving around the dishes and gifts sitting on my island. I hear the doorbell ring, and Andie yells that she'll get it. Before long, I realize Linc was just messing with me.

Me: You're gonna get it. I actually went and looked!

Abraham L: <insert laughing emoji> Well, maybe it was yours. You sure are a wet one, when I get you all…

I don't even finish reading the text because Andie is calling my name. With a huff, I jam my phone back in my pocket, grab the bottles needed, and bring them back out in the living room. Someone clears their throat and I jerk my gaze over to see my next-door neighbor's daughter in my doorway.

"Hi, Reagan? Stephanie, my mom Judy, lives next door." I greet her and swap all the bottles to one hand so I can shake her hand. "I'm sorry to bother you, but there were a few packages delivered to my mom's house by mistake. They have your name on it but the address seems to be wrong." I take a peek at the boxes, wondering what they are. I don't remember ordering anything lately. "I feel horrible. She's had them for over a month. I came across them in the garage. So I just wanted to, uh, return them." She looks almost uncomfortable, which makes me even more curious as to what they are.

"Oh, no problem. No one's gonna punish you for it!" I try and make a joke, but Stephanie just seems to become more uncomfortable.

"Okay, well, again, my apologies. I'll uh, just let you go back to your party." She turns and is gone.

"What's her problem?" Andie asks, bending down to examine the return label.

"No idea." I shrug. "Maybe she's not a people pers—"

"Demi's Dildo Domain? What the fuck?" Andie reads the tag and pushes the box over to read the next one. "Orgasms 'R Us… *Penny's Punish 'N Pleasure Warehouse*? Ummm…what in God's name…"

I must look just as horrified as Stephanie did. I bend down, the bottles slipping from my grip. I try to snatch the boxes away, wanting to get rid of them, but Andie is already ripping the boxes open. "Uh, maybe we shouldn't open those. Those have to be a mistake."

My suggestion falls on deaf ears as Andie rips the first box open and pulls out a leather strap with a red ball holding it together.

"Okay. I have to ask, man. What. The. Fuck?" I'm asking myself the same damn thing. I watch her drop the ball and reach for another item. She pulls out the largest tube of… "Oh God, is this *lube*?" Yep, it is. How…

When…oh, crap. That one night I had too much to drink. I got on those dirty websites and ordered a bunch of random stuff. I forgot all about those. Ack!

Andie pulls out a flogger with little tiny spikes attached. "Jesus, Reagan, no wonder why she turned pale when you told her you weren't going to punish her."

Dani lets off a giggle. "I think I just saw something like that on the History channel. But it was in regards to medieval torture to the poor fellow who stole from the king. Can I assume that's not for punishing thieves?"

Oh boy, if they only knew.

"Guys, honestly I have…"

"Jesus, are you and my brother into this shit?" Andie squeals, standing and holding a container of lube large enough to satisfy a sex colony.

"It's not really…" I start, but Dani steps in.

"Wait, she knows about you and Linc?"

"Well she kinda…"

"Of course I know. He's my brother," Andie argues back.

"Yeah, and I'm her soon-to-be sister-in-law," Dani counters.

"I'm *already* her sister-in—"

"ENOUGH!" I shout, startling them both. "Yes, you both know and found out at the same time. And yes, but no, it's not what it looks like. But, shoot, it is. I don't know! I was drunk and wanted to experiment. Linc was a willing participant and…" What the hell am I confessing here! Is this where I spill the beans on how much sex we have? How incredible Linc is, in and out of the bedroom? Do we all discuss sizes? *Ew. Okay, I actually blanch at that.* Those two can keep their measurements to themselves.

"Rey, it's okay. We're not judging you. But, please… Do tell us how exactly you plan on using all this stuff?"

We all stare at the lube and flogger Andie's holding up, then bust out into a fit of laughter. "Oh my God, the look on my neighbor's face." Another fit of laughter, and before we know it, we're all in tears.

Andie drops the items back in the box and says, "Okay, so I will regret this two seconds into the conversation, but you need to fill us in. What's the story with you and Linc?" She twirls the flogger in the air. "All of it."

"Okay, open mine next!" I push forward my big, pretty bridal bag full of *Just Married* leggings, taffy I had shipped in from Silver Dollar City, and random pieces of lingerie.

Both girls trapped me by planting me in between them on the couch—while passing the peach schnapps back and forth—and made me spill. And that I did. I kept the personal details to myself and underplayed the sex. It was for the best, but by the time I was done telling mine and Linc's story they were both in tears. And so was I. Because our story is special. Unique. We are the thieves to one another's hearts, holding the other captive. After I got it all out, we drank, and played a few bridal games, which ended in us sitting on the couch, Dani wearing a choker with handcuffs, Andie sporting some sort of weird domination mask over her head and myself with nipple clamps hanging from my shirt. What the hell was I thinking when I ordered all this stuff?

Dani finally gets all the stuffing out of the bag and makes it to the good stuff.

"Oh, I *looove* them!" she squeals, pulling out the leggings. And I knew she would. She makes it through the entire bag offering a louder squeal at each item. Turning her entire body to me, she says "Reagan, I love it all. I love you. This whole day has been so much fun. I can't think of two more amazing girls to call my sisters. Thank you." She leans in and gives me a hug. I don't deny her and wrap my arms around her.

"Hey, don't leave me out of this," Andie grumbles and wraps her arms around me. The three of us, drunk and covered in sex toys, sit on my couch and embrace in the best soon-to-be sister-in-law tripod ever invented. It's not until the sounds of car doors slamming that it clicks. For all of us.

"They're baaaack," we sing in unison.

Oh shit. "Get this stuff off, now!" We pull apart and all jump off the couch. I pull the nipple clamps, and dammit, they are more willing to put holes in my top than snap off. Andie is twirling around in circles trying to pull the black latex mask off her head while Dani struggles to unclasp the choker around her neck.

"Oh my God, it's stuck! I can't get the clasp off!" Dani shrieks, clawing at her neck.

"Fuck," I cuss. "Turn around!" I'm still trying to assist Dani with her dilemma while Andie is still struggling with the mask. She steps backward and trips over the coffee table.

"Holy fuck!" she yelps as she falls over.

Oh God, this is not happening.

We have less than thirty seconds before that door opens and we are drunk and covered in strange sex toys. My brothers are going to kill me.

Just as I hear the door jiggle, the latch unlocks from the choker.

And with three seconds to spare, I panic, trying to throw my shirt over my head.

Chapter Fifteen

Linc

Anal Cherry Pop

"YOUR MOM IS SO STUPID, SHE PUT HER PHONE up her ass to make a booty call," I call over my shoulder to dumbass Roman as we walk into Reagan's.

He glowers at me. "Your mom is so stupid, she put cat food down her pants to feed her pussy."

Ram snorts and I laugh. But the moment I take in the scene in the living room, my chuckling turns into full blown laughter.

"What the actual fuck, Andie?" Roman demands, his hands on his hips.

His wife—my crazy sister—shrugs from the floor, wearing a fitted black latex mask that covers her entire head with two nose holes cut out and a round opening for her mouth. Dani stares at Ram with a guilty-as-fuck look on her face as she attempts to pull off a slave collar that is latched tight enough that her face is turning slightly purple. She's unsuccessful because she's wearing a pretty expensive shackle set on her wrists that's making it hard for her to do anything. Reagan's face is beet red as she tries to shove a nipple clamp chain between the cushions of the couch. The room smells like liquor and Christina Aguilera's "Dirty" is blaring through the speakers.

"I can explain—" Reagan starts, but Roman cuts her off with a wave of his hand as he turns down the music.

"Hell," I say through my tears of laughter, "if I knew bachelorette parties were like this, I sure as hell would never have gone fucking golfing. This looks like a lot more fun."

Ram shakes his head and stalks over to Dani to assist her before she passes out. Roman simply stares at my sister like she's lost her damn mind. She wiggles her tongue through the hole, making her husband growl.

"What is all this shit?" Roman grumbles as he sits on the coffee table and starts trying to peel the mask from Andie's head.

"Girl stuff," Andie huffs, her words slightly slurring.

Roman rolls his eyes. "I can't leave you alone for ten minutes."

At this, she sticks her tongue out of the hole again.

"Come on, Rey. I think we need to get some food into you guys. A little help in the kitchen?"

She nods rapidly and accepts my offered hand. I tug her along behind me until we're out of eyesight and then I pin her against the refrigerator. Her lips part as she looks up at me with wide, innocent eyes. What just happened in the living room was far from innocent.

"I missed you," I whisper and press a soft kiss to her mouth. "Looks like you went shopping for toys without me." My teeth find her neck and I nip at her flesh. "Do you even know what half of that stuff is?"

She whimpers when I suck on her throat. Her palm roams down to my dick and she grips me hard. "I guess I went shopping while I was drunk. I'm afraid to look at my credit card statement." Our mouths meet for a deep kiss. "I do want you to show me how the nipple clamps work, though."

I slip my hand under her shirt and bra before pinching her nipple. "You'll like them, dirty girl. I promise."

"I'm going to order pizza—Oh, for fuck's sakes!" Ram groans.

Reagan jerks away from me, and I do my best to try to hide my hard-on.

"Pizza sounds good," I offer, my voice dancing with amusement.

"I hate"—Ram gags—"you guys."

"I'll be right back," Reagan squeaks before bolting.

"Is Dani going to live?" I ask him, my brow arched in question.

He shudders, still clearly suffering from the image of my hand up his little sister's shirt. "Choker has been removed, but the damn girl stole it and stuffed it in her purse." He smirks a little. "Now *that's* a better image."

I laugh and slap him on the shoulder. "Get the pizza ordered. I need to go check on your sister."

Before I have to endure any more of his gagging, I stalk through the living room where Andie has taken to slapping Roman as he works at removing the mask but apparently keeps pulling her hair. She's still stuck. He keeps trying to peel up the front and she screams that it's tugging her hair. I don't stop to tell them there's a zipper in the back. I'll let those two knuckleheads figure it out themselves.

I find Reagan hiding in her bathroom. Pushing through the door, I don't bother kicking it closed behind me and pick up where we left off. She slaps at the light switch to shroud us in darkness while I start ripping off her shirt. We probably only have a few moments before they come looking for us. Long enough for me to put my cock inside of her.

"Want to add having sex while your brothers are in the other room to your list?" I ask, my teeth nibbling at her ear as I unhook her bra.

"They'll kill you," she says but fumbles with my belt. "You better fuck me before they tear you apart limb by limb."

"You got it, babe." I rip the rest of her clothes off because I fucking love her naked. My pants only get shoved down to my thighs, but I do manage to throw my shirt off. In the next moment, I have her bent over the counter and am slamming into her from behind. She moans loudly, so I cover her mouth with my hand.

Something crashes in the other room and then Reagan's brothers start yelling at each other. If I wasn't fucking my tight girlfriend, I'd be laughing my ass off about now.

"You like being a dirty girl. Don't you?"

"Mmmm-hhmmm."

"You like when I fuck you where anyone could watch us, huh?"

"Mmmm-hhmmm."

"You're going to let me fuck your pretty ass tonight, aren't you?"

"Mmmm-hhmmm."

From the angle I'm driving into her, she seems to unravel quicker than usual. Soon, her cunt is strangling my cock as she screams with my hand still pressed to her mouth. I let out a grunt before spilling my seed deep within her.

"How romantic," Dani sighs.

Dani?

What the fuck?

I jerk my head to the doorway to see her lying on Reagan's bed, staring up at the ceiling, a dreamy smile on her drunk face. The light from Reagan's bedroom is enough to have given her quite the show, if she were looking. Something tells me she looked, all right.

"Don't worry," Dani whispers loudly. "I created a diversion so they wouldn't know you were back here having sex. Sorry about the mess, Reagan. Andie doesn't know what she's talking about. I can keep secrets, too!"

I slide out of Reagan and quickly yank my jeans into place. She scrambles behind me as she hunts for her clothes.

"What kind of diversion?" I ask Dani as I scoop my shirt up and tug it back over my head. I offer her my hand before pulling her drunk ass from the bed to her unsteady feet.

"I 'accidentally,'" she says, using exaggerated air quotes, "knocked all of the glasses out of the kitchen cabinet and onto the floor."

Reagan groans from behind me before stumbling

into the wall. "All of them?!"

"Yep!" Dani says, beaming proudly. "Ram told me to leave the kitchen before he gave me a spanking." Then she loud whispers again. "It was hard to leave because that was super tempting. Ram's kinky, too, you know. He once did this thing with his tongue while I was—"

"Enough, Dani," Reagan screeches. "Ack. No more. Gross."

"—tied to the hood of the car—"

"Lalalalalala! I can't hear you—"

"—and the hood ornament got me right in the—"

"Noooooooo!"

"—I'm pretty sure I got third degree burns on my hiney from the hot metal—"

"Stahhhhp!"

"Were there witnesses?" I interject, amused by Dani's drunk storytelling.

"Like fifteen!"

"Don't encourage her, Lincoln Carter!"

"What's going on in here?" Ram grumbles as he enters Reagan's room. He takes one look at Reagan—as she tries to redress behind me—and my disheveled state before he starts gagging again.

"I even waved to Jimmy Franklin. That's your mom's pastor friend. We saw him driving by—" Dani gets cut off when Ram covers her mouth from behind, squeezes his eyes shut as to not see any more glimpses of his sister behind me, and drags his blabbing soon-to-be wife from the room.

"I can't wait to be a Holloway, too," I tease with a chuckle.

Reagan slaps my ass from behind. "The guy doesn't take the last name, nerd. I'd be Reagan Carter. You wouldn't be Lincoln Holloway." She shuffles past me and shakes her head.

"Lincoln Holloway has a nice ring to it," I muse aloud.

It's then we lock eyes. We're being playful but an awareness seems to prickle around us. One day I *am* going to marry this girl. I just don't think either of us fully realized it until this moment.

I snag her wrist and tug her to me before giving her a quick kiss. When she pulls away, love dances in her eyes.

"You're impossible, Mr. Carter."

I smirk and flash her a panty-melting grin. "That's Mr. Holloway to you, missy."

"They've been going at this all goddamned day," Ram groans his explanation for Reagan, who sits closely beside me on the sofa. Despite being annoyed, he's loosened up after a few shots of tequila. Dani got cut off hours ago and is sleeping soundly up against his chest.

"Your mom is so stupid she brought a bible to Church's Chicken," I toss back at Roman, ignoring Ram's complaining.

Andie snorts. "He'll never stop, babe. Where do you think *I* learned it? My big brother over there." She flashes me a proud smile. Her hair is messy as shit but at least they finally freed her from the latex mask.

"*I'll* never stop either," Roman grumbles. "Your mom is so stupid she tried to put M&Ms in alphabetical order."

"You guys are *both* so stupid, I think I'm going to claw my fucking eyeballs out if you don't quit," Ram complains.

"*You're* so stupid, you wore a coat to Dairy Queen because of all the blizzards," Roman says and then starts laughing his ass off at his own joke.

"These were 'your mom' jokes," Reagan reminds him, trying subtly to defend me.

I give her a wink that tells her I've got this. "You're so stupid, when your doctor said you needed more iron, you planted your *nine iron* in your sister's garden."

Reagan and Andie gasp.

I flash Roman an evil grin. "I got you, motherfucker."

"I fucking knew it!" Roman roars as he jumps to his feet before charging out of the house.

"Oh my God! Linc!" Reagan screeches. "You asshole."

"You are so dead," Andie huffs. "You do realize this, right? Dead. He's going to kill you."

Laughing, I rise to my feet and trot after him. Andie and Reagan are hot on my heels with Ram pulling up the rear while Dani sleeps on the couch. When I make it into the backyard, Roman is rummaging around in Reagan's shed where I hid all the shit from the garden and cursing every time he sees something that belongs to him.

"Assholes! The both of you!" he hollers.

Reagan and Andie are chattering. Ram is laughing.

"You kind of deserved it," I say, shrugging. He launches his shaver at me, but I duck out of the way. "Okay, so you definitely deserved it."

When he goes back into the shed, losing his fucking mind, I turn and give Reagan a thumbs up. She smiles and shakes her head at me. “I can’t believe you, punk.”

I shrug. “It’s funny.”

“Oh, shit,” Ram barks. “Duck.”

Dropping to a squat, I narrowly miss the swing of a golf club.

Fuck.

So, he’s really pissed.

I take off running but that football-playing motherfucker tackles me. We roll around in the grass, each doing our best to pin the other. He may be slightly bigger and more of an asshole, but I’m fucking scrappy as hell.

His fist hits my ribs, but I clock him in the jaw with my elbow. Ram and the girls stay out of our way, letting us have at it. I manage to pin him on his back with my forearm crushing his throat. Then, I lean in and spill more secrets.

“I’m going to marry your sister.”

My whispered words send him into a homicidal rage because with strength I didn’t know he even possessed, he flips us over, and the last thing I see is his fist before he pops me right in the face.

As the darkness swallows me, I smile because Rey is worth it.

She always has been and she always will be.

“I told him you were kidding,” Reagan tells me, her hot breath tickling my chest. “Always have to be provoking that beast, don’t you?”

But I wasn’t kidding. It was the honest to God truth.

I stroke her hair and grin in the darkness. “He likes

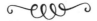

it when I poke at him."

She laughs. "He so does *not* like it."

After Roman knocked my ass out cold, Ram managed to drag me into the house and toss me on the sofa. Since everyone was drunk as hell, they all stayed over. Andie and Roman took the guest room while Dani and Ram took Reagan's room. She told them she'd sleep on the loveseat, but as soon as everyone went to bed, she climbed under the covers on the couch with me.

"Do you think they're going to have sex in your bed?"

"Dear God," she groans. "I hope not. I still can't believe she saw us having sex."

"We put on a good show. Five bucks says she bones your brother in your bed."

"Ew. Yuck. You're sick."

But not too sick because she straddles my waist. She's long since changed into some shorts and a flimsy tank top that both have me wanting to rip them to shreds to get to her.

"Take off your shirt and let me see your pretty tits," I whisper.

Even though the living room is dark aside from the moonlight pouring in from the window, she still looks around to make sure nobody is watching…like no lurking Danis in the corner. When she's satisfied we're alone, she peels away the tank, baring her breasts to me. I shove my hand between the cushions and hunt around until I find the chain that had been hidden in the couch earlier.

"Move your hair," I instruct, my voice husky.

She pulls her dark hair back into a ponytail and

holds it there so that her breasts jut out at me. I grip her sides and pull her closer.

"Will it hurt?" she asks, her plump lip sliding between her teeth.

"When I pull the chain it will."

Her eyes widen but she doesn't move away. I lean forward and tongue her nipple until it's erect. Then, I pinch it with the clamp.

"Ow!"

I grin up at her. "Don't be a pussy. You're a tough girl."

She rolls her eyes but leans her other tit toward me. I attach that clamp once I've licked that one hard too. The chain is shaped like a "Y" once the nipples are clamped. I take the end of the chain that hangs down to her belly button and give it a pull. She lets out a sharp breath.

"How does it feel?"

She looks down at her breasts. I have the chain pulled just enough that her nipples are stretched slightly. "It hurts but kind of feels good too."

I tug harder and she cries out. "Too much?"

"No," she breathes. "I like it."

"Know what else you'd like?"

Her head shakes. "No. What?"

"I'll show you. Why did you buy that entire box filled with different kinds of lube?" I'd nosed around earlier, while everyone was getting shitfaced, and found more lube than she and I could probably use in our lifetime.

When she doesn't reply, I tug at the chain, making her yelp. "I thought we could try stuff."

"*Butt* stuff?"

"Oh my God, Linc," she squeaks. "What if one of them walks in on us? We could get caught doing the nastiest of the nasties." But despite being embarrassed and fearful of her brothers catching us, she starts rocking against me. Nasty little girl. "Maybe."

Thought so. We've been working for weeks to get to this point. Now, she can easily take three fingers after some stretching. I can't wait for my cock to fill her instead.

"Take off the rest of your clothes," I order, giving her chain a little yank. "I need you naked for what I have in store."

She climbs off of me and starts stripping. The moonlight hits her creamy skin. She's gorgeous as she dances in the darkness. I stand and peel away my shirt. It gets tossed to the floor on my way to the box full of lube. After rummaging in the dark, I find one with the bright red lid that says Anal Cherry Pop.

When I turn to look at Reagan, I grin at finding her sitting on her knees on the sofa as she inspects the nipple clamps. Fuck, she's hot. I unbuckle my pants and lose the rest of my clothes along the way back to the couch.

"Someone might see," she challenges but makes no moves to dress.

I smirk and point toward the guest room. "That headboard has been bumping the wall for the past five minutes. I think they're a little busy."

"Ew," she says but then giggles. "What now?"

"Now, you bend over, put your sexy little ass in the air, and let me fuck you."

She gasps. "B-But..."

"No buts. Well, aside from the butt I'm about to own. This is happening. Besides, you promised earlier."

She huffs. "Why do I get turned on when you act all bossy and growly?"

"Because you're addicted to sex, Reagan Carter," I tease, using the name I'm going to give her one day.

"I am not addicted to sex. I'm addicted to you, Lincoln Holloway."

We both chuckle, but then things grow serious when she gets on her knees and offers me her ass. I flip the cap open and pour a generous amount of cherry-scented anal lube down the crack of her ass.

"That's cold," she whines.

"I'm about to warm things up…"

I coat my finger and begin sliding it up and down along the crack of her ass until she's pushing it toward me. In goes a finger from me and out comes a moan from her. I let her fuck my finger until she's begging for more. Two and then three, her ass easily takes me. We've used regular lube in the past, but this shit is extra slippery—made especially for a cock in the butt.

"Ready, baby?"

"I am," she purrs. "Wait."

Her body stiffens as she listens. One of her brothers snores loudly. The other is attempting to bang his woman right through the bedroom wall.

"Okay," she breathes. "It's safe."

Slipping my fingers from her, I lubricate my cock. When I begin to push against her tight hole, she lets out a whine.

"It's okay," I assure her as I caress her hip. "It'll feel

better than my fingers. We'll go slow."

I ease myself inside of her tight channel as slowly as I can possibly go. Her body is hot and grips the fuck out of my cock. I sure as hell won't last long because it feels way too good.

"We're doing this," she whispers. "Oh, God. We're doing this." Just like she does on my fingers, she slides up and down, controlling the pace. "This feels better than your fingers."

I drive into her a little faster and reach around for the chain to her nipple clamps. When I pull at the chain as I thrust against her, she cries out.

"Touch your clit, beautiful. I want you to come hard."

She obeys and pretty soon, she loses control. Her body is meeting mine thrust for thrust, her moans aren't even quiet despite her brothers being nearby, and her body is trembling with pleasure. It's taking everything in me not to come too soon.

"Linc," she moans, her entire body seizing with a sudden orgasm. Her ass clenches hard around me, and I come with a loud grunt. My release surges into her perfect little ass that's no longer a virgin.

When she stops shaking and my cock softens, I slip out of her and give the chain a quick tug.

"Same time next week, Rey?" I tease and slap her ass before heading toward the kitchen to get something to clean her up with.

She looks over her shoulder and flashes me the sexiest look ever. "Same time tomorrow?"

"You bet your ass, baby."

Chapter Sixteen

Reagan

You Two Big Idiots

Is it cliché to want to sing "It's a beautiful day in the neighborhood" while I drink my morning coffee and wave at my next door neighbor, whom strangely just ran back into her house? They really need to get over those boxes.

Things have just seemed to be so much brighter lately. Happier. Perfect. The weekend wrapped up, and Dani couldn't have been happier with the turn out. There were a few headaches and a black eye casualty, but other than that, major success.

We all spent the morning sipping on coffees and eating the breakfast Linc picked up, which was super yummy. He knows exactly what donuts I like so, if nothing else, at least I enjoyed the spread. I can't say Roman enjoyed his morning since he spent it giving Linc the death glare the entire time, and Linc didn't help the situation by grinning every time.

When everyone got sick of Roman's constant

growling, we decided to call it a wrap. Dani hugged me big, thanking me for everything, even the extra stuff, and her and my brother were gone. Andie practically threw Roman out and waved, telling me she would call me later. That left Linc and I, a whole uneaten box of donuts, and the entire day to ourselves.

"You know, you're gonna have to find a way to get along with my brother," I state taking a huge bite of my apple fritter.

"Yeah, I'll get right on that," he replies with an eye roll. He pops donut hole after donut hole into his mouth. That man can eat anything and still look like a God. I don't get it.

I chuckle and finish my fritter. *This thing is seriously worth the month in calories.* I get up, grabbing my latte, and snuggle next to my man. *My man.* I love the sound of that. What I loved even more was our little banter about being a Mr. and Mrs. I know we were both drunk, but our eyes told a very sobering story. That we were very much in love. And this love, it's not something that ever plans on going away.

"What do you want to do today?" I ask, stealing a donut hole. Okay, so maybe a month and a half worth of calories. Linc wraps his arm around me, bringing me close to his chest. I love being able to hear the beating of his heart.

"The day is ours. Whatever you want." He places a kiss on top of my head and turns on the TV. "What do you want to watch?"

"Anything that doesn't turn either one of us on. I'm going to admit, I'm a bit sore today."

I feel Linc's chest vibrate. "Is my girl throwing out the white flag? Giving up on her wild adventure throughout the sexual unknown?" The fact that there is still *sooo* much unknown tires me but then excites me all the same. One thing's for sure, Linc surely hasn't let me down when it comes to fulfilling my sexual curiosity. What he's done is help feed this new beast in me that, as of late, craves more. And more. And more.

"Definitely not throwing in the towel," I argue. "I have two full boxes of leather, chains, and something that resembles a taser that we need to test out."

Linc bellows with laughter as he hugs me tight. Another kiss to my head and he flips through the channels until some zombie flick fills the screen. "Here, dead people on the hunt to suck each other's brains. Nothing sexy about that." And he's right about that. Goo and slime dripping from eyeballs and dead zombie creatures chewing on human flesh. Yuck.

I would make Linc change it, but my mind drifts away from the show and more onto our last conversation about the whole past literally crashing into us. *You need to trust me*. I keep replaying those words in my head. Do I trust him? Yes. Without a doubt. And that's the thing. It's not about the trust. It's about how worried I am that he's in trouble and he's trying to hide it from me. He says he protecting me. But from what? Who? No one would have to say that unless they *were* in trouble.

And of course, me being me, I just want to help him. Fix whatever problems he may be having. If it were money, I have it. I would help him. But after our talk, I know he would refuse. If he were in trouble, I wish he would confess to someone. Maybe Ram. Ram would be able to help him. Talk to the police. Help get him out of any trouble he's in. I don't doubt Linc had a rough past. He has never hidden any of that from me. But he *is* hiding something that's happening in the present, and I'm struggling with not knowing just how deep in trouble he is.

"Hey, Linc?"

"Yeah, baby?" He lifts his hand to caress my hair.

"About that night..." I immediately feel him tense. Feeling defeated before I even start, I wish I never brought it up. But I just need to know. I've never been one to just sit around when I could possibly be of help. And I feel deep down that Linc, admitting it or not, needs that. So I push through the conversation. "I just wanted you to know I trust you fully. And I get that there are some things you can't share. I don't understand, but I get it. But if there was something I could do to help you, would you please let me?" I lift my head so he can look into my eyes and see the sincerity. The devotion I have for him. "I'll never judge you. I never have and never will. But I want to be there for you. And right now I feel like I can't."

He raises his palms, cupping my cheeks.

"You *are* there for me. Rey, I can't even begin to explain what you've already done for me. You've given me a reason to be better. To get my shit together. Before you, I had nothing. I was bound for jail, or probably six-feet underground."

At that comment, I gasp. To think Linc would not be in my life immediately crushes me.

"But I'm not," he continues. "I'm here because you changed my life. I was nothing before you. And now, I'm everything. I'm doing what I need to do to make sure I'm the man you can be proud of."

I grab for his face, pressing our foreheads together. "Linc, you *are* that man for me. You're everything. I couldn't take it if something were to happen. Please. Thick as thieves, remember? Let me in. If you're in trouble, please let me help." I'm beginning to panic, and the events from that night start to come back.

Linc presses his lips to mine, calming me with his soothing mouth, his hands working their way to my hair. "Trust me. That's all I can ask right now. Soon, it's going to be me and you. Bonnie and Clyde, minus all the illegal crap, because I'm a good man now. We're going to ride this life out together. I promise you. When my bullshit settles, I'm going to make some moves to make you fucking mine. Permanently."

We kiss frantically, sealing his promise to me with such an intense kiss, I can feel it all the way down to my toes. Eventually, yet all too soon, he pulls away.

I reopen my eyes, my lids heavy with building lust. "Why are you stopping?"

"Because of the way you're looking at me right now," he groans, as if he's frustrated for even having to say the words. "If we don't start watching more brain-eating zombies tearing through flesh, you're going to end up naked while I suck on your flesh. Then I'm going to fuck the Sunday right out of you. *That* is why I'm stopping." He gives me a playful wink and runs his thumb across my bottom lip.

I take a moment to stare into his smoldering green eyes. Ones that tell me that if I don't make a decision soon, there's no stopping what he has in store for me. And as much as I want him to take all of me, I wasn't kidding. My body needs a time out.

"Okay. Good call. Flesh-eating zombies it is. But it's fair game after our Sunday nap."

With a smile, he pulls me back down for a three-hour zombie marathon.

"You're going to do great." I cheer Linc on as I watch him attempt to tie his tie. After I've gotten a good laugh, I give up and help him.

"I'm going to do great because you're going to be sitting next to me," he says with a low growl. "And most likely, my fingers will be up this naughty skirt you have on the entire meeting."

I finish knotting his tie and slap him on the shoulder. "No funny business while we're in there. If you do well and land the client, I'll give you a private treat in my office." I lick my lips suggestively and step away, but he's too quick. He wraps his arm around my waist, crushing my body against his.

"Looks like I'm going to nail this meeting then. And once I'm done, I'm going to nail you and that pretty ass of yours."

I blush instantly at his ass reference. I never thought that doing something so crazy would have been so sexually exhilarating. Not only did we take our sex a step farther, but we did it with a full house! The horror of what might have happened if one of my brothers walked out. But the thrill. God, the thrill of what we were doing knowing at any moment we could get caught was what made it even better.

"What are you thinking about, beautiful?"

Such a troublemaker, this one. He knows exactly what I'm thinking about. His phone vibrates in his pocket, though, and it kills the mood. It went off all day yesterday and into the night. Linc ended up turning it off. I didn't pry. But my simple question on who kept calling was met with vague replies.

I push away from him and hurry into my bedroom to finish getting ready. "That you need to hurry before you're late in prepping with Ram before the client meeting."

"Are you sure you don't want to just ride together?" he asks. "Save on gas? Better chances of road head for me on the way to and from the office?"

Laughing, I toss a pair of pantie hose at him. "Go, Linc."

He flashes me a wolfish grin and prowls over to me for a naughty kiss that ends with him groping my butt. "Fine. I'll see you in the office."

He whistles, looking every bit the beautiful businessman with his new leather portfolio tucked under his arm. His butt is downright bitable in his charcoal grey slacks.

I smile at his retreating form, until I hear the door shut and the sounds of his car fade away. My mind is immediately back to the excessive phone calls. That's when my smile slightly falls. Those darn calls. "Oh Linc, what are you hiding?" I whisper as I finish getting ready, pack up my laptop, and head to work.

Whoever is calling him clearly wants to talk to him. I lost count after the fifth call. Once the text messages started popping through, he shut his phone off. I wanted to ask. No, I was *dying* to ask, but he told me to trust him. So that's what I had to do. But the calls never stopped. I'm not sure when he turned his phone back on. I assumed it was when I had him order the pizza, because late last night they started again. Linc was dead to the world, but when I rolled over to grab his phone, he immediately awoke, distracting me, so I never was able to see who it was.

I had to believe that he was doing what he thought needed to be done, but it also unnerved me. Who called that many times? And who didn't answer? Was he hiding someone? A woman? My gut drops to my toes at the mere thought of him having another woman in his life. *He wouldn't do that to me.* Ashamed to even think that, I hop in my car and pull out of my driveway.

How could I even think that? He has never lead me to believe there was anyone else but me. But the feeling that something is wrong just won't fade. I simply don't know how much longer I can go on with just the faith of trust to keep my worries at bay. I drive down my street and wave at one of the neighbors jogging by when I catch a strange gold town car driving behind me. I try and get a good look at the driver but the windows are heavily tinted. Even in the front. Feeling unnerved, I try to remember the car from that night. I can't say I saw it though because I had had too much to drink. "You're being paranoid, Reagan." I try and shake it off and turn right out of the neighborhood. I would feel better if the car went left. But he doesn't.

"You're not the only one who goes this way to work," I chide myself, trying not to freak out. I wish this feeling I have were for nothing, but the strange calls combined with having gotten almost run off the road a few weeks ago, and I can't rid the nerves. I pick up my phone and reverse the camera so it's facing me pointing backwards. I snap a few shots, hoping to get the plates so I can show Linc when I get to work. If I see any sort of reaction from him, I'm making him tell me what's going on. If whatever's going on with him puts me in danger, then I have the right to know.

I speed up and change a few lanes, seeing if the car stays with me. I'm not an expert at tailing so I'm not sure if he is or if it's my paranoia. He doesn't keep right up on me, but at the last yellow light, I sped up, which caused him to blow through the red. I'm about to pull up to the office when the car suddenly pulls in front and speeds past me.

"Fuck," I curse, which is completely out of character for me. I don't realize I've been holding my breath until I see his headlights in front of me. I park and grab my stuff and head upstairs. I'm praying that Linc and Ram are in a place where I can grab Linc and talk to him. Sadly, when I enter the office, Clara is waiting for me, an anxious frown on her face.

"Hi, sorry, but they're ready for you. Linc and Ram just finished the morning prep. The client showed up early, so they're already in the conference room. I have the presentation and the account profile. Everything you should need is in here." She hands me the folder and grabs my laptop bag to drop off in my office, so I can go straight to the meeting. I'm feeling a bit shaken up and need to pull myself together.

I walk into the conference and see Roman in front with the client, while Ram and Linc take the back seats, allowing Roman to begin the morning presentation.

I offer Linc a smile but it doesn't reach my eyes. Linc notices it immediately.

"What's wrong? You look like you've seen a ghost."

I want to tell him what just happened. Show him the photos. I look forward and see Roman finishing up his spiel and know I don't have much time.

"Linc, when I—"

His phone rings, distracting me. I quickly look at his screen to see who it is, but he ignores the call. Two seconds later, the phone vibrates again.

"Who's calling you? Why don't you ever answer?" I whisper frantically. I need to know. And now.

"Babe, I told you, it's nothing. Bill collectors probably. I'm fine. What did you want to tell me?"

"When I was driving to—"

"Linc, did you want to come up and present your graphics?" Roman cuts us off, and Linc quickly pats my thigh and stands, heading to the front of the room.

I try and sit through Linc's presentation. His drawings are amazing. And he is a natural with people. I watch as our client hangs on every word, practically drooling over his ideas. I begin to settle, enjoying watching him in his element, when his phone rings again.

Leave it be, Reagan. Trust him.

God! I just can't. I lean over and see a random number. It tells me nothing, which means he could be telling me the truth. Bill collectors call day and night from random numbers. *Dang, relax, girl.* I take a deep breath and sit back in my chair, eyes back on Linc. He's well into nailing this sale when his phone dings again, this time indicating a text.

None of your business.

Ignore it.

He would tell you if…

Oh, to hell with it. I lean forward just as another slew of messages come through.

Detective Dickhead: I know you see my calls. Answer.

Detective Dickhead: We made a deal. Screw me and I take everything from you.

Detective Dickhead: It ends tonight. This is the end of the line for you, Carter, if you fuck it up.

I gasp at the messages I'm reading. What deal? Who is this? What has Linc gotten himself into? I lift my head, finding Linc's eyes. He knows I'm reading something I shouldn't be. The look on my face resembles the look on his.

Worry.

His phone dings again. I look down to another text.

Detective Dickhead: 7pm by the docks. You're the bait. Play your part. It's your life if you mess up.

My hands go over my mouth at the last message. Oh

my God.

"Well, I am sold, sold, sold!" our client boasts and stands. I can barely pull myself together to shake his hand, telling him that we'll be in touch to finalize the financial portfolio, before Ram is walking them out of the conference room. Linc is by my side instantly.

"Rey—"

"Don't you Rey me, goddammit," I snap. "You've been lying to me. This!" I jab at his screen filled with message after message. "This is *not* nothing! This is someone threatening your life!"

He attempts to bring his arms up to comfort me, but I slap him away. "No. You're not going to smooth your way out this with your kisses and tender words."

Linc ignores my fight to keep distance and wraps his large hand around shoulder. "Baby liste—"

"Get your fucking hands off my sister," Roman barks from across the room.

Linc ignores him as he fights for my attention. "Rey, look at me."

"You're lying to me," I accuse. "You're in trouble. Big trouble." My voice cracks. "Am *I* in danger? Was the man following me today one of these people who are out to get you?"

Linc's eyes darken. "What man?" he demands. "Who was fucking following you?"

My eyes fill with unshed tears and fear claws at my throat. He's been hiding this from me the whole time when in reality things have not been okay. "Linc, you need to tell me, now, who that is texting you. We need to go to the police!"

"NO!" Linc snaps back, just as Roman rips Linc's hand off me. "Touch my sister again like that and you're a dead man."

Linc's eyes flicker with rage, the growl leaving his lips straight up dangerous. He takes a threatening step toward my brother. "You know what, motherfucker?" he hisses. "Open your goddamn eyes. If you weren't so worried about what *you wanted,* like the selfish prick you are, you'd realize that Rey *wants* me. Me. And for the record, I'm going to touch her. All of her. And there isn't a damn thing you can do about it." He shoves Roman into the table. My brother retaliates and charges after him.

"Stop! Both of you stop!" I scream. "I can't take this anymore!"

Roman pauses, mostly shocked at my outburst.

"Roman," I say much quieter. "I'm sorry if this is going to put a rift between us, but I'm with Linc. Heart and all."

He scowls. "You have to be fucking kidding me. Him, Regan? *Him*?"

"Approve or don't but it's what I want," I clip out. "Stop trying to decide what's best for me. Because I've already chosen for myself."

Roman gapes at me in shock. He turns from me to Linc. This time Linc isn't egging him on. Linc's nostrils are flaring with fury.

"And you," I snap, pointing at my boyfriend. "We're going to the cops. Now. And you are going to tell them what sort of trouble you're in. You're going to do it for me."

Linc's chest heaves with each angry breath. The

tension between the three of us is thick. With narrowed eyes, I stare at Linc, waiting for him to agree. To tell me he will do it. For me. But the words that fall from his lips are not what I expect.

"I fucking can't." His green eyes flicker with regret.

My heart plummets. "What do you mean you *can't*?"

"I can't do that," he mutters, scrubbing his cheek with his palm. "I told you to not worry. I have this under control. I'm not going to the cops."

God, he is so stubborn!

Roman steps in. "If you're putting my baby sister in danger, you piece of shit, I'll fucking gut—"

Roman doesn't get to finish, because Linc tackles him. Swings are being thrown. My screams and pleas for them to stop aren't being heard.

I know better than to get in the middle of those two unless I want a matching black eye like Linc's.

"You two big idiots!" I scream, my voice breaking with emotion. I've had enough. I grab my purse and throw it over my shoulder. "Fine, if you won't do what's right, I will," I state and storm out of the room.

Linc bellows my name just before Roman slams his fist into his gut. I run out of the office, the tears flowing heavily.

I knew I should have trusted my instincts. Something was wrong. He was *not* okay. *Oh Linc, what have you done?* I step onto the sidewalk, trying to wipe my face so I can see where I'm going. I must look a mess to anyone walking by on the street.

The police station is just a few blocks away, so I'm not going to bother getting my car. I need the time to calm down anyway….

“’Scuse me, miss?”

I halt at the sound of a heavily accented male voice. I turn to see a man standing at the curb.

“Um, yes can I help you?”

“Yes, I’m a little lost, sweetheart. I’m in town, visiting a friend and I seem to have gotten all turned around. My GPS keeps taking me in circles.” He taps at his device. “Can you tell me where this address is?”

“Sure, of course,” I say, walking up to him so I can take a look at his phone. Looking at the location, I notice it right away. “Oh, that’s in my neighborhood. You just want to go left…” That’s when I feel a sharp pinch in my neck. I throw my hand up to the skin just as I watch the man pull a needle away from my neck.

“What…what did you jus…” I fade off as my words begin to slur, my head feeling like dead weight. I attempt to push away from the man, but my legs give out. He catches me in his arms. I open my mouth to scream, but nothing comes out as he shoves me into the back seat of his car.

That’s when life goes black.

Chapter Seventeen

Linc

Think, Linc

"YOU"—PUNCH—"ARE"—PUNCH—"A"—punch—"fuck up!"

I roll Roman onto his back and narrowly miss his fist. I'm about to knock his big head right off his shoulders when strong arms yank me from him. Roman is on his feet ready to charge at me when Ram bellows at him.

"Enough! Stop acting like goddamned children!"

Roman glares at me before storming off to his office. Ram slams the door of the conference room. I scrub at my face and instantly hate how I behaved. Roman and I can't stand each other but we lost our shit, at the office of all places. Reagan is pissed at me for the whole Louie crap—that I can't even tell her about—and now probably for fighting with her brother at her workplace as well.

"I'm sorry," I groan and drop into one of the leather chairs.

His hard gaze softens as he sits across the table from

me. "Care to tell me what the fuck is going on?"

I clench my jaw and shrug. "I can't."

He leans back in his chair and shakes his head. "That might fly with Reagan because she's nice and sweet and gullible. But it does *not* fucking fly with me. You're going to tell me what the hell is going on. Every bit of it. Whatever you're hiding. Your past. All of it."

I glare at him. "After tonight, it won't matter anyway."

"So, if it doesn't matter, tell me. What is going on?"

A huff of frustration escapes me but I resign myself to spilling it to Ram.

"When I lived in New Jersey, I got involved with the wrong crowd. At first it was simple errands for this guy I knew. Pick up money from one guy and then deliver it to another guy. That guy would take it to the big boss, Louie. Easy stuff. A little too easy. I started to learn that I could skim anywhere from five hundred to two grand off each run without anyone noticing."

Ram's eyes widen. "Oh, shit."

"It started out innocent enough. I just wanted to see if they would notice. I'd had all these grand ideas that I was like Robin Hood. I'd steal from them and then do things like help my mom or my sister out. Just fun. And since nobody noticed the first five thousand I took and funneled away, I kept on skimming." I lean back in my chair and loosen the knot of my tie. I hate wearing this shit. "Before I knew it, I had nearly twenty-five thousand dollars stuffed between my mattress and box spring at my apartment. I'd been bored and lonely in New Jersey. With all the money, I felt like I could come back to North Carolina and settle down. Start over. It's not technically stealing if you take from the bad guys, right?"

"Wrong," he mutters. "It's worse than stealing."

I sigh and nod in agreement, ignoring my phone that continues to buzz. I'm sure it's Detective Douche blowing up my phone still. "I'd barely made it out of town when my phone started ringing over and over again. My friend who hooked me up doing the money running in the first place warned me Louie had figured out I'd managed to embezzle a shit-ton of money from him. I took my piece of crap car to the dealership, traded it in and added some cash for a new one, and hightailed it out of the city. I figured Louie wouldn't suspect I'd come here. And for months and months, everything was fine."

"He's here?" Ram asks, his eyes wide. "Your mob boss is here?"

"Yeah," I groan. "I saw him awhile back. I'd evaded him but he saw me. I traded in my new car for a different one and have been lying low ever since. But don't worry, I have a plan."

His eyebrow arches. "A plan, huh? So who the hell has been blowing up your phone then? This mobster guy?"

I motion for my phone and he picks it up to pass it to me. "Nah, it's this guy I call Detective Douche but really he's a—"

"FUCK!" Ram roars as he glares at my phone. "FUCK!"

I yank it from his grip and stare down at the picture. My entire world shifts beneath my feet and spins out of control.

No.

No.

Fucking no!

"He's got Rey." I stare in shock at the picture of Reagan gagged and bound in the gold-leathered backseat of a vehicle with her eyes closed. The text was sent from her phone but it's most definitely Louie. "He's got Rey."

Rey: No more hiding, thief. I've found you and I took something precious from YOU.

Ram bolts from the room, and I stand, tapping out a quick reply.

Me: Don't you dare fucking hurt her, Louie.

The dots move as he replies.

Rey: How do you know I haven't already? Meet me at the following address in fifteen minutes. We have much to discuss. If you comply, your pretty girlfriend might not suffer the consequences of your actions.

I don't wait for him to text the address and I'm already running from the office. Ram calls out after me but I'm on a mission. Soon, two pairs of thundering footsteps are behind me as we run outside. Ram points at his Mustang.

"My car," he grunts. "It goes faster."

Roman flashes me a murderous glare as he climbs into Ram's backseat. I take the front and barely have my door closed before Ram's peeling out of the parking lot. The engine roars as he blasts down the road. After I rattle off the address I've been given, I text Detective Douche.

Me: Plans have changed. I can't make our date later. It's happening now.

"I knew you were trouble," Roman snaps. "The only

reason I put up with you was because you're related to my wife."

I jerk my head over my shoulder and snarl. "Not the time for this shit. I get it. You hate me. Big fucking deal. Right now, all I care about is getting Reagan back from New Jersey's biggest mobster."

Ram's grip on the steering wheel tightens. "We need to call the police."

"If we call the police, we'll waste time explaining things. Louie said fifteen minutes. I don't know what the hell he'll do if we don't make it in time..." My voice is raw with emotion. I won't even allow myself to consider what he'd do to her if we didn't show up. Louie is a bad man—someone you don't mess with. I not only messed with him, but I fucked him over. He's itching to teach me a lesson.

We're all on edge, imagining the worst.

Fuck, this is all my fault.

"I'm going to get her out of there," I vow. "And when I do, I need you guys to be ready to take her and bolt. He wants to punish me—maybe even kill me for what I've done to him. None of that matters as long as she's safe." I attempt to rub the tension from my neck. "Promise me you'll stay out of sight. I'll find a way to get her out of there, but if you go in with me, you're as good as dead, too."

Neither of Reagan's brothers makes any promises, and I can sense their hesitation. On one hand, the last thing either of them want to do is get involved in my mess, but on the other hand, my mess has involved their sister.

Ram barrels down the street, and we eventually turn onto a road that leads to an old abandoned factory on the edge of town.

"Stay here," I instruct. "I'll walk the rest of the way."

Ram throws the car into park and gives me an exasperated look. "So we just fucking wait?"

"Yeah, that's exactly what you do." I pull my phone from my pocket. "Here, hold on to this. You'll need it."

He gives me a confused stare, but I don't waste any more precious seconds. I've just wrenched open the door when Roman reaches past me.

"Take this with you."

I gape at the Glock in his hand. "What the fuck? You carry?"

He growls. "Ever since that asshole Frank nearly killed my wife, I've been packing. You never know when you might need to use it. And apparently my hunch was correct."

I take the gun and chamber it. "I'll get her out of here. And if something happens to me…" I hang my head in defeat. "Let her know that living with her the past couple of months was the best time of my life. Tell her that I loved her."

"Wait, you two were living togeth—" Roman starts.

I slam the door shut and start running down the gravel path. I untuck my dress shirt and shove the gun into the back of my pants. The road winds, but when I round the corner, I see a familiar gold Town Car parked in front of a side door of the factory. The door stands wide open, but it's dark inside.

"Fuck," I utter under my breath. When I woke up

this morning, I did not expect to be meeting with Louie to try and trade myself for my girlfriend before lunch. This was not the plan.

"Well, if it isn't the thieving little shit Lincoln Carter himself," Louie's raspy-from-cigars voice grumbles within the dark doorway. The light of the cherry on his cigar reveals his location. But it's not his location I'm worried about. It's hers.

Stopping dead in my tracks, I put my hands on my hips. "Where's the woman?"

I don't dare tell him she's *my* woman, but he's not an idiot. Still, I don't offer any extra information.

"Your girlfriend is sitting quietly, listening to all kinds of stories I have about you." He laughs until it becomes choked coughing. I hope he dies of lung cancer. "Why don't you come inside and join us?"

Gritting my teeth, I step over the threshold. As my eyes adjust to the darkness, I see Louie standing with a gun in his hand, pointed straight at me. Beside him, one of his giant thugs holds a very limp Reagan in his grip with his hand over her mouth. Her eyes are wide and teary.

"You can have me. Just let her go. She has nothing to do with this," I say as calmly as I can.

"Do you hear that, young lady? Your boyfriend here thinks I should let you go." He steps over to her with his gun still pointed at me and gropes her breast through her shirt.

"Don't touch her!" I snarl, taking several steps toward them.

He turns the gun to her temple and shakes his head

at me. "Not so fast, thief. You're not the one barking orders around here. It's me. I'm the fucking boss." He motions for his goon to move his hand and free her mouth. "What do you think, sweetheart? I pop him right in the skull and let you go? Win-win for everyone?"

She shakes her head in vehemence as tears roll down her cheeks. "N-No," she slurs as if she's been drugged. My hackles raise at that thought. "I-I'll g-give you m-money."

I close my eyes for a brief moment before pinning her with a serious stare. "Rey. Don't."

Louie presses the barrel of his gun into her temple hard enough to make her cry out. "Again, thief, this is not your show. I do the goddamned ordering around. And I want this pretty little thing to tell me what she thinks she has to offer that'll make me forget how much money you stole from me."

A sob escapes Reagan and she trembles. The gun at my back is useless as long as there's one pointed at her head. He'd shoot her before I could even put my arm behind me.

"I'll g-give y-you d-double," she says slowly, each word as though it's sticky on her tongue.

He smirks at me. "She's cute. Little problem solver we have here. Just pay the bad guy back—with interest, I might add—and we can live happily ever after." He uses the barrel of the gun to lift her chin. "That right, sweetheart?"

She nods and more tears roll out. "P-Please."

Louie flashes me a dark, wicked smile. "Now that's more like it. Mario," he says to his goon, "what do I love most?"

"A beggar."

"That's right. I love to see you useless people begging and groveling at my feet. I'm the god and you're my fucking minions. I control you all. Right, pretty little thing?"

Her eyes flit to mine and terror flickers in her stare. "I, uh, p-please…"

"So hot," he murmurs as he plucks at her top two buttons.

"Stop," I thunder, my hands fisted in rage. "Just let her go and fucking kill me already. This is bullshit. She didn't do anything."

He shoves the gun against her stomach hard enough that she starts coughing in pain. "You. Are. Not. In. Charge. Here." His face is screwed up in anger.

I clench my jaw and wait for my moment. The next time he turns away, I'm going to shoot him in the goddamned face. His eyes remain fixed on me, though, as he continues to unbutton her shirt with the gun pressed against her belly. The moment her shirt falls open to expose her lacy bra, I nearly lose my shit.

Be smart, Linc.

Don't go fucking wild and get her killed.

Think.

"You need me," I bark out, startling both Louie and myself with that statement. "If I could skim the money right out from under your nose, imagine what else I could do. I'm slick and smart and people trust me."

"I don't fucking trust you," he snarls, his nostrils flaring.

"Not yet. I'll do anything for you if you'll just let her go. Need me to rob the goddamned Federal Reserve? I'll do it. Just name your fucking price and it's yours. If your price is my head, then fine. Let her go, though."

He snorts with laughter. "Can you believe this guy, Mario? Fuckin' balls, this one."

I grit my teeth and stare at Reagan with every ounce of love I have for her. A look that says, *I'm sorry*. A look that says, *I love you more than anything*. A look that promises, *I will get you out of here, no matter what*.

She nods. She fucking loves me too. And she believes me. Trusts that I'll do exactly as I promise.

Think, Linc.

"I'm your guy," I continue as I slide my hand to my hip. "I'll do whatever you need me to, man. Just release her and let's talk."

Louie glowers at me. "I'm not one of your little cons, thief. You can't waltz in here and avoid the inevitable by running your stupid mouth. This isn't a negotiation, and I don't fall for tricks." His lip curls up in an evil way. "I know exactly how to punish you. You can watch me as I put my fat cock inside your little girlfriend. Watch her scream as I split her right open. And when she can't take anymore, I'll cut her throat. She'll bleed out with her panties around her knees and her bloody ass in the air. It'll be all your fault."

I growl and ease my hand behind me underneath my shirt. "You're a dead man."

"No," he snaps. "*You're* the dead man. Before the life has even left her eyes, I'll tie you to a chair and peel your flesh straight from your body until you're begging to join your cunt girlfriend in the afterlife. But it won't be so easy, will it?" He laughs harshly. "No. I want you to suffer. You can watch while Mario fucks her dead body as I carve out your organs one by one and feed them back to you."

My grip tightens around the metal. "Not on my fucking watch."

His eyes go wide when he sees me swing the gun around. He's standing slightly in front of Mario, who has Reagan still in his tight grip. I'm not a good enough shot to not accidentally hit her instead. I take a chance at his knee, though, to distract him.

Pop!

He howls in pain.

Pop! Pop! Pop!

I'm able to squeeze off one shot but Louie manages three. What feels like punches of fire on my chest instantly immobilizes me. Reagan screams at the top of her lungs as I clutch my rapidly bleeding wounds. I fall to my knees, my breath wheezing from me.

Pop! Pop! Pop!

Those shots don't hit me though.

I pray to fucking God they don't hit her either.

Voices. Yelling. More gunshots. Scuffling.

Falling forward, I'm barely able to catch myself from landing face first by throwing my palm out in front of me. My eyes jerk to find her running clumsily toward me, stumbling over her own feet. But she's free. Fucking free.

"Linc!"

Her warm scent envelops me a second before her loving arms do. I crash forward and land on my shoulder, my cheek slamming against the concrete floor. The pain is excruciating and blackness swarms around me. Her perfect hands are running all over me as she shrieks out words that I can't seem to comprehend.

"I l-love you. Oh m-my God, Linc. I love y-you. P-Please don't leave m-me."

Blinking away the darkness, I latch onto those words. They're still slurred but she's with me. She's safe, *I think*.

"Rey…"

"Linc," she sobs.

"I..I…"

"Shhh. Don't talk."

"L-Love…"

"I know. I know. Linc, I know."

"Y-You."

The room spins, and it's like I'm falling in a black hole.

A dark, never-ending hole where the sun doesn't exist.

Hell.

Any place without my fucking Rey of sunshine is hell.

I don't want to go without her.

Goddammit, I can't leave without her.

"Rey…" I call out in the darkness. I reach for her. "Rey…"

She's gone.

She's fucking gone.

And where the fuck am I?

Black. Black. Black.

Chapter Eighteen

Reagan

You Promised

"I don't care!" I shriek. "You have to know something!"

"Reagan, they just told you he's still in surgery." Ram tries to pull me away from the doctor, but I fight out of his arms. I barrel into the doctor, grabbing at his coat.

"Tell me something," I demand tearfully. "Anything. I need to know what's happening!" I begin to sob again, Ram pulling me off the man. All the doctor offers is a solemn apology before escaping my hysteria.

"NO! Don't let him go back there! He has to know something! COME BACK HERE!" I scream fighting Ram, but he has me in a strong hold.

"You need to calm the hell down," Ram grits out, his iron grip on me unbreakable. "They told us as much as they know." I battle until Ram loosens up just to allow me to turn around, facing him.

"They told us nothing. They told us that he is

fighting for his life. They never told us if he is going to make it. They needed to tell us he's going to make it." I break down sobbing in my brother's arms. My knees buckle and he catches me, while I grab onto his shirt, gripping for dear life. I cry so hard I choke on my own severed breaths. This is not happening. Linc is not fighting for his life right now. There was so much blood. So many shots fired. How does someone live through that?

"Sis, you need to breathe. You're having a panic attack. Please, just calm down." He cradles me in his arms. I feel him sit. He's probably taken me back to the waiting room. I try catching my breath. "Reagan, you're scaring me. Please calm down." But that request seems impossible. I can't calm down knowing Linc is fighting for his life.

"I asked the nurse to give her a sedative," I hear Roman say from behind me and I whip my head from Ram's now-soaked chest.

"You're not drugging me! Why are you even here? To hope Linc dies? Get what you finally want since you hate him?!" I instantly feel regret the moment those words leave my lips. I watch Roman blanch. "I'm… I didn't mean that… I'm so…" I can't even finish without going into another fit of sobs. I hang onto my brother as tight as I can, feeling like if he lets me go, I'll break down and never recover.

I feel Roman's large frame kneeling in front of us, his warm hand on my shoulder. "Reagan, I… God, I don't hate him. I just wanted what was best for you. I'm sorry I was so blind. Please don't hate me for just wanting to protect you. I would never want something like this for Linc."

I take in a deep breath and lift my head to turn to my brother. It's then we all hear the familiar shriek.

"What the FUCK?! Where is he? Is he alive?" We turn to see Andie, disheveled and barging into the emergency room. Roman stands to comfort his wife, but she pushes him away and makes direct eye contact with me. "Is he alive?" Her words are blunt but strained. She doesn't want it candy coated. She wants the truth.

"We…we don't know. He's st-still in surgery." I have to stop because I can't say anything else without the fear of losing it again. I can't tell my best friend that her brother is fighting for his life because he was shot trying to save my life.

Andie comes at me and we embrace, both breaking down. After a few long moments, she pulls away.

"Honey, are you hurt? Is this your…" She looks at me, and it reminds me that I'm still covered in blood. Linc's blood.

"No…it-it's not mine." Oh God. Why haven't they come out yet? We've been waiting for over an hour. They should know something. "Andie, I'm so sorry, he tried—"

"You stop right now. This is not your fault. Linc is a stubborn shit and he'll pull out of this just to laugh about it. Have faith. We all just need to have faith." I want to believe her. Hang on to her every word, but the shakiness in her voice and the wetness in her eyes tells me she isn't even sure of her words. "I called Lana. She and Dad are on their way. Roman told me you won't let the nurse check you out. Honey you were drugged, you should have someone—"

"Excuse me, Reagan Holloway?"

We both turn to see a tall African American male, suited with a badge hanging from his side. "I've already told the police what I know. I have nothing more to say to you people," I snap, turning away when he halts me.

"I'm sure you have. My name is Drake Jenkins. I was the FBI agent working with Lincoln on this case." That gets my attention along with Andie's as we both whip our heads back.

Detective Douche, as Linc had him labeled in his phone, I'm assuming.

"You what?"

"Mr. Carter was working with us to bring down Louie Romero."

At that Andie grabs my hand and tries hauling me behind her. "My brother wouldn't work with the Feds, nice try. You need to leave."

Roman steps up, looking ready for a battle. "You need to back off, you—"

"Lincoln was in quite a bit of trouble. Seemed like he was in town trying to run from it. Good thing for him, he'd already cut ties with Romero and had bailed. Bad thing is, his past caught up with him. We've been tracking Romero for the past three years. Mr. Carter hit our radar because stealing from Romero was enough to drive the old man from his secure environment where we had nothing on him. Outside of Jersey, we stood a better chance of nailing him. Romero killed a small-time drug dealer while here, Larry Brown, in a Dairy Queen parking lot of all places, and he was out for Linc's blood, too." Both Andie and I gasp, and Roman cusses.

Agent Jenkins continues, "Lincoln, being the reformed thug, made a deal. He would help us take down Louie. In return he would be exonerated for his previous illegal activities. Assuming he could stay out of trouble after that."

I'm in shock. Andie is shaking her head. "No, I don't believe you. Linc would never—"

"It's true." Ram steps up. "He confessed this right after Reagan took off. He wanted to make things right. Wanted out. He didn't expect for them to take Reagan. He blames himself for it all."

My heart breaks even more, knowing he was putting himself in harm's way just to make things right. He told me he wanted to be better. But this shouldn't have been the way.

When I first woke up in the dark warehouse, I was confused. Unsure why I was taken. Worried it was from an angry client. Someone who knew Holloway Advertising had a lot of money, so a ransom would be easy. I even thought Chase had something to do with it. But then that man Louie started talking.

He thought he would disgust me with all the bad things Linc had done. But it just made me hurt for him more. I knew Linc regretted his past. There was always such sorrow in his words whenever he spoke about it. His life growing up. The things he did to make do, people he hurt because *he* was hurting. The life he lived knowing he could be dead at any moment and welcomed it.

Then he showed up, offering his life for mine. Not caring that this psychotic man wouldn't think twice about shooting him dead. He didn't care. He just wanted me safe. And the look… The look he gave me telling me he would do just that.

I break down again. The echoing in my head of gun shots sends me into another attack. I start pulling at my hair, needing the banging to stop. "Make it stop. Make it stop!" I scream and Ram grabs for me. Andie begins to sob, while Roman grabs for her to comfort her.

Linc can't die.

He can't come storming into my life and steal my heart just to leave me.

"He can't die. He just can't," I wail bringing my hands up and taking my closed fists to my brother's chest. I feel myself sliding down Ram's chest when he scoops me up.

"Shhhh… He's not going to die. Stay positive."

I wish everyone would stop saying that. It's like the most cliché thing to say when someone is about to die. As if saying it means it'll make the situation less glum. I want to be hopeful. I want to believe Linc wouldn't leave this world without me. That he loves enough to fight. But the blood. There was so much blood.

I tense, remembering. I pull away from Ram, startling him. I look down at my blouse, completely covered in red. My arms are red, and my nails are stained red.

All I see is red.

"S-s-so much blood. T-There w-was s-so much blood. He w-was losing s-so much blood. How does someone live!? HOW!? He was bleeding everywhere! THERE WAS SO MUCH BLOOD!" I lose it. I start scraping at my skin, trying to rub the dried blood off my arm. I'm pulling at my shirt. I need it off me. I need to not see all this blood.

I start screaming.

Ram fights to keep me in his arms. I hear him yelling for Roman, but I can't stop seeing red, the sound of gunshots, and the look on Linc's face as he fell to the ground. I've lost all control over myself as I go completely mad in Ram's arms. I hear Roman along with a voice that doesn't sound familiar near me. I hear Ram apologize to me, just as I feel a small pinch in my arm. I slowly turn, seeing a nurse holding a small syringe in her hand.

"I'm sorry, sis. You're scaring us. This is just going to help you calm down."

I slowly turn back to Ram, one last thick tear flowing down my cheek. "Why would he do this? Why would he risk his life? Why would he want to leave me?" I feel the drug flow through my veins calming my body and mind instantly. I take in a deep breath, feeling my shoulders relax, the need to rest my head on his shoulders immediate.

"Let's get her admitted and into a room to rest," I hear the nurse instruct just as things, once again, go black.

"You can't just take things that don't belong to you, you know. One day it's going to catch up to you," I say with a grin as Linc pulls out a golf glove he apparently stole from Roman's golf bag.

"Sure I can. I stole your heart, didn't I?" he teases playfully before winking, causing me to blush like a darn school girl. Linc puts on the glove, and starts to perform a Michael Jackson skit. I bust out laughing.

"You are seriously ridiculous," I say, wiping the tears from my eyes. He comes at me, causing me to squeal as he wraps his arm around my waist. Pulling me close to him, his mouth just a hairsbreadth away from mine.

"You, my little thief, are just as guilty." He presses his lips to mine, then pulls away.

"Guilty of what?"

"Stealing."

"And what exactly is it that I stole?" I'm very curious about his answer. I'm not the one taking Roman's dumb crap all the time.

"My heart." His brows furrow together as his eyes flicker with what I hope is love. All playfulness is gone. "You stole my heart, Rey." He pauses for a second allowing his words to sink in before he continues. "Two thieves, you and I. Forever."

I'm struggling with how to respond. His admission tugs at my heart strings, tearing open any doubts I ever had about us. He only speaks the truth. We do have each other's hearts. We have since the day we met. I take in a deep breath, fighting off the tears. "Forever, huh?" I say, my voice hoarse.

"Forever. We're in this together. For life, thief."

I like the sound of that.

My eyes open, the fogginess in my head still heavy. I look around at my surroundings and realize I'm in the hospital. I must have been dreaming. I notice I've been changed into scrubs. My arms are no longer covered in blood. I lift my head which seems too heavy and then bring myself back down to my pillow.

"Sweetie, just relax." I acknowledge Dani's voice and turn to see she's seated next to my bed. "Hi, how are you feeling?" she asks, her voice laced with concern.

It doesn't take long before the reason why I'm here slaps me in the face. "Linc…how's Linc?"

I watch as Dani's face fights not to show emotion, but I know she has no game face. Her eyes fill with tears as she grabs my hand.

No.

"No…" I pull away trying to sit up but the dizziness wins out again and brings me back down.

"Oh, honey, he's alive. It's just… It's not good." She begins to cry. I stare at her in shock. I needed her to tell me he was out of surgery and waiting for me to wake up. That he was going to be fine. "He made it out of surgery but there was extensive damage. The next twenty-four hours are crucial, but the doctor told Lana that she may want to get his affairs in order. I'm so sorry, Reagan." She breaks down crying, holding my hand. I can't help but stare at her. My mind refuses to process what she said. Because he promised me. He promised me forever.

I tug my hand away. "I want to see him. I don't believe you." Dani jumps at my harsh tone. I don't care. She's lying to me. She's been told wrong information. And I won't believe otherwise until I see him for myself. He just needs me to wake up.

Dani wipes her face and stands. I refuse to make eye contact with her, but she nods, and tells me she will let my brothers know I'm awake and want to see Linc.

It takes a few minutes, but eventually a solemn

looking Ram comes in to help me. I refuse his help until I realize I'm still too weak and need his help walking through the halls. Stepping out of my room, I notice Lana in the arms of her husband Roger, weeping. I turn away because I don't want to see the pain, sadness, loss in her eyes. I say nothing while Ram guides me to Linc's room and ignore him when he warns me about tubes and bandages.

When we make it to his room and Ram holds the door for me, it feels like someone takes a bat to my gut. All the air in my lungs escapes me when I see him. I wobble on my feet, and Ram catches me before I faint. I tell him I'm fine and request that he leave.

It takes me a moment to remember how to breathe. I grab his hand. No one could have prepared me for this. To see a tube helping him breathe. To see half his body wrapped in bandages that aren't nearly thick enough because I can see the red staining through. His eyes are closed, but they look sunken, his skin so pale.

I want to be strong for him, for me, but I fail. I start to cry. I hold his hand to my face, hoping my warmth will help his coldness.

"Always wanting to steal the show, huh? Just wanted to be the damsel, didn't you," I say, trying to make light of this dark situation. I wait for him to laugh and tell me that he would look amazing in a dress, and that he would let me save him as long as it came with hero sex, but he doesn't move. His eyes don't open and he doesn't offer me his perfect laugh.

"Please, just wake up so I can tell you how stupid you are for trying to play the good guy." I squeeze his hand pressing a kiss to his palm.

"These doctors here think you're not doing well, but I know you. Faking it for the attention. I know you just want to pretend you're sleeping and let everyone confess how much they love you so you can wake up and hold it all over their heads." My cheeks are soaked, and my words are interrupted by hiccups of emotion.

"If this is what you had to do to get me all sappy, then so be it. I love you, Lincoln Carter. A love so thick that I can't even begin to explain the deep, solid emotion of what my heart feels. I loved you the moment you stepped into my life. The moment you made me feel like I could be someone's forever. *You* made me feel that way. I want us to be that forever. The one you promised. You told me you were never going to leave me so just wake up, okay? Wake up and tell me more about how you want to take my last name, like the goofball you are." I have to pause. I can barely see him through my tears and my chest feels like it's going to explode.

"Don't you leave me, Lincoln Carter. Come back to me and be my forever like you promised. Please… Please. I need you to wake up. I love you and I need—"

The loud sounds of the monitors interrupt me. I'm startled and look to the machines—his heart rake spiking—then watch as the heartbeat line quickly drops.

The machine plays a solid tone and indicates a straight line.

And that's when I begin to scream.

Chapter Nineteen

Linc

The Past…

The Chaos is My Calm

"You suck," I tell my little sister as I take a hit of my joint.

She huffs and tosses the spray can into the dumpster. "I don't see your dumb ass doing any better. It's a pretty heart."

I pass her the roach and pick up the untouched black spray can. She used the red one until it ran out. Ugliest fucking heart I've ever seen. "Watch and learn, loser."

She punches me, and I laugh. Truth is, she's not the loser. I am. Well, was. When Mom married Roger, and Andrea came to live with us, the ever-present ache in my chest seemed to loosen its grip. Andrea didn't look at me as though I was a fucked-up teenager like my teachers and parents did. She saw through to me. Became my friend and loved me in spite of the fact I had no future in front of me.

I shake the can and toss the cap at her. She grunts, which makes me chuckle. My sister is a mean ass. Gives my step-dad Roger a helluva time. It's funny as shit. "Five bucks says my heart will be better."

"If your heart looks better than mine, I'll buy you a Big Mac and *a chocolate shake," she agrees, but her tone is smug. She's pretty fucking proud of her ugly ass heart.*

I start tagging the back wall of the old abandoned grocery store and zone out. When I paint or draw, I get lost in the moment of it all. My bedroom is littered with dark drawings. Portraits of myself, two people in one. Smiles and fucking sunny on the outside. Broken and messed up on the inside. And just like those drawings, I put my own heart on this wall.

Smooth and strong on the outside.

But the tear in the middle of my heart reveals the twisted wreckage within.

The heart is huge, just like my own, and takes up nearly a six foot by six-foot space. It's giant, anatomically correct, and tries desperately to do its job correctly. But the peek of the inside is enough to see that it's a mess. It is broken. It doesn't understand how to be healthy and whole.

When I finish, I drop the can to the concrete. With my fingers, I steal some of the blood red runoff from Andrea's heart and smear it along the outer curve of my black one. It's poetic, really. A direct parallel to my real life. I desperately take from others what I hope to somehow restore within me. Andrea is hardened and sad but within she is good and loving. If I could have one ounce of her goodness, maybe my own heart wouldn't be so fucked-up.

"Linc." My sister's voice is shaky with emotion.

I step back and blink away my daze. When I dart my eyes to hers, she's crying. This is what I do. I make them cry. My mother. My step-sister. My teachers. I'm not whole like they want me to be. I'm a shattered mess inside, barely tied together in a shiny package. Those sharp edges bleed through, and everyone sees my imperfections. Late at night, I vow I'll be a better person the next day. But when the next day rolls around, I'm back to stealing or lying or fighting. The chaos is my calm.

"You win," I say gruffly and kick the can toward the dumpster. "Your heart is better than mine."

I stalk off toward McDonald's, which is a half-mile up the road. Andrea's footsteps can be heard behind me as she runs to catch up. I'm stopped dead in my tracks when her skinny arms hug me from behind. Her cheek rests against my back.

"You're wrong, big brother," she whispers tearfully. "Your heart is beautiful and strong and the only thing that keeps me alive most days."

My chest pounds with her words which are no longer about the artwork. "My heart is dirty and ugly."

"You're wrong," she murmurs again. "So wrong."

I scowl but make no moves to break from her hug. I love Andrea more than anyone in this world. One day she's going to go off and do great things. She'll meet some cool guy and have awesome kids. I'll be the dumb uncle that can't keep his shit straight.

"You're wrong, Linc."

Her words keep echoing inside of me, giving me the slightest inkling of hope. Hope isn't an emotion I'm familiar with. Hope is fucking stupid. And yet…here it is, blossoming inside of me, like a contagious disease. I'm infected by it. Andrea seems to love me despite my shortcomings. Maybe one day I'll find a girl who sees straight inside me to my jagged little heart and thinks it's beautiful and strong, just like my sister says.

"So what you're saying," I say, my voice tight with unshed emotion, "is I'm the best motherfucking artist you know and you'll be glad to buy me a Big Mac."

She chuckles and sniffles. "I'm saying," she teases back "that I let you win sometimes. I can't always be the best at everything. Don't want my big brother to go home and cry to his momma."

I reach back and tickle her until she squeals, running away.

"Asshole!"

I grin at her and take a bow. "I'll take that as a compliment."

She's beaming at me. My sister isn't one for smiling much since she's come to live with us. When she does smile, she lights up a room. I may not be good for much but I am sure as fuck good at making her laugh. And that's something I can be proud of.

"Let's go, punk," she orders as she starts marching down the road to the restaurant.

I trot to catch up to her and sling an arm over her shoulders. "Thanks, Andrea."

"I meant every word," she says, her tone solemn once again. "You were wrong. One day you'll realize that."

Fucking hope multiplies inside of me again.

God, how I want to believe you're right, little sister.

Chapter Twenty

Reagan

The End

LIFE IS A PRECIOUS THING. SOMETHING THAT MOST take for granted. We spend our entire lives almost blind to how beautiful it really is, and we walk through it ignoring the small signs. Signs that implore us to stop for a second and enjoy it. To take a look around and freaking notice all the beauty around us—because in an instant it could all be gone. Fragile and not promised. But people rarely do that. They don't stop. They don't take the time to be thankful for the life they have or the love they're surrounded by. I didn't stop. I just went along my merry little way. Those moments were there for my grasping all along. I ignored them because I thought I had time to enjoy more of them. But I didn't. Just like everyone else, I took them for granted. I let the beauty pass on by without ever taking the time to fully acknowledge it. I won't ever make that mistake again.

This is what fills my mind as I sit in the hospital

chapel. Thinking about the years, hours, minutes, even seconds of life I've taken for granted. I think about all the time Linc and I fought against our feelings. How much time we wasted fighting what we knew was right from the start.

I think about how life is never guaranteed. No matter what promises people make in life, nothing is guaranteed. Linc promised me forever. I promised him I would always be there for him. Promises that will soon mean nothing. Because he won't be here long enough to give me that forever he promised.

Linc flat lined while I held his hand begging him to come back to me. My screams, along with the sirens alerted staff and I was quickly pushed aside while they worked on him. The horror of watching them take a machine to his chest to revive his heart. The yelling, the orders, the unbelievable feeling that it was the end. For him. For us. A nurse tried to escort me out of the room, but I refused. I wasn't leaving if he was about to take his last breath. I owed him that much. The least I could do was stick to my word and be there for him.

Feeling as if eons of time had passed, eventually the room filled with the small beeping sounds of a heartbeat. He hasn't left me. Not yet.

I broke down, and this time allowed the familiar hands of my mother to pull me out of the room. I wanted to stay. I begged to, but my mother convinced me I needed to let the doctors do their work. It was a short time later when the doctor came out to talk to us.

"He's stabilized. We were able to get his heart going again, but his organs are struggling to function. We will keep him comfortable, but I won't lie. His situation is grim. To be safe, you might consider saying your goodbyes to him before it's too late."

I watched his mother collapse into her husband's arms. Andie howled as if it was her own heart that was stopping. I just stood there, my universe feeling as if it stopped. Watching the reactions of people as if they were already letting go, when he was still alive. He would pull through. He was Linc. He wouldn't leave me. He promised.

But promises are just words. And I'd quickly come to realize that you can promise the world, it doesn't mean you can actually deliver it. Within the room of hurting loved ones, a retched scream breaks through. It's when everyone turned to me that I realized that sound was coming from me.

How could he do this to me? How could he just leave me? Make my life feel so loved and whole. He lied to me. And now he is going to leave me feeling empty and lost. I took off, away from the worried eyes of my family, and eventually found solace in the chapel.

I sit in here, the silence comforting. Away from the sobs and the looks. The way everyone tries to comfort me as if that's going to fix the hole being torn inside me. As each one holds their loved ones, knowing they will go home with them tonight. Unlike me, who will go home alone.

"I will never forgive you for this, Lincoln Carter," I whisper to no one, feeling sorrow so deep in my soul. I wipe at the tears that won't stop. I fear they never will.

They want to me to go say goodbye. And I just don't

know how to do that. How can I say goodbye to the one person who showed me how it felt to finally live?

"I'm not jumping off this ledge, Linc. You're crazy. Plus the water has to be freezing!"

"I'm not crazy, beautiful, I'm adventurous. Plus, I wouldn't bring you here and make you jump, unless I knew it was safe. You're my prized possession, remember? I can't let anything bad happen to you." He leans in and kisses me, helping me forget about the levy below us and the high rock cliff we're standing on. Finally pulling away, I feel breathless and free. Almost careless enough to take his word and jump off the cliff into the frigid lake.

"Hey, you're the one who said you wanted to feel high without the help of illegal substances."

I laugh, smacking him in the arm. "Yeah, but I kinda crossed that off my list after the romp we had with the choker and clamps. If I felt any more pleasure, my eyes would have popped out of the sockets." His smile is absolutely infectious as it spreads across his face. Such a typical male, loves hearing what a stallion he is in bed.

"Well, thank you for the kind words. I will make sure to let Chef Cock know you approved of the meal. But in the meantime, this is different. You said you wanted to feel free. This will hit the spot."

Linc always throws me off by how observant he is. He listens when even I'm not paying attention to myself.

"Rey, I want to do everything with you. Experience life to its fullest with you. And I promise to do my best to make sure all your dreams and aspirations are met. Just

stick with me, okay? Don't give up on me."

I wrap my palms around his cheeks, bringing his lips to mine. "I'll never give up on you, Lincoln Carter. Even if you think about giving up on yourself."

Our eyes scream with so much meaning, you can feel the echo of emotion against the rock levy. My nerves have suddenly calmed and I know I trust Linc with my heart, my soul, my life.

I grab his hand. "Never give up."

"Never give up." And with that promise, we both take a huge leap off the cliff.

I pull myself back from the memory, feeling the vibrations of my phone. I know they are looking for me. I know I can't hide in here forever. I check my phone and find a text from Ram.

Ram: Don't put it off any longer. He would want you to say goodbye.

No.

He would want me to fight for him.

But it seems I'm the only one doing that. Am I being foolish? Unwilling to see the truth?

No one ever prepares for death. No one leaves their house in the morning on their way to work, saying, today I'm going to die, make sure you kiss your loved ones and tie up any lose ends.

Linc left the house today the happiest I have ever seen him. And now he is lying in a bed, fighting for his life. Or maybe even letting death win. I'm not sure anymore. I lift my eyes to the statue of Jesus, offering him one last plea, before turning and making the long trek to Linc's room. With each step, my legs feel heavier. A force almost fighting me. If I don't go in there, then he won't die. He wouldn't leave this world without letting me at least say good bye, right?

It's when I turn the corner that I run into Lana. I try turning around, but she calls my name.

"Reagan, please. Just a quick word?" I want to pretend I don't hear her. Keep going until I can make my way out of this hospital and keep walking until I can disappear away from this life, this pain, this emptiness quickly filling my heart.

I take in a breath for strength and continue walking forward. Two, three, four more steps closer to goodbye.

When I make it to Lana, I see the loss in her eyes. I look away. I refuse to let go.

"I just wanted to say thank you. Thank you for loving my son. Giving him what he ached for his entire life. For making him feel like he wasn't such a burden."

I don't want to cry.

I'm sick of crying.

It does nothing to help Linc.

I allow her to wrap me in her arms and hug me, offering me warmth. She releases me, trying to offer a small smile for courage. "He's all yours," she says patting me on my shoulder, walking back towards the waiting room. I begin walking, when I turn and call for Lana.

She turns and I speak. "He was happy. He smiled and laughed and loved. But it wasn't me who showed him how to do that. It was him showing me. He always knew how precious life was. He just needed reminding himself." Then I turn back and head toward the end of my future.

The beeping of the monitor fills the quiet room as I take my seat next to his bed. He looks the same as before. As if he's sleeping off one of our fireball nights. But this time his silence has nothing to do with having too much to drink. I take his still hand in mine, pressing the top of his hand to my cheek. The hairs on his hand brush against my skin, and I close my eyes, trying to memorize the feeling.

"I remember the first time you touched me. Well, not really touched me, but the first time I felt your skin on mine. Remember Roman's office, when you were trying to be suave with me? Complimenting my hair? I about swooned the moment your finger brushed against my cheek. So silly, right?" I laugh at the memory. "I know Roman wanted to murder you, but I couldn't get my legs to leave. I just wanted to get you to keep talking. For some strange reason, I was so entranced by your voice. I was willing to do anything to spend more time with you, but then you offered to take me to a movie. You didn't even know me and asked me to sneak into a movie without paying." I laugh again, shaking my head at how hard he had to convince me to go. "You told me I needed to live a little and then started to spit out fake statistics on how beneficial it was for the economy when people didn't pay for movies." And he did. He went on and on about why we were doing society a favor by not paying, then ended up spending the cost of a ticket and then some on snacks and sodas.

"Everything you ever did, made me see life more

brightly. From the moment you convinced me I was doing my civic duty by stealing from the movie theater, to showing me how it felt to truly love." I wipe the tear running down my jaw, fighting to stay strong. "You taught me to be whoever I wanted to be and not worry about what others thought. You always acted like you never knew how it felt to live. But you were wrong. It wasn't until you came into my life that I ever truly lived. Every day with you was life."

I can't say it. I can't say goodbye.

But it's time, Reagan.

"Goddammit, Lincoln Carter. Why are you leaving me? Why are you making me say goodbye when I feel like I just said hello?" My tears are starting to soak his cradled palm. "We have a future planned. A life. And I can't do it without you. I won't. You promised me forever, dammit, why are you giving up?"

I feel weak and ashamed that I'm crying so hard. I wanted to be strong for him, but I can't. I can't walk out of this room knowing it's the last time I'll see him.

"I will never forgive you. If you leave me, I won't forgive you. Do you hear me? I love you. If you say you love me as much as you do, show me. Wake up! GODDAMMIT, WAKE UP!"

I grip his hand, resting my head on the edge of his bed, not wanting to hurt him. As if it would matter. I try catching my breath, so I can pull it together. I need to…

I lift my head up quickly, staring at the hand I'm holding.

"Do it again," I whisper, praying it wasn't in my head.

I wait.

And I wait.

Then it happens again.

I feel the small twitch of his hand inside mine.

"Oh God, I knew it. I love you, please, come back to me. Come back to me."

The movement in his hand gets stronger at the same time the monitors start to react. I stare at the heartrate monitor, watching the pace pick up. I'm holding my breath, waiting for it to flat line again.

"Come on, baby. Give me another sign. Come back to me."

The machines go nuts.

I almost drop his hand as the sudden beeping startles me. I'm not sure what's happening, but I start to yell for the nurse.

It's then that I watch his eyes open, locking directly with mine.

Chapter Twenty-One

Linc

Six weeks later…

Yes

"IN A MINUTE," I SAY, MY FOCUS ON MY SKETCH PAD.

Reagan huffs, and I can't help but smile. "You said that ten minutes ago."

"Surprises have to be timed just right."

I steal a glance at her. She's beautiful today in a silky cream-colored shirt and fitted black skirt. With her brown hair twisted in a messy bun, she reminds me of a naughty school teacher or librarian. My dick twitches.

"How are you feeling?" she asks as she comes to sit on the edge of my desk where my feet are propped up.

"Like a million bucks."

Another huff.

Every time she asks me, I give her the same reply. And it's the truth. I may have been pumped full of lead but I made it through. I had to. She was waiting on the other side for me.

"Okay, done. Whatcha think?" I ask and pass her the notebook, ignoring the pain that streaks across my chest at the movement.

She stares down at it and her lip trembles. She loves it. I knew she would. "Oh, Linc."

I lift a brow at her and reach forward to pat her knee, my new tattoo visible on my forearm that's exposed with my dress shirt sleeves rolled up. She runs her fingers along the words—words that match her forearm exactly.

Thick as thieves.

"Yes," she tells me firmly without hesitation.

"It was a rhetorical question," I say in a smug tone and wink at her. "I already knew the answer."

She laughs and slaps at my hand. "You're too much."

"I'm not enough." My words are somber. Often, I worry that's the truth. Especially since I've had to rely on her to do everything for me the past few weeks. Driving. Laundry. Hell, at one point, showering. My sweet Reagan has had to fucking take care of me. It's annoying as hell that I can't sling her over my shoulder and have my way with her. I'm still too weak and only recently have I been feeling more like myself. A collapsed lung, punctured intestine, and shattered spleen will bring a strong man to his knees. It nearly took me to my grave.

"You're everything," she says in the fiercest tone.

Our eyes meet and she almost knocks me over with the love shining in her eyes. "I love you," I blurt out. I don't ever refrain from telling her anymore. I've been made well aware that life can be over in the blink of an eye, and you can't waste a minute of it.

"I love you, too." She leans forward to kiss me, and I

pull her into my lap. "Linc! You'll hurt yourself."

Smirking, I brush some hair away from her face. "I'm fine. You were there at this morning's appointment when Dr. Adams said I was fine…" I trail off and palm the inside of her thigh before inching my hand up under her skirt. "I'm fine for *everything*."

Her cheeks blaze red and a shy smile curves her lips up. "Everything?"

My fingers brush against her panties. "Everything. Even anal."

She giggles, and I'm trying to sneak my fingers into her panties when my office door swings open. Roman groans and covers his eyes.

"Really, man? We give you an office for what? So you can have a quiet place to feel our sister up?" His words are amused despite his grumbling.

"I specifically told you both that this office would be used for shenanigans with the CFO. You and Ram chose not to believe me," I say in defense.

Ram walks in after his brother and gags. "Fuck, man." He shakes his head and glances at Roman. "But he *did* say that."

Reagan scoots out of my lap and stands. She hugs the sketchbook to her chest. "You'll live. The both of you." Her eyes are warm and full of love as she regards me. "You ready?"

"Ever since the day I met you," I say with a wink.

"Now?" Roman asks. "Like right now?"

"Yep," Reagan huffs. "We're leaving and that's that."

"You're still going to do this? Have an impromptu vacation two weeks before my wedding?" Ram asks in astonishment. "Is it even safe for you to travel?"

I sit up and wince slightly. Ram frowns but I brush it off with a smile. "I'm fine. Besides, we're not flying."

Roman's eyes fly to his hairline. "You're driving all the way there? Goddamn, it'll take you the whole two weeks."

"We'll be back before the wedding festivities," Reagan assures them. "Linc and I need this vacation."

The room grows quiet, everyone undoubtedly recalling that fateful day a month and a half ago. I wonder if she'll show them the drawing. A part of me hopes she won't. She makes no moves to bring it from her chest.

Looks like she loves her secrets as much as I do.

"When you get back, Andie wants to have dinner at the house one day before the wedding," Roman says, his eyes finding mine. "She'll want to celebrate…"

He knows of course.

It makes me wonder if my sister knows.

It's all my fault. I asked him and he said yes. The motherfucker said yes. I still can't believe that one.

"To celebrate you being back," he tells me, assuring me my secret is still safe.

I give my him a tip of my head in thanks. "Tell her to make me that coconut cake I love. The one where she puts actual rum in the cake mix," I instruct and pat my stomach.

Reagan laughs and looks over her shoulder at me. "You're not supposed to drink."

"I'm not supposed to do a lot of things," I tell her, my palm sliding up the back of her thigh. "But I do them anyway."

"And on that note," Ram groans. "I'm out."

"Me too," Roman agrees. "Be safe. Be good."

I snort and Reagan laughs.

"Fuck it. Have fun," Roman says, chuckling.

"We are not stopping here," Reagan says, her smile wide and breathtaking.

"I have it circled on the map. We're stopping."

She puts on the blinker and is shaking her head. "You do realize this is the most ridiculous spot to stop."

"We're having a picnic."

I guide her to Lake Dardanelle State Park in Arkansas. We find a camping area that has several picnic tables and an unobstructed view of the glistening lake. And…

"A nuclear power plant," she says as she unpacks the cooler and tosses me a sandwich.

Shrugging, I unwrap my sandwich and grin at her. "Ever watch *The Simpsons*? I've been dying to see one of these in real life." I point at the steam coming out of the reactor. "Stunning view."

She laughs. "We're probably getting radiation poisoning as we speak."

"My love for you is nuclear," I jest. This earns me a piece of lettuce to the face.

We finish our lunch and then she leans up against me. The sun is high on this cool December morning, but we're warm. Everything about this day is perfect. I'm not in a rush to get out west. We have all the time in the world. These small moments with her are the best. It isn't the destination with Reagan Holloway, it's the mother-fucking journey.

"It really is beautiful in a bizarre kind of way," she admits. "Even if we are exposing ourselves to chemicals that will make us grow extra body parts."

Chuckling, I kiss the top of her head. "Those are steam clouds. Water vapor. Don't worry your pretty little head. Besides," I tease. "If I grew an extra dick, I seriously doubt you'd complain. Mark that off your bucket list. Double penetration by Lincoln Carter."

"You're ridiculous."

"You won't say that when you've had both my dicks at once."

"The view is gorgeous. I love it here," Reagan chirps as she throws herself on the giant king-sized bed at the Bellagio. "Those fountains are so pretty."

My view is breathtaking as well but I'm not staring out the window like she is. My gaze is following the curves of her body in her silky pale white dress. The way it pools around her like she's sitting in a cloud. An angel. So fitting. Her dark hair is a stark contrast. It's pulled up in a fancy do, but she releases some pins and it falls down behind her, brushing against her shoulders.

I loosen my tie and toss it away. Apparently, you have to be fancy here. I don't normally do fancy but I'd be fancy as fuck if that meant making Reagan happy. And boy is she happy. Unimaginable, but it's true. She's on top of the world. I put her there.

She toys with a strand of her hair as I pluck through

the buttons on my shirt. I shed the shirt, wincing only slightly when I pull my arms back to tug it away from me. The wife beater goes next and then my pants. When I'm naked, I crawl in behind her and stare out the picturesque window with her. It's dark out, but the fountains are dancing and lighting up with many different colors.

"You're naked." There's a smile in her voice.

"You should be, too."

I kiss her soft throat and roam her breast over her dress with my palm. She rolls onto her back and runs her fingers through my hair before pulling me down to kiss her mouth. This trip has been unrushed and exciting. We've done exactly what we've set out to do. Live in the moment. Enjoy each other. Laugh. Make love.

She's mine forever.

Even if my forever ends tomorrow.

I'll have had her fully and all encompassing for every second that's left in my life.

"You make a lot of serious faces lately," she says when I pull away from her lips. Her brows are crashed together in concern. "Where's my smiling man?"

My lips quirk up on one side. "Sometimes I have to take a minute and appreciate how lucky I am. It's a sobering fact."

Her brown eyes pool with unshed tears. "I'm so lucky you didn't leave me. I wouldn't have…" She swallows and a tear leaks out. "I don't think I could have survived losing you."

I press a soft kiss to her perfect mouth and swipe away her tear before slipping my hand under her dress. I'm pleased to find she's bare beneath the fabric. Slowly,

I run my fingers between the lips of her pussy and massage her clit.

Despite not being able to have sex until recently, I've still been unable to refrain from touching her. Two days ago, the doctor said I was cleared for sex, but she's been hesitant this entire trip. Tonight, we're going to make it work. I don't care if I die in the process. I'll have my sweet Reagan again.

"Ready to get fucked, Rey?" I growl as my finger enters her tight sex.

She moans and shakes her head. "No."

I frown but continue to tease her between her thighs. "Why not?"

She gently pushes my shoulder until I'm on my back. Her brown eyes that were sad moments before now flicker with wickedness. "My sex bucket list. I was thinking about it on the way here. There's something I want to try. You're usually too busy manhandling me to let me."

I smirk and hold my hands up in defense. "Well, I certainly can't manhandle you now, so I guess you'll get to have your pretty little way with me."

She straddles my hips and starts to peel away the white dress, but I stop her.

"Leave it on. You're sexy as hell in it," I tell her, a grin tugging at my lips.

Her fingers go to her neck and she unties the halter top. When she pulls the fabric down just below her tits, I get an unobstructed view of them. The material of her dress still hides the rest of her from me.

"Actually," I growl, my dick impossibly hard and eager. "This is better."

With her eyes on mine, she lifts her dress with one hand and uses the other to guide my throbbing cock inside of her. Once she's settled on me, she doesn't move.

"I'm pretty sure you've ridden me at least once," I observe, my palms sliding up her thighs under her dress.

She grabs my wrists and pins them to the bed beside my head. Her lips are parted and her eyes are dilated as she starts working her hips. "Not like this. You're under my control, Lincoln Holloway. I'm woman-handling you."

I smile and drink in this gorgeous vixen, fucking my cock like she owns it. Hell, she does. Hottest damn thing I've ever seen.

"You're mine," she says, mimicking something I say to her all the time. The possessiveness in her tone makes my dick twitch inside of her.

Her eyes grow sad again as she runs her fingertips over my still healing wounds. They're angry and agitated, but she's tender as she touches them. Tears well in her eyes again. We both know how close we were to losing each other. It's something we think about a lot each day. Not long after I came home with her from the hospital, she spent an entire day crying while curled up beside me in the bed. I teared up, too, but never let her see how fucking emotional I was. Truth is, I was fucking terrified. Seeing her with Louie cut my soul deep. The crushing responsibility I'd felt over putting her in that position is something I'll never be able to fully recover from. It haunts me in my nightmares. A scenario that plays out more horrifically than what happened. And because of that, I walk the straight and narrow for her. It's easy being good when you follow around an angel all day.

"Oh, Linc," she whimpers, her tears splashing my chest.

I pull from her hold on me and reach up, ignoring the pain tearing across my muscles, and grip her jaw. Her eyes are wide as I pull her down to my lips. I may not be able to toss her around and own her like I want but I can do this. My lips power over hers. I let her know with a kiss that I'll always protect and cherish her. That I will love her with every ounce of me that I have. Those are my vows.

"I love you," she murmurs between kisses. "So much."

I slide my other hand into her silky hair and kiss her hard. "I love you more, Rey. I always have."

"Stop babying him," Reagan teases, her pretty mouth curled into a smile. "He's eating this up. Aren't you, babe?"

I clutch my chest. "Owwww. Andie, please give me another slice of coconut cake." I give my sister my best puppy dog eyes. She's growing soft in her old age because her face crumples.

"Of course. Don't move, Linc."

Reagan shakes her head at me. "You're impossible."

Molly shrieks as if to agree with her. Roman laughs and pats her back. "The kid agrees. *I* totally fucking agree."

Andie slaps his shoulder before leaning across the table to hand me the plate. She gave me an extra big piece. "Leave him alone, guys. He's still hurt."

I wink at Reagan and flip Roman off. They both groan.

"I can't believe Dani is getting married Saturday. Pretty soon, you two will be next." Her blue eyes are lit with happiness as she teases us. It's such a good look on my sister. Pride thumps in my battered chest.

Roman makes a grunting sound and wears a smile like he's the cat that ate the fucking canary. Reagan shoots him a warning glare.

"Rey," I say after I polish off my second helping of cake. "Can you help me go to the bathroom?" I shrug. "I'm practically an invalid."

Andie's mouth parts, and I swear she's about to cry. "My poor big brother."

Reagan laughs. "Oh my God. He's not helpless. Trust me on this."

I turn my puppy dog eyes on my woman this time. "Please, angel. Help me upstairs. I might need to rest a moment."

Andie shoos us away. "We'll clean up down here. Help him, Reagan."

I play the part of wounded victim as Reagan helps me from my chair. When I twist a little too quickly, the hiss of breath and wince are real, though. Reagan senses this and her arm wraps around my side. She guides me upstairs. I point at my sister's room.

"In there."

She frowns up at me. "Why?"

"I'll show you."

We shuffle down the hallway. Once we make it to their room, I shut the door and lock it before flashing her an evil grin.

"Wanna fuck on their bed?"

"Lincoln!" she screeches but she's already peeling away her shirt.

"I knew you'd be down, bad girl."

She tosses her jeans and panties to the floor as she backs up to their bed. I shove my jeans and boxers down my thighs far enough to pull my hard dick out. She sits on the edge of the bed. I give her a tiny push until she's on her back. Then, I grab her hips and yank her toward me. The motion has me gritting my teeth because it hurts like fuck, but I power through it and hope to hell I'm not grimacing. When I tease the tip of my dick at her entrance, I'm pleased to see she's wet and ready. With a quick thrust, I'm inside of her. I fuck her as roughly as I can without hurting myself too much while I finger her clit. The moment she comes, I spill my seed deep inside of her.

We're all smiles and jokes as we clean up and redress.

While she smooths out her hair, I pick up Roman's big expensive watch from the dresser. "Who even wears something this big? It's an old man watch."

Reagan laughs. "Mom got that for him."

"Of course she did," I say, my lips twitching. "It's big as fuck. Like it should be a mantel clock. In fact…"

"No."

"I think—"

"No."

"—it would look great—"

"No."

"—on the mantel, next to the picture of him and

Molly we took last time—"

"No."

I laugh as I set the watch back down. "What? You act like taking his ugly watch and doing him a fashion service is the worst thing we've ever done to your big brother. I'm pretty sure me fucking you on his side of the bed was right up there in the number one slot."

Her face turns bright red and she shakes her head. "You're crazy."

"Crazy for you," I challenge.

"Fine."

"Fine?"

She picks up the abomination and shoves it in her pocket. "How long you think it'll take him to notice?"

"Oh, I imagine tomorrow morning, he'll be over with the sunrise and another laundry basket to collect his things," I say, my chest rumbling with laughter.

"We won't answer the door." She grabs my hand and beams at me.

"You know he secretly likes when we steal his shit."

"You just like to live dangerously. And if we keep swiping his stuff, he's going to kill us."

I pull her into my arms and kiss her forehead. She hugs me tight. Our eyes meet and say so many things our lips never seem to be able to express properly.

"At least we'll die together," I tell her. My hand strokes through her hair and my thumb brushes along her cheek.

"Thick as thieves," she murmurs, her eyes full of love and adoration. "In it until the end."

My mouth crashes to hers and I kiss her with that

very promise. She's mine until the end. And then she's still fucking mine because that's the way love is.

It's selfish and powerful.

It's ridiculous.

It defies reason or logic.

Love follows no rules.

I'm smirking as we kiss. The realization hits me like a ton of bricks.

Love is a fucking rebel.

Epilogue

Wedding Day

It's Just the Beginning, Baby

Reagan

I'M RUNNING THROUGH THE CHURCH HALLWAY, dodging guests left and right. Dani pulled me aside earlier asking if I could do her a favor and to keep it between us. With no thought, I agreed, being the good bridesmaid I am.

I almost make it back to the bridal suite when I spot Linc. He's standing in a huddle with the other groomsmen, laughing at something Ram just said. I take a quick moment to watch them. Ram looks happy. Anxious, but he's been waiting for this moment since the day he met Dani. Linc looks beyond handsome in his tuxedo. He lifts his arm to pat my brother on the shoulder when his newest tattoo pops out through his linen shirt sleeve. The view causes me to smile, lifting my fingers to graze down my own arm.

Thick as thieves.

A symbol that tells us that no matter what obstacles we face—good or bad—we'll face them together. Because we are a forever thing. That's our promise.

I know Linc senses me, so I duck out before he sees me. I don't have time to get tossed into the broom closet and lose a few sequins off my dress. He already caught me this morning trying to sneak out of the house, letting me know I'd forgotten something.

I'm sneaking back into the bridal suite just as Mom is helping Andie into her dress. I find Dani sitting at the parlor table while the stylist finishes curling her hair. I bend down, slipping her what she needed, and whisper in her ear. "In and out. Like a ninja."

She offers me her sweet smile, her wedding day beauty radiating. "Thank you."

I give her a kiss on the cheek and head back to Andie, who seems to be having some trouble getting her zipper up.

"Sweet girl, just stay still, it's probably just stuck," my poor mother says as she looks at me, giving me that *it's not stuck, it's too tight* look.

"How hard is it to make a dress that fits? That dress tailor was not listening to me!" Andie gripes as she sucks in another breath before my mom attempts another tug. Relieving her of her duty, I nod to Mom to move aside as I take over wrestling with the zipper.

"Mine was tight, too. Don't worry. We just need to wiggle it a bit. Ready?" We both count to three and with a big suck of air in, the zipper cooperates and slides

up, allowing me to clasp it at the top. "There y
Perfect."

Andie turns around and we both look at ourselve
the full-length mirror. It's almost impossible not to ma
fun of the disco dresses Dani picked out. With each ray
of sun that assaults us through the window, we turn on, creating a 360-sparkle show.

"You both look *so* beautiful." We both turn to see Dani, her eyes beginning to fill with tears. She's the one who's beautiful. Her dress that lies on her perfect little form as if it was made just for her. I think about what Ram is going to do when he finally sees his bride and it causes my eyes to fill as well.

"Oh Jesus! No crying right now! We just spent a shit ton on makeup, and if someone has to fuck with these fake eyelashes one more time, I'm going to flip out." We both laugh at Andie who also seems to be fighting back tears.

I take a step closer to my soon-to-be sister-in-law. "You look absolutely breathtaking, Dani." Might not have been the right thing to say, because the first tear falls from her cheeks. "I'm sorry, please don't cry. This is a happy day." She grabs me and hugs me tightly. I embrace her, feeling such love for my growing family. "This is going to be the best day ever. I'm so excited for you."

She pulls away as we both wipe at our wet cheeks. "Reagan, I have no doubt that your day will be coming very soon—"

"Already has," Andie mumbles under her breath.

We both whip our head to Andie.

"What is that supposed to mean?" Dani asks.

Linc. She simply beamed at me and told me she couldn't be happier. Maybe it has something to do with the fact that Linc is a suck up and they cook together now for family dinners, like they're on their own little cooking show.

"You're married," Dani utters in shock. "You're really married? Oh my goodness! You're married!" She starts jumping up and down while still holding my hand. I have no choice but to follow my hand and jump with her.

"You're not mad, are you?"

Dani stops. "Mad? Why would I be mad? This is the happiest news I've ever heard. Reagan, I love you. I've loved you as a sister ever since the day you came and talked me off my ledge. If it weren't for you, Ram and I might not have found our way back to one another. I owe you so much. I pray at night for your happiness. All I wanted was something wonderful for you, and I know Linc is that kind of wonderful."

I barely allow her to finish before I'm throwing my arms around her. "Thank you," I whisper, fighting off the heavy tears. Looking back, it's been such a long road for all of us. Pain and loneliness all wiped away by great men. We all started at the same place. And in the end, we all found our happiness. We found our forever. Together.

I think I could continue hugging Dani forever, but the sound of weeping coming from next to us has us breaking apart.

"Are…are you okay?" We both ask Andie, trying not to laugh. Being the toughest girl we know, she sure has turned into an emotional mess this past year.

"Yes. Shit. No. Shit!" She wipes at her face and turns to go walk into the corner of the room.

"What are you…" Dani tapers off as if something clicks.

"I should have known the second the gas issues began."

"You're not…" Dani breathes out.

A guilty look washes over Andie's face. "Fuck, I am! I don't even know how this happened! Roman just won't leave me the fuck alone!"

"Wait…you're pregnant again?" Shocked, I watch as Andie swipes at the air around her butt and walks back over to us.

"Yeah, I can't even believe it myself. I thought I was just moody because of the lack of sleep, but with my past experience with Molly, the second I started getting bad gas, I knew it. Your damn brother knocked me up again."

We both squeal, going in for a group hug, jumping up and down. "Oh my God! That's wonderful news! Another princess to spoil. Or prince! Do you know what you're having? When did the gas start? Is that a common sign of pregnancy…"

That's when *my* words taper off.

And something else clicks.

I stop jumping.

And I slowly turn to Dani.

"You…" I point at her, accusingly. "Wanna tell me why you had me get you Gas-x earlier?"

Linc

"It's a dick, isn't it?" Ram questions, his lips quirked into a half-grin.

Roman snorts, which makes Molly jump in his arms. "It's worse."

I start laughing but don't take my hand from my pocket. "It's none of your business."

Ram tugs at his bowtie, which looks like it was purchased to go to a discothèque, and darts his gaze to the back of the chapel. "What's taking so fucking long?"

Molly whimpers, but Roman pats her small back until she falls back asleep. "I'm pretty sure she's planning her escape."

I point out the window behind him. "Wait. Is that her running through the parking lot? She's going to get frostbite in that snow."

Ram jerks his head backwards and nearly topples over the steps at the front of the chapel. "Fuck you, Linc."

Roman and I both start laughing.

"The minister is giving you the stink eye," I warn.

Ram rolls his eyes and tugs at his shiny bowtie again. "I hate this thing. I'm itchy and need out of these clothes."

"Slow down, killer," I say, laughing. "Honeymoon is after the wedding, not before."

"Do you think Andie is going to kill me?" Roman asks suddenly, uncertainty flickering in his eyes.

Ram laughs. "Wait. You haven't shown her yet?"

Roman's jaws clench. "Not exactly."

"Pussy," Ram and I both mutter at once.

"At least I didn't get a dick tattooed on my finger," Roman shoots back at me. This makes Ram chuckle.

"It's not a dick, fucker. It's an image of your mom's—"

"Gentleman," the wedding coordinator interrupts. "The ladies are running a few minutes behind. Looking good." She grins and bounces off, hissing in her earpiece.

"What is it really?" Ram demands again.

"It's not a gay-ass Christmas tree, that's for damn sure."

Ram starts to flip me off but Roman swats him away. "She likes Christmas," Ram huffs in defense.

I gesture at the chapel that has more holiday decorations than Macy's the day before Christmas. "Clearly, man." I turn to regard Roman who looks serene as hell holding my niece. We may have had a fucked up start, but Roman is growing on me. I still like giving him shit, but at least he doesn't want to kill me anymore. If anything, he treats me like a special agent who's supposed to help me get Andie to not kill *him*. As if I know secrets about her that unlock the mystery that is her. I don't think anyone will ever figure that woman out. "She'll like yours. It's badass."

He smiles. He'd gotten his first tattoo last night with Ram and I. While the girls stayed at the house working on favors for the reception, the guys went out for drinks and then tattoos. The girls weren't privy to that part. Ram got a dumb Christmas tree in the middle of all his other tattoos. Damn tree only had one ornament on it. That one, I did *not* design. That was all Ram. There's no way in hell I'd own that shit.

But Roman's?

He asked me to design something that would have meaning to Andie. I'd sketched from memory the big red heart she'd tagged the grocery store with long ago. But then I drew barbed wire that was wrapped around it in an iron grip. Her and Molly's names are written inside the heart. Fucker was proud as punch when the artist finished the tattoo I'd sketched. That is…until Ram reminded him that Virginia was going to flip her shit that her perfect, untouched son now wore ink, like her other two kids.

Big guy turned fifty shades of pale as fuck.

But what matters is that Andie will love it. The heart. The meaning. His intentions. All of it. I can't wait for her to see it.

As for mine…

"It's a dick," Ram huffs. "Definitely a dick."

With a smirk, I yank my hand from my pocket and flip him off. Of course that shows the small amount of new ink I had done on my ring finger. Ram gapes at the "R" on my finger. I'm not about jewelry. I figured the tattoo would keep all the ladies off my junk and proclaim that I belong to my beautiful wife. Reagan Carter.

"You slick motherfucker," Ram mutters. "And you knew about this?"

Roman shrugs. "Sucks being the last to know shit, huh?" He turns to look at me. "This noble asshole had the balls to ask me for our sister's hand. How the fuck was I supposed to tell him no? Andie told me that you can't make eye contact with him. The puppy dog eyes are the devil. Her words, not mine." He clasps my shoulder and laughs. "Welcome to the family, Carnie. Don't fuck up or I'll fuck you up."

Andie

"Get the fuck OUTTA HERE!" I shriek. I know that look. That's the look of my best friend who just got caught! "You're *pregnant*?"

Dani's eyes skim back and forth between us girls, even shooting a guilty eye toward Virginia. "Oh, shoot yes. I don't even know how it happened!" she exclaims.

Reagan and I both burst out laughing. "Well, normally when you insert the penis into the vag—"

"I know *how*, silly." She slaps my shoulder.

I stare at my best friend since childhood. The first day we met was the first day I realized what true friendship was. "I… I… We get to do this together," I state, fighting back the emotions and failing. We all seem to have ruined our makeup already, so what's one more round of tears.

"I know. Can you believe it!? I'm hoping that I'm not as hungry and moody as you were, though." I bust out laughing while smiles brightly at her joke.

"Excuse me, ladies, are you ready? I have a group of antsy groomsmen and one very inpatient groom." We all nod to the coordinator.

We pull ourselves together after one final hug. Today marks the beginning of the complete Holloway clan.

Three women connected to three wonderful men. I never thought this is where life would take me. I never saw happiness, a husband and child, and now a group of six of the most amazing people that I can proudly call my family. I squeeze Dani's hand one last time and we all file out of the bridal room and line up behind the closed church doors.

"I can't believe that on the other side of those doors is my soon-to-be husband."

We all gush over Dani's words, knowing soon, she will be wedded to her soulmate. It brings my thoughts to Roman, the only person on this planet who is able to tolerate me. And he does it with such ease that it almost hurts to know how much I love him.

Because I have no patience, I step forward and open the door a tiny smidge to take a peek. I spot Ram first, tugging at his bowtie, looking nervous as shit. I see my brother, and in between them is my husband, holding our daughter. The plan is to have Virginia snag her once she walks up the aisle, but I have a feeling Roman will have a hard time letting her go. He cradles her sleeping form in his arms, rocking her. I watch as he places small kisses to the top of her head every three seconds. My heart swells with so much love for him, my daughter, my life.

Before I get yelled at, I take one last look at my version of a happily ever after, and shut the door. I take my spot in line, just in front of my best friend.

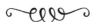

Roman

My mom slips through the chapel doors just as the music starts playing and holds out her hands. I shake my head to let her know Molly is fine in my arms. Truth is, that's where I'd like to keep her always. Andie may have been the best thing that ever happened to me, but then I got knocked on my ass the moment I held my little girl for the first time.

Apparently, happy endings aren't endings at all.

They just get happier and happier as time goes on.

"You're going to have a little brother or little sister soon," I whisper against Molly's hair. Andie doesn't know I know, but it's hard to hide fifteen pregnancy tests crammed in the trashcan that I empty. Not to mention, she's been acting a lot like the woman I fell so madly in love with.

Psychotic.

Hormonal.

Emotional.

Crazy as fuck.

Jesus, I love her.

The doors open again and Reagan steps out. Her dress is shiny and as obnoxious as our bowties and vests. She holds a bouquet of some kind of red Christmas-looking flower. But what has her drawing everyone's eye is the brilliant smile she wears. *For him.* I steal a glance at my brother-in-law two times over who's grinning like he got the toy out of the cereal box. Goofy ass.

At one point, I hated this guy. But then something shifted. Deep down, I knew he was in love with my sister and that the feeling was mutual. She's been hurt so many times though. I didn't want Linc to be on the long list of people who stole pieces of her heart.

The troublemaker shocked me though.

His loyalty and devotion to Reagan is admirable.

He made some mistakes, but hell, haven't we all?

All that matters is that he loves her. He was barely out of death's door and that punk was asking me if he could whisk away my sister and marry her. I'd felt honored he'd asked me instead of Ram, especially since we had bad blood between us.

I just want my sister to be happy.

And somehow, Linc is the one who makes her that way.

The door opens again and my attention is stolen once more.

My wife.

Goddamn she's beautiful.

Her eyes are teary and her cheeks are tearstained. That swollen bottom lip I love to suck on is wobbling as she walks toward us. Our eyes are locked. I see the nervousness in her eyes. The same unsure look she'd given me when she told me she was pregnant with Molly.

This time, I don't fuck it up.

"I'm pregnant," she mouths to me.

I wink and mouth back. "I know."

Brilliant beautiful adoration shimmers in her blue eyes. I'll always take care of her and our kids. The fact that she felt even a flicker of worry has me vowing to do better. To show her she's my everything.

"I love you," I mouth at her and kiss Molly's head.

A tear streaks down her cheek and she nods before giving me a shaky smile.

She knows.

Dani

Once upon a time, there was a girl who sent a text message to the wrong guy. That message blossomed into the most beautiful, loving relationship two people could ever share. At times, finding the right words to express how deeply they felt for each other just seemed impossible. It didn't seem. It just was.

As the doors open, and my father laces his arm into mine, I see *him*.

My soulmate.

The love of my life.

The reason for every breath I take.

For him.

Ram stands there, his brown eyes locked on mine. It's how it's always been between us. A room full of people, but we only see each other. I knew one day I would marry. It's a girl's dream. The planning, the colors, the perfect dress that would make the bride feel as if it were made just for her. But as I walk down the aisle, none of that truly even matters. It's not about the dresses or the flowers. The perfect playlist or the hors d'oeuvres.

It's about the man who stands at the front of the altar ready to make me his wife and vow to love and honor me until our last dying breath.

My father kisses me on the cheek and states his honor of giving me away. Andie takes my bouquet, and in no time, I am standing at the altar, face to face with my life. My happily ever after.

"You take my breath away," he whispers for only my ears, his eyes flickering with emotion.

Before I can respond, the minister begins.

He tells our tale of finding love. How today is the day we unite to start our future. Build a family and spend our days loving one another.

Roman hands us our rings, while juggling our niece, as we both repeat our vows.

Ram struggles through his, the emotion in his voice thick with each promise he makes to me. I take labored breaths trying to hide my own emotions as Ram slips the custom-made band on my finger. I look into the eyes of a man who fell into my life by mistake, who has turned into my rock. A man who would lay his life down to make me happy.

"I now pronounce you man and wife. You can kiss the—"

Ram doesn't wait for the minister to finish. His lips are on mine, offering me the sweetest, most powerful first kiss as husband and wife.

Ram

"Would you just look at everyone?" Dani sighs, her voice dreamy in quality.

I push the plate of food away and scan the reception hall. Reagan and Linc are dancing too slowly to a fast song. His palms are on her ass and he's whispering things to her that make her blush. Meanwhile, Roman keeps grinning at Andie while she nurses Molly. I can see his mouth moving every so often. She tries to kick him from her chair, but the motherfucker is quick these days and steps out of hurting distance. They're both feisty as hell but they're also perfect for one another.

"You did this."

My wife—*God, do I love the sound of that*—jerks her head to stare at me. Her lips are painted a pretty pink color that I'm dying to suck off later. The dark hair she normally wears down or in a messy bun has been pulled back in a sleek bridal do with curls hanging down the back that looks too fancy to touch. But later, I'm going to pluck every damn pin from her head and run my fingers through her hair that I love so much.

"Did what?" she asks, her cute nose scrunching. "Plan the best Christmas wedding ever?"

I grin and sling an arm over the back of her chair so I can lean in close to her. "No, Buttercup. This." I point at Linc and Reagan and then Andie and Roman. "Them."

This close, I get a whiff of some new perfume she's wearing. Smells sweet, like the taffy she loves so much.

"W-What?"

I run my fingertips along her bare outer arm, making her shiver. "You. The little Christmas angel. Sprinkling her dust all over and making miracles happen."

She laughs, and fuck do I love the sound. "You're crazy."

"Think about it. Had you not texted me, impressing me with you're *The Princess Bride* knowledge, none of this love would exist." I nuzzle my nose against her throat and press a kiss to her soft flesh. "It all started with you."

She sniffles and takes my hand. "You always say the sweetest things, Mr. Holloway."

I nip at her throat and hope Mom doesn't give me an ass whipping later for trying to eat my wife at the reception in front of her church friends. "I speak the truth." My palm finds her stomach and I rub it reverently. A few weeks ago, we found out she's expecting. Fucking finally. I've fucked her bare the entire time we've been together and we'd yet to get pregnant. I knew it weighed heavily on Dani. We'd even promised that after the new year, we'd see a doctor so we could start planning a family. Out of the blue, she turned up pregnant. A Christmas miracle. "You think the baby will like Branson?"

She sighs happily. "Our baby will *love* Branson. Silver Dollar City is the best. I know you've only been the one time with me, but just wait until we get there tomorrow. Best. Honeymoon. Ever. This time of year, it's decorated so beautifully. They even make fake snow!"

I suckle on her throat. It'll only be a matter of time before Mom is over here lecturing me about PDA. I will have to steal my moments while I can. "But who will fold the towels in your absence?" I tease.

She sucks in a sharp breath and slaps me. "Don't even joke around about that," she huffs. "Mary is going to destroy that entire color-coded section with her lazy ways. I just know it."

I hear my mother call my name in the same tone she'd take with me when I'd be up to no good during my teenage years. Quickly, I pull away and flash my mom an innocent smile. She shakes her head at me and goes back to talking to one of her friends.

"Just think how satisfying it will be to fold all the towels in the store and make them right again. Glass half full, wifey."

Dani taps at her bottom lip thoughtfully. "Well, now that you put it that way…"

Her cheeks glow with happiness and her smile is wide. I catch myself staring at how perfect she really is. She's mine now in every sense of the word.

Grabbing her hand that bears my ring, I bring her knuckles to my lips and kiss them. "I have a new favorite thing to add to my list."

Her eyes twinkle with excitement. "Oh, yeah? What's that?"

"My pregnant wife."

She laughs and lets out a sigh. "Whoever thought that our accidental start would end like this?"

I slide my palm to the back of her neck and draw her to me so that her forehead rests against mine. "End? Not even close." I press a kiss to her sweet lips. "It's just the beginning, baby."

The End

Want more? Stay tuned for Molly's story in 2025.

Not really.

Go away, we're done here.

Dear Reader,

We hope you enjoyed this series and thank you for taking the time to leave a review! If you're wondering, K Webster wrote Linc's chapters and J.D. Hollyfield wrote Reagan's. The epilogue, K wrote the boys and J.D. wrote the girls. It was fun and we look forward to writing more stuff together in the future (but not Molly's story…gah, get over it already)! Hope you check out our future projects as well! K is trying to convince J.D. to write something dark…ha!

If you want to have more fun with us, come find us in our active reader groups on FB. We like popping into each other's groups and harassing each other from time to time (legit always)! See ya there!

K&J

Acknowledgements

K WEBSTER

A huge thank you to my amazing friend J.D. Hollyfield. You're such a great friend and I love you. You cheer me even after that one time you made me cry when you tried to take my anal scene away. I'm glad we went through this 2 Lovers journey together!

Thank you to my husband, Matt. I love you more than words can describe. Your support means the world.

I want to thank the people who read this beta book early and gave us incredible support. Elizabeth Clinton, Jessica Viteri, Amanda Soderlund, Amy Bosica, Shannon Martin, Brooklyn Miller, Robin Martin, and Amy Simms. (I hope I didn't forget anyone.) You guys always provide AMAZING feedback. You all give me helpful ideas to make my stories better and give me incredible encouragement. I appreciate all of your comments and suggestions. Love you ladies!

Also, a big thank you to Vanessa Renee Place and Ella Stewart for proofreading our story after editing. You ladies rock!

A big thank you to my author friends who have given me your friendship and your support. You have no idea how much that means to me.

Thank you to all of my blogger friends both big and small that go above and beyond to always share my stuff. You all rock! #AllBlogsMatter

I'm especially thankful for my Krazy for K Webster's Books reader group. You ladies are wonderful with your support and friendship. Each and every single one of you is amazingly supportive and caring. #Cucumbers4Life

I am totally thankful for my author group, the COPA gals, for being there when I need to take a load off and whine. Y'all rock!

Vanessa Bridges and Jessica D. from Prema Editing, thanks so much for editing our book!

Thank you Stacey Blake for always being so flexible. I love you! I love you! I love you!

A big thanks to my PR gal, Nicole Blanchard. You are fabulous at what you do and keep me on track! And also thank you to The Hype PR gals for sharing the love!

Lastly but certainly not least of all, thank you to all of the wonderful readers out there that are willing to hear my story and enjoy my characters like I do. It means the world to me!

Acknowledgements

J.D. HOLLYFIELD

Thank you first to my bomb ass husband. Who always puts me before himself. I know it takes a lot to deal with a writer. So thank you for all those times you've questioned my sanity at two in the morning, and just turned and walked away. Since they haven't invented a word strong enough for how much I love you so we will stick with the four letter word for now.

To K Webster. Thanks for being the most beautiful, talented, smart woman I know. Did you ever know that you're my hero? Did you ever know that you're the wind beneath my wings? Will you marry me? Your anal scenes are on point. I want to be you when I grow up. I want to have all your babies. From now on, call me J.D. Webster.

Thank you to my editor Vanessa Bridges and her team at PREMA for their efforts in this story. Thank you to my amazing Beta team, and all the ladies who offered their eyes on this project. Amy Wiater and anyone else I missed who took the time to jump on my story and work together to make it what it is today. I appreciate you all!

Thank you to All by Design for the amazing cover! You nailed it. As you nail everything else. (Not everyone. Whole nother conversation…)

Thank you to my awesome reader group, Club JD. All your constant support for what I do warms my heart. I appreciate all the time you take in helping my stories come to life within this community.

A big hug and wine clink to Stacey at Champagne Formats for always making my books look so pretty.

And most importantly every single reader and blogger! THANK YOU for all that you do. For supporting me, reading my stories, spreading the word. It's because of you that I get to continue in this business. And for that I am forever grateful.

Cheers. This big glass of wine is for you.

About K WEBSTER

K Webster is the author of dozens of romance books in many different genres including contemporary romance, historical romance, paranormal romance, dark romance, romantic suspense, and erotic romance. When not spending time with her husband of nearly fourteen years and two adorable children, she's active on social media connecting with her readers.

Her other passions besides writing include reading and graphic design. K can always be found in front of her computer chasing her next idea and taking action. She looks forward to the day when she will see one of her titles on the big screen.

Join K Webster's newsletter to receive a couple of updates a month on new releases and exclusive content. To join, all you need to do is go here (www.authorkwebster.com).

Facebook: www.facebook.com/authorkwebster

Blog: authorkwebster.wordpress.com

Twitter: twitter.com/KristiWebster

Email: kristi@authorkwebster.com

Goodreads:
www.goodreads.com/user/show/10439773-k-webster

Instagram: instagram.com/kristiwebster

Books by
K WEBSTER

The Breaking the Rules Series:

Broken (Book 1)

Wrong (Book 2)

Scarred (Book 3)

Mistake (Book 4)

Crushed (Book 5 – a novella)

The Vegas Aces Series:

Rock Country (Book 1)

Rock Heart (Book 2)

Rock Bottom (Book 3)

The Becoming Her Series:

Becoming Lady Thomas (Book 1)

Becoming Countess Dumont (Book 2)

Becoming Mrs. Benedict (Book 3)

War & Peace Series:

This is War, Baby (Book 1)

This is Love, Baby (Book 2)

This Isn't Over, Baby (Book 3)

This Isn't You, Baby (Book 4)

This is Me, Baby (Book 5)

This Isn't Fair, Baby (Book 6)

This is the End, Baby (Book 7 – a novella)

2 Lovers Series:

Text 2 Lovers (Book 1)

Hate 2 Lovers (Book 2)

Alpha & Omega Duet:

Alpha & Omega (Book 1)

Omega & Love (Book 2)

Pretty Stolen Dolls Duet:

Pretty Stolen Dolls (Book 1)

Pretty Lost Dolls (Book 2)

Taboo Treats (Standalones):

Bad Bad Bad

Easton

Standalone Novels:

Apartment 2B
Love and Law
Moth to a Flame
Erased
The Road Back to Us
Surviving Harley
Give Me Yesterday
Running Free
Dirty Ugly Toy
Zeke's Eden
Sweet Jayne
Untimely You
Mad Sea
Whispers and the Roars
Schooled by a Senior
B-Sides and Rarities
Blue Hill Blood by Elizabeth Gray
Notice

About
J.D. HOLLYFIELD

Creative designer, mother, wife, writer, part time superhero…

J.D. Hollyfield is a creative designer by day and superhero by night. When she is not trying to save the world one happy ending at a time, she enjoys the snuggles of her husband, son and three doxies. With her love for romance, and head full of book boyfriends, she was inspired to test her creative abilities and bring her own story to life.

J.D. Hollyfield lives in the Midwest, and is currently at work on blowing the minds of readers, with the additions of her new books and series, along with her charm, humor and HEA's.

Read MORE of J.D. Hollyfield

My So Called Life:
Life Next Door
Life in a Rut, Love not Included
Life as we Know it
Faking It
Unlocking Adeline
Sinful Instincts
Passing Peter Parker

CONNECT WITH J.D. Hollyfield

Website: authorjdhollyfield.com

Facebook: www.facebook.com/authorjdhollyfield

Twitter: twitter.com/jdhollyfield

Newsletter: http://eepurl.com/Wf7gv

Pinterest: www.pinterest.com/jholla311

Instagram: instagram.com/jdhollyfield

Made in the USA
Monee, IL
18 July 2021

73830906R00174